Cruising

Desiree Day

POCKET BOOKS

New York   London   Toronto   Sydney

POCKET BOOKS, a division of Simon & Schuster, Inc.
1230 Avenue of the Americas, New York, NY 10020

ISBN-13: 978-1-4165-0351-4
ISBN-10:   1-4165-0351-X

This Pocket Books trade paperback edition September 2006

10 9 8 7 6 5 4 3 2 1

POCKET and colophon are registered trademarks of
Simon & Schuster, Inc.

Manufactured in the United States of America

For information regarding special discounts for bulk purchases,
please contact Simon & Schuster Special Sales at 1-800-456-6798
or business@simonandschuster.com.

In loving memory of my mother

Acknowledgments

I would like to thank my agent, Bob DiForio, for all his help and continued support. Thanks, Bob!

Big thanks to my editor, Amy Pierpont, and her assistant, Megan McKeever, for all their suggestions on this novel. I truly appreciate it.

Erica Feldon, you're a wonderful publicist. Thanks to you my book tour occurred without a hitch.

Thank you, Carly Sommerstein, you're an awesome copyeditor.

And a trillion thanks to my family, friends, and Georgia Romance Writers, your continued support buoys me up.

And a very special thank you to my readers. Y'all are phenomenal!

Cruising

Chapter 1

". . . nine, ten, eleven . . . and twelve." Madison DuPree took one last look around the restaurant, then smiled triumphantly. "Twelve gay men, but that's not including the one who doesn't know what the hell he is. Check him out," she said before nodding toward the bar. As usual, Leonard's was crowded, but it seemed even more so for a Thursday evening.

Squished in between a nightclub and a strip joint, the restaurant was the first thing people noticed because of its shocking purple brick front and cotton-candy-pink trimming. It was in downtown Atlanta within walking distance of Centennial Olympic Park, an arm's length away from the CNN Center, and a quick jog from the Georgia Dome.

But it wasn't too packed to figure out who Madison was talking about. Honey-hued and with the black man's requisite bald head, he was flitting between men and women as though he was at an all-you-can-eat buffet and he wanted to sample each one.

"He could be bi," Lauren Hopson offered in a dry tone, then rolled her eyes and took a sip of her apple martini.

Madison turned around in her seat and scrutinized him. After a minute, she concluded, "You're right, he's bi."

Blair Ricci turned wide green eyes on her friends. "Do you think he knows . . . that he's bi?" Even though she was white and a housewife from the suburbs, in all the years that they'd known one another, she'd never been uncomfortable with asking them questions. In some ways the three of them were closer than her own sisters.

Madison gave a loud snort. "Hell yeah, the dude knows he's bi. After all, this is Atlanta, where the dicks play double duty."

Blair swiped a handful of red hair out of her face before glancing at the man. He had moved on to a woman and was whispering something in her ear that caused her to blush. "I don't know . . . now he looks totally straight," she said, bewildered. This whole bi-gay thing was confusing.

"Oh Lord," LaShawn Greene groaned and fingered the Bible in her lap. Their level of conversation had sunk to a new low.

Madison shot her a look but continued. "That's all part of their plan . . . to fit in and play both teams without anyone finding out. I bet Leonard would know."

"I bet he would," Blair answered as she gazed around the restaurant. The owner of the club was easy to spot. He was the only two-hundred-pound, six-foot-four black man dressed in a gold sequined dress and Jimmy Choo shoes. "Oh, he's busy," she said, disappointed, spying him at the front door greeting customers.

"Thank God," LaShawn muttered, relieved as she relaxed against the leather cushions of the spacious booth. Not even the half-eaten birthday cake, gifts, and wrapping paper that littered the table could make it feel cluttered.

It was Thursday, and like every first Thursday for the last five years, it was their official Screw Men Night *and* Blair's birthday.

On Screw Men Night families were forgotten, worries were nonexistent, and fun reigned. They were teenagers again. Mortgage-paying, suburb-living, pedicure-loving, thirty-something-year-old teenagers. In a town where beautiful women were as common as succulent peaches, they held their own.

But it was Laura's, Madison's, Blair's, and LaShawn's beautiful coloring—slick brown, luscious red, luminescent pink, and vibrant yellow—that made one think of M&M's. In the crowd of chalk-colored blondes, ashy brunettes, and muddied-down grays, they stood out like splashes of sunshine against a black canvas.

They had met five years ago at a yoga class. In the middle of twisting their bodies into shapes that made them look like human pretzels and stretching their limbs to what felt like the ends of the earth, they had become fast friends.

"Why do you insist on doing this every time we go out?" Lauren hissed at Madison.

"You guys weren't talking about anything interesting," Madison answered in a defensive tone. "Besides, all this gay stuff reminds me of my same-sex experience," she boasted and a loud groan went up. They all had heard the story hundreds of times.

Lauren shook her head and sipped her drink. "Are you talking about the time you got shitfaced at Mardi Gras and tongued that blond chick?" she asked, but didn't wait for a reply. "I wouldn't call that a *same-sex experience* . . . it's just another slutty moment in the life of Madison DuPree," she finished and everybody laughed, even Madison. "Speaking of Madison's slutty moments, isn't that Keith?" Lauren asked, and then nodded toward the bar. He had sauntered in, carved his way through the crowd, and made a spot for himself at the bar.

"What? Where?" Madison asked. She dared a look over her shoulder and groaned. In a city where people tried on relationships as easily as sweaters, Madison had worn more than her fair share.

"Shit!" she muttered, then eased down in her seat. Not that that would've made her less noticeable; at five-ten, a hundred and thirty-five pounds, skin the color of spiced cinnamon, and the face of a model, Madison was noticeable. Less than ten yards away was the man she had dated four months ago. She wouldn't even call it a relationship. Three dates: First was dinner, second was movie, then came playing finding the booty.

She grinned at the memory, but when she sneaked a second look, her heart nearly stopped. Next to him was Robert, whom she'd dated right before Keith. "Dammit, this city is getting too fucking small," she groaned and scooted farther down in her seat.

Lauren smirked at her friend's distress. She was wiggling faster than a fish caught in a net. "Weren't you dating Keith the same time you were dating Robert *and* Carlton? You and Keith were getting hot and heavy there for a minute. Wow, girl, what happened between you two? You never did tell us. Did you give him one of your breakup speeches?"

She fired the questions rapidly at her friend. Madison's breakup speeches were a running joke with the group. Madison cocked her head and gave her a blank look. "You know what? Maybe I should call him over and ask him. I'm sure Keith will spill the beans," Lauren teased, then motioned as if she was getting up.

"No!" Madison and LaShawn shouted at the same time. LaShawn glared at her friends. "Why can't we go out and have a good time? It's the same thing every time we go out, bicker, bicker, bicker. You guys fight worse than four-year-olds," she scolded. "You've always been like that. Remember that first yoga class?" Madison rolled her eyes in response. "Y'all fought over the yoga mats."

"It was my mat, I had just bought it. I had set it down for a second, then when I went to pick it up, Miss Sticky Fingers had taken it."

"It was *my* mat!" Lauren insisted.

"Stop it, you two!"

"I'm sorry. I guess we get carried away," Lauren said. "We'll be good," she promised, then reached into her purse and pulled out a white medicine bottle. Without glancing right or left, she flipped off the lid and popped two quarter-size pills in her mouth, which she quickly followed with a swallow of her martini.

Madison's love life was forgotten as LaShawn, Madison, and Blair shot furtive glances at one another. Madison raised her eyebrows at LaShawn, who jutted her chin at Blair. "What's wrong, sweetie? You sick or something?" Blair asked.

Lauren shook her head. "Not really, I've had this headache for a couple of weeks now and it won't go away," she answered, then glanced over at Madison, who had by now inched her way up in her seat, but was still occasionally glancing over her shoulder toward the bar.

"Oh Lord," LaShawn groaned, as she discreetly glanced down at her watch. It was getting late and she needed to call her fiancé for their nightly prayer session. "We all hope you feel better. Let's pray," she announced and bowed her head, thus missing the annoyed looks from her friends. "Heavenly Father," LaShawn began, "please free Lauren from her pain. Please take away her affliction so that she can walk through life with a clear and unencumbered mind and spirit. Fill her soul with peace and happiness. And please, Lord, bless everyone here tonight, especially Blair on her birthday. In Jesus' name we pray, amen," she finished.

Madison turned to LaShawn. "So how's Calvin doing? Did you finally decide to give him some?" she asked.

"Madison!" Lauren and Blair shrieked. LaShawn's decision to be celibate wasn't something they talked about. It was like crazy relatives. The whole family knew they existed, but they were never mentioned.

"What?" Madison asked, feigning innocence. "As if you guys weren't thinking it. Come on . . . do you really think she's gonna wait until the wedding night?" Blair and Lauren couldn't meet her eyes. Madison turned her attention back to LaShawn. "So?" she pressed.

LaShawn swallowed a retort. Three years ago when she walked in on her then fiancé, Troy, screwing his secretary on his office couch as though they were two rabbits on crack, she had dumped him. After that, she decided to wait until marriage before any man even got a glimpse of her goodies. There was only one force strong enough to make her keep her resolve: God.

"Calvin is fine, and my celibacy is fine," LaShawn answered prissily, but she breathed a little bit easier. She'd known Madison would get around to asking her about her sex life some time that evening, and at least now it was done and over with. Now they could move on to another topic.

Lauren shook her head at Madison before she looked across the table at LaShawn. "Hey, girl, how're the wedding plans? Is there anything we can help you with?"

LaShawn smiled brightly at the question. "Naw, everything is fine. My sister is a big help. I can't believe that in another six months I'll be Mrs. Calvin Worthy," she whispered dreamily.

Madison snickered and Lauren toed her, the pointy tip of her shoe digging into Madison's shin, Madison inhaled a short yelp. "Did you all get fitted for your dresses?" LaShawn asked nonchalantly, but she stared pointedly at Madison. Something told her Madison hadn't even tried on her bridesmaid dress. Lauren and Blair nodded and Madison mumbled under her breath. "What did you say, Maddy?"

"I'll do it next week," she said. Madison hated the bridesmaid dress. It was lemon colored with yards of ruffles and made her look like a canary. "So are we all going to yoga this week?" A chorus of protests went up. "Come on, y'all, don't be so lazy. Besides, where else can you touch your nose with your toes?" Madison quipped, then turned to LaShawn. "I bet that's something Calvin will be thanking you for on your honeymoon."

Just then Leonard traipsed over to their table, his wife Thomaseena at his side. She preferred to be called Thomas and dressed in men clothes.

"How are the finest ladies in Atlanta doing tonight?"

Leonard asked and smiled so brightly that it blanketed them all in its warmth.

"Hi, Miss Lenora!" they chorused together as they took in his appearance. His fingernails were polished a sultry red, his makeup rivaled any *Essence* magazine cover model, and he rocked his blond wig as though he had been born with it.

"I'm loving the shoes," Madison said as she admired the three-inch-heel, strappy stilettos.

"Thanks, gurl," Lenora gushed. "Outlet mall . . . let me know when y'all got time, we can roll up there. I'll show y'all where all the bargains are. But it all depends if Tommy lets me get away," he giggled and shot "Thomas" a coy look. She winked in response.

"Bet!" Madison smiled, but as soon as the couple was out of earshot, she turned to her friends. "I wonder who's the man in bed."

"Madison!" LaShawn reprimanded.

"I was kinda wondering that, too," Blair admitted, then turned to Madison since Lauren and LaShawn could care less. "Maybe they switch off."

"Maybe." Madison considered the idea. "Do you think that he dresses up in lingerie and stuff?"

Blair shrugged. "I bet he does . . . he's already in full drag." She glanced across the room at Leonard, who was greeting some customers. "Check out his makeup, it's fabulous."

"I know. Do you think Thomas uses a dil—"

"Okay, enough of this!" LaShawn hissed. "Can't you find something more enlightening to talk about? Why does it always have to be about sex with you, Madison?"

"It's not *always* about sex," Madison snapped. "I was just curious. And I bet you all are, too," she said, only to be met with silence. "Well, I'll stop talking about it then." She was quiet for a moment, then drawled, "Soooo, Blair, what are you and Rich doing for your birthday? Some horizontal action?" she teased, then gyrated her pelvis as if she was making love.

Blair reddened, drawing attention to her freckles, which looked like flecks of brown paint. "We're going to *Europe*," she said airily. "We're going to tour Rome. I can't wait. We were supposed to go ages ago, on our honeymoon, but you know how things happen. He said if we had time, we'll hop over to Paris." She shrugged nonchalantly, then stuffed a piece of her birthday cake in her mouth.

"Go 'head, Rich!" Lauren said. "I'm so jealous. Cleve and I haven't been on a real vacation in years. Between his business and my job we don't have the time. I wish we could get away," she said wistfully. "You two have the perfect marriage, the perfect house, and the perfect kids. You got it all, girl." Lauren sighed, then reached over and clasped Blair's hand.

Blair smiled weakly. "Oh, thanks. But I think *we* all have it all," she said, glancing around the table and then raising her cup. "We should make a toast." Blair cocked her head and studied her friends. Her green eyes flicked over the ladies she loved like sisters. Like her momma used to say, they were tighter than a gaggle of geese. "To our perfect lives," she murmured.

There was a moment's hesitation before a round of cheers went up. The friends shot furtive glances at one another before gulping down their drinks.

Chapter 2

Blair slid behind the wheel of her Volvo and began her drive home. "I'm such a liar. 'Oh, he's taking me to Rome,' " she said, mimicking her earlier comment. "Yeah, right!" She laughed bitterly. "I'd be lucky if he'd take me to Rome, *Georgia*. And what was 'hopping over to Paris if we have the time' all about?"

She glanced in her rearview mirror and was startled to see a pair of dull green eyes staring back at her. Her stomach lurched and she quickly shifted her gaze back to the road. "Perk it up!" she demanded. "It's your birthday!" she shouted. "And you're the prettiest, luckiest, and happiest lady in the whole wide world," she said, then grinned until her mouth hurt. "Yep, sweetie, keep telling yourself that and maybe you'll believe it," she muttered, and her smile faltered.

"At least I got my girls," she whispered and managed a genuine grin. The gifts from her friends were neatly packed in an oversize gift bag. It was all there: the edible strawberry-flavored panties from Madison, Susan Taylor's *In the Spirit* from Lauren, and a personalized Bible from LaShawn. Her happy feeling lasted until she got home, then it deflated like a boob job gone bad.

She pulled into the garage. The spot where Rich's Mercedes should've been was empty . . . again. She sighed and hurried into the house, where she was met by the roar of the TV and the sight of her children sprawled out like crash test dummies all over the living room. Five-year-old Ariel was on the floor, twelve-year-old Caitlyn blanketed the couch, and fourteen-year-old Richard hugged the chair. She clicked off the TV and began the cleanup.

"Everybody up!" Blair demanded, nudging them with her foot. "Go on up to your own bed!" she ordered and was met with cries of protests. "If you don't, you're gonna wake up tomorrow with kinks the size of boulders in your neck." Mumbling under their breath, they all sleepwalked upstairs to their bedrooms.

"Hola! You're home!" Maria, the housekeeper, hurried into the room. "They promised they were going right to bed, but you know how they are."

"No problem," Blair responded. "And I do know how they are."

"How was your birthday dinner?" she asked slyly. Blair always kept Maria up-to-date on her friends' lives, which were better than *Guiding Light,* especially Madison's.

"It was nice," Blair answered in a distracted tone. "So where's my hubby? Did he call?" Blair asked, her green eyes wide and expectant. Maria shook her head no. Blair slumped a little and Maria's heart hurt for her.

"I'm sure he'll be home soon," Maria optimistically offered.

"Yeah," Blair answered sadly. Maria, sensing her distress, offered to fix them both a cup of herbal tea, but Blair waved her away. "Won't Jorge be waiting for you?" Blair asked.

"We've been married for ten years. He can wait another hour or two."

"Well, it's settled." Blair made herself comfortable in one of the kitchen chairs and watched while Maria moved around the room.

Minutes later Maria placed the steaming cups of tea on the table. "So what did your friends get you for your birthday?" she asked, curious. Blair filled her in and Maria roared. "That sounds just like your friends," she said and Blair readily agreed. They were silent as they sipped their tea.

"He wasn't always like this," Blair said softly. "When we first got married he got me 'just because' gifts. Every day there was something special on my dresser waiting for me. And when I had the children, you would've thought they were solid gold the way he carried on. He lavished me with diamonds, gold jewelry, and designer gowns . . . he's changed. Now he's hardly home. I bet the kids were trying to stay up to see him."

"He's a hardworking man," Maria offered weakly.

"He shouldn't be working so goddamn hard that he forgets my birthday," Blair retorted hotly, then set down her teacup. "Has Jorge ever forgotten your birthday?" she asked.

"Once. And I'll tell you, it didn't happen ever again," Maria answered and Blair quirked an eyebrow. "We had just started dating," Maria began. "And everything was wonderful." She smiled at the memory. "So on my birthday, me and my friends were expecting Jorge to do something romantic. So that morning when I didn't hear from him, I wasn't worried. I just thought he was going to do something in the afternoon. He didn't. By nine o'clock I hadn't heard anything from him, and I tell you, I was heated. The very next day, I broke up with him and started dating his cousin, Jose. For three months Jorge didn't exist to me."

"Oh no! What did he do?"

Maria grinned. "What didn't he do? He started courting me again. I tell you, he was like a bitch in heat. And you know what?" Maria asked, and Blair shook her head. "I made him cry like a bitch, and he came crawling back to me," she bragged. "He hasn't forgotten my birthday since. And he'd better not, he knows better. Jose lives just around the corner from us," she joked.

They laughed and talked a little more. When Maria thought that Blair felt a little better, she left.

Blair pretended to be asleep when her husband crept in at two o'clock in the morning, pulled off his clothing, crawled into bed beside her, and drew her to his side. Can I make Rich cry like a bitch? she fumed silently.

Chapter 3

Madison slowly navigated her Lexus through her subdivision, cruising past quarter-million-dollar houses whose owners were her age or younger. Her headlights splayed over professionally manicured lawns, brick homes, and an occasional Jaguar or Mercedes.

Never in her wildest dreams did she think the little girl from upstate New York would be living large; getting *the* job offer of a lifetime and moving to Atlanta turned out to be the best thing that ever happened to her. And the fact that her auntie and cousins were already happily settled in Atlanta was the ultimate cherry on top.

Nestled in a cul-de-sac, her four-bedroom brick house was the largest in the subdivision. With its white shutters and doors and velvety brown bricks it looked like an over-size gingerbread house. Getting her MBA had bigger dividends than she had ever imagined.

"Not bad for a nappy-headed girl from Buffalo. You did very well for yourself, young lady," Madison said, chuckling mirthlessly. The stress and embarrassment of seeing her exes had worn off like a bad hangover, leaving a dull ache. "Girl . . . one day you're gonna get into a whole lot of trouble. But they're gonna have to catch you first."

She pulled her Lexus into the garage. Designed for two cars, the garage's other half was filled with items from the past. Last year's Christmas tree, boxed-up clothes that needed to go to the Salvation Army, and dozens of unopened cans of dog food from six months ago when she got the urge to buy a puppy, but changed her mind when she realized how much work it would be.

She stared at the mess, wondering how to get out of her car without scratching the door. Taking a deep breath, she inched the door open and eased out backward, butt first. "Mission accomplished," she said, and grinned once she was standing in the garage. Her smile of accomplishment lasted until she spied the slice of birthday cake on her front seat.

"Crap!" she muttered, breathed deeply, reversed her steps, grabbed the cake, then slammed the door shut. "I really need to clean out this garage—ooooh!" The garden hose had caught her heel; she pitched forward and before she knew it she was kissing the cement floor. "Double crap! I *really* need to clean up this booby trap!" She groaned as she kicked off her pumps and gently massaged her right ankle. Instinct told her that it wasn't sprained, but it hurt like hell.

Next to her was the birthday cake. She slipped the box's top open and peered inside to see that it had stayed intact during the fall. "You'll go perfect with a glass of white wine," she murmured, eyeing the cake in anticipation. Clutching her shoes and with the cake box tucked under her arm, she pulled herself up, then tested her ankle before hobbling into her house.

Tossing the pumps into a growing pile of shoes next to the door, she reached out and felt the wall for the light switch. Instead of the switch she connected with something soft and fleshy. It grunted and Madison let out an ear-splitting scream.

Chapter 4

LaShawn stepped into her modest apartment and turned the deadbolt. Her place was smaller than she wanted, a one-bedroom with a thumbtack-size living room, but it was the right price. With what she was saving on rent, she was able to sock away an extra eight hundred dollars a month toward the wedding-and-new-house fund. So far, her bank account had swollen to twenty thousand dollars.

Where's Calvin? she wondered as she went over to the window and pulled back the curtains to peer worriedly into the night. He had promised to stop by. Three phone calls to his home and five to his cell phone turned up nothing. He was another brother MIA. Turning away from the window, she took the five steps necessary to walk through her living room and into her bedroom. This was the third time this week that he had missed their nightly prayer session.

They had met two years ago at Bank of America, the guardians of her money; he was keeping guard over the building. Early into their relationship he wooed her with surprise picnics, dates to the drive-in, and impromptu trips to the mall.

He showered her with so many compliments that she was convinced that he couldn't sleep if he didn't hear her voice before he went to bed. And best of all he had signed on with her decision to be celibate, stating simply that she was worth the wait.

What's going on with him? she mused. Settling on her bed, she dialed his number and immediately got his voice-mail.

"Whadup, y'all. This is Calvin. I'm not here right now, or maybe I am and don't want to talk to you, but you know what to do . . . later!" LaShawn left a quick message for him to call her, then hung up.

LaShawn gave the telephone one last look before reaching for her great-grandmother's Bible. She lovingly kissed it before peeling it open to her favorite verse.

For forty minutes she read about serving Him and the words filled her spirit and cleared her mind. It wasn't until her eyelids started drooping that she set the Bible on the nightstand.

She pulled off her knee-length skirt and long-sleeve blouse and headed into the shower. Fifteen minutes later, she made her way back to her bedroom and knelt on the side of the bed and prayed.

As soon as she said "amen," she guiltily walked over to the closet and reached to the top shelf to pull out an old tattered shoebox. Out of the box came the paperback, filled with erotic stories, and her lubricating gel. A blissful expression came over her face while her body shivered with anticipation. Floating across the room, she settled on the bed in her favorite position. Once she was on her back with her legs splayed wide open, she quickly glazed her fingers with the gel. With the book in her left hand, her right hand automatically drifted to her clit.

Flipping through the pages, she came to her favorite piece, a ménage à trois, involving two men and one woman. Her mouth formed a small O and her eyelids became slits as the cool gel connected with her hot spot. Her fingers, slick with her juices and gel, roamed gently through her soft folds. Soft whimpers escaped through her parted lips as she read the familiar story. Her hips rocked up and down with her fingers.

Before she could finish the story, the book fell from her hand and she reached up and began stroking her breasts. It was as though she had a private lover. Her hand danced over her breasts like gentle kisses, caressing, fondling, and rubbing them until her nipples became hardened bits of chocolate.

She moaned softly as she tenderly inserted her finger and her hips swirled slowly. Suddenly her fingers breezed over her clit and she gasped out loud at the pleasure and her back arched. Her hips moved up and down as if pulled by an invisible lover. When the climax came, it was long and hard. She gasped as her body shuddered and her toes tingled. Her eyes suddenly widened in embarrassment and she turned her face into the pillow.

Chapter 5

Lauren padded into her bedroom and found her husband, Cleve, in his usual position, stretched out on their king-size bed with his laptop computer. She always teased him that one day his body was going to lock up in that position and she would have to take over his computer consulting business.

"Were the kids okay?" She had peeked in on them as soon as she had gotten in and found them sleeping harder than two extra firm mattresses.

He continued to peck at the keyboard and didn't bother to look up. "Oh . . . they were fine," he answered absentmindedly.

"Oh really? I would like to see that. You sure we're talking about the same two children?" she asked, surprise in her voice. At twelve and ten they weren't bad, but they hardly qualified for the Kids of the Year Award.

"Hey, how're the girls?" he asked in a dry voice, expecting the standard "they're fine" response, but Lauren surprised him.

"Maddy was being extra mean tonight. Acting like she

wanted to beat up the world. I hope she's okay." She worried about Madison; not that she'd ever tell Madison that. "LaShawn was LaShawn, Bible and all. She was excited about her wedding." Cleve glanced up from the computer and watched his wife as she undressed. Off came the red power suit, stockings, and bra, then the jewelry, leaving her wearing a pair of plain white cotton drawers.

"I wish you would get some decent panties," Cleve muttered. "Why don't you wear the ones I got you for your birthday? You'd look good in them."

Lauren shook her head. The pair of eye patches that Cleve called panties were teeny enough for her daughter to wear. "Floss really should be used for your teeth . . . not your butt," she retorted, but with little steam; the day was catching up with her.

Today had turned out to be one of those days that made her feel as though she was on a nonstop roller coaster. Being vice president of public relations for a Fortune 500 company was the job she had dreamed of ever since she graduated from Spelman. After ten years of fighting off backstabbing coworkers and sacrificing time with her family, the title was hers, and she wore it the same way a soldier wears his uniform, with dignity, pride, and a touch of arrogance.

She scooped up a pair of ratty sweatpants and a T-shirt and threw them on. Then came her laptop, her third hand. "Rich is taking Blair to Europe for her birthday. I'm *so* jealous. When was our last vacation?" she asked as she slid into bed and plopped the computer onto her lap.

Just as Cleve powered off his laptop, Lauren turned hers on. Jumping out of bed, Cleve started to remove his clothes. He was six-foot-five, the color of watered-down mustard, with a muscled body that would cause a twenty-six-year-old man to double his weight-lifting routine. "Last year . . . in Milwaukee, for my family reunion," he answered before sliding into bed next to his wife.

"You call that a vacation? That was pure hell. A week with your family . . ." her voice trailed off. "I mean a *real* vacation, just the two of us, no kids, no Uncle Hezekiah, and no family members trying to wear us down for a loan. It would be nice . . ." she said wistfully.

Before Cleve could answer, she bent over her laptop and all thoughts of a romantic vacation were forgotten. A marketing agreement was due tomorrow and she hadn't even begun working on it. Her fingers were flying over the keyboard when she felt Cleve's hand caressing her thigh.

"Cleve!" she protested. "I really need to get this done, it's due tomorrow," she murmured and gently pushed his hand away.

"I'll do it really fast," Cleve reassured her.

"Honey," she cajoled. "I'm really tired, I can barely keep my eyes open, and this needs to get done. Why don't we make plans to do it this weekend? We can spend all day Saturday in bed."

"I can't wait until then . . . I want you now," he pleaded as he slipped his hand underneath her T-shirt and began stroking her breasts. "You don't even have to move," he promised, then tugged at her pants.

"Take your hands off me! This really needs to get done tonight!" she barked and Cleve's hand froze, then he yanked it away. Squaring off like two heavyweight boxers, they glared wordlessly at each other, each wondering when their marriage had been reduced to this.

Chapter 6

"Dad?" Madison squeaked when she finally found her breath. Staring at her with a sheepish grin was her some-times dad. Ever since she was a little girl, he'd drop into her life whenever he needed something. Madison stepped back and peered up at him. At six foot six, one hundred and ninety pounds, and shrouded in Rocawear, he looked more like her older brother than her father. She quickly scanned his face. Whatever he needed this time must be a doozy; he was wearing the shamed look of someone who had farted in the middle of church service.

Neither made a move to hug the other. Madison frowned and crossed her arms over her chest. "What are you doing here?" she asked harshly.

Lucius stared at his daughter, who looked like she was two minutes away from kicking him out on the street. "What's wrong, baby girl? Can't a father visit his daughter?"

"How did you even get in here?" She had changed the locks after his last visit.

The sheepish look returned. "I remembered where you hid your spare key," he admitted.

"That wasn't a goddamn community key! Don't you ever—"

"Thank you for letting us stay here."

Madison jumped and turned toward the voice.

"I'm Mosaquiema, Moe for short. You have a very beautiful home," she answered in a voice so cultured that it left Madison speechless. In the past her father's friends ranged from forty-year-old ex-convicts to twenty-year-old strippers. Moe, who was staring wide-eyed around Madison's house as though she had died and ended up in P. Diddy's crib, looked like a person barely grasping the straws of sophistication, despite her fancy drawl.

Her hundred-dollar designer jeans were so tight that she looked like all the air had been sucked from her legs and pumped into her stomach. Her spiky haircut, which tried hard to mimic Halle Berry circa early 1990s, made her look like a rooster instead. And her artistically but caked-on makeup made her thirty-something face look like a *Glamour* don't.

"Umm, thanks, I like it," Madison muttered as her anger simmered to irritation. She glanced down. Her slice of cake had fallen out of the box and was lying in a pile in the middle of her floor.

Her father caught her looking at the now-ruined dessert. "Baby girl, I'm sorry about the cake. I'll buy you a whole one. What kind was it?" he asked, but both of them knew that he wasn't going to replace it.

"Carrot," she mumbled, playing along. Madison shook her head, then busied herself with cleaning up the cake.

She crooked her finger and pointed to the kitchen table. "Whassup?"

"We're here to visit Moe's people. Yep, down in the A-T-L, where the playas play."

Madison shook her head; he was never going to grow up. "How did you get here? I didn't see a car when I drove up."

"Her brother, Coot, dropped us off. He got some business to take care of, but he should be rolling through here in a little while to scoop us up."

Coot? Madison bit her tongue. Instead she asked, "How long do you plan on staying?"

"Not long, a week . . . or two," he stuttered, then sneaked a peek at her reaction. Seeing Madison's neutral expression, he felt safe enough to turn to Moe and say, "Didn't I tell you my little girl was da bomb?" Moe yawned loudly. "You tired?" he asked and fussed over her as if she was a child. "I'll be right back," he said to Madison as he practically carried Moe up the stairs to the guest bedroom. Madison could hear him noisily tucking her in, their laughter wafting down to the kitchen.

While her father was upstairs, Madison pulled two beers out of the refrigerator for them. She was sitting at the table, arms crossed and ready for answers, when he ambled into the room. It wasn't until he demolished his third beer that he announced why he had come.

"She's pregnant. And I don't want the baby," he stated before he popped open the fourth beer.

Chapter 7

Blair was standing at the stove, putting the finishing touches on dinner when Rich strolled into the kitchen, twirled her around, and kissed her cheek. Blair laughed softly, as her lips melted against her husband's. The pain from her forgotten birthday was long gone; he'd sent four-dozen long-stemmed red roses to her the day after, and all was forgiven.

She quickly scanned her husband of fourteen years. He looked the same as he did in college. Six foot two, one hundred ninety-five pounds, curly hair so black it glistened, and a smile so devastating that if the receiver wasn't prepared, she'd swoon. Just like she did the first time she'd seen him, on her first day of college.

He and half the football team had rumbled past her like an avalanche, but he paused long enough to toss her his crotch-warming smile.

Later that week she had found a single long-stemmed rose along with his name and phone number propped against her dorm room door.

During their college years he had wined, dined, and sexed her so well that just the mention of his name got her wet. Blair sighed softly at the memory, then she refocused on Rich. She tilted her head to the right; something wasn't right. It took her half a minute to figure out what it was.

She lightly stroked his chest. "Hon . . . you weren't wearing this shirt when you went to work this morning . . . what happened?"

"I was wearing it," Rich answered easily.

"No, you weren't," Blair argued. "You wore your light blue with the white pin-stripes. I remember because you asked me to help you find your cuff links."

"Umm, yeah," Rich said, then smacked his forehead. "I spilled coffee on it, that's what happened. Bob and I went out to lunch and I splashed coffee on it. Then I ran over to Macy's and got a new one. This one." He grinned and pointed to his shirt.

"Oh." She turned her back to him and picked up a big wooden spoon and began stirring the pot of spaghetti sauce. "So what happened to the one with the coffee stains?" she asked softly.

"Mmmm, I threw it away," he said, grinning sheepishly. "It didn't make sense to keep it . . . it being stained and all."

"I could've washed it for you," Blair squeezed out, between clenched lips.

"You do way too much around here as it is," Rich answered. He had snuck up behind her and began kissing her favorite spot, right between her shoulder blades and the nape of her neck. Her body automatically relaxed against his.

Rich pulled away and turned her around so that they faced each other. "I didn't bring home any work tonight," he winked and Blair blushed. "I'll go see what the kids are up to," he said, then gave her a heated stare. "Mrs. Ricci, after dinner you're all mine," he promised.

Blair giggled, but as soon as he turned away, her eyes narrowed as she watched him saunter out of the kitchen, her eyes on his new shirt. Her only thought: *Why couldn't you bring home the dirty one?*

Chapter 8

LaShawn stuffed a forkful of lettuce in her mouth and chomped down so hard that her teeth rattled. The night wasn't going the way she had planned. Instead of being bathed in soft candlelight, she was drowning in harsh fluorescent lights. Instead of being wooed by the sensual sounds of jazz, she was being assaulted by misogynistic rap. Worst of all, instead of being romanced by the love of her life, she was becoming nauseated. Her night of romance had turned into a night of a hundred horrible jokes. Sitting across from her was the culprit, Malcolm Bowers, Calvin's best friend.

Malcolm personified everything LaShawn despised in a man. He lacked education, couth, intelligence, and ambition.

She snatched up a roll and slathered it with butter. Neither Calvin nor Malcolm noticed when she groaned loudly and slouched in her chair. They were too busy guessing the waitress's bra size. Her jaw dropped with amazement when Malcolm called her over, and it nearly hit the floor when Calvin egged him on.

LaShawn silently regarded her fiancé while slowly chewing her bread. I'm watching a Dr. Jekyll and Mr. Hyde show, she thought. It never failed; whenever Malcolm came around Calvin's personality changed faster than Atlanta's weather. Before Malcolm's arrival Calvin was the perfect gentleman. An hour ago, before Malcolm joined them, Calvin had held her hand and looked deeply into her eyes as they talked about their wedding day. Now he acted as though she was an irritating rash.

Malcolm sneered when LaShawn blurted out an excuse and practically ran to the ladies' room. After reapplying her lipstick and whispering a soft prayer for strength and understanding, she walked calmly across the restaurant and slid into her seat.

Calvin kissed her cheek, then turned his attention back to Malcolm, who was voicing his admiration for a lady sitting across the restaurant. It took LaShawn one glance to determine the woman was out of Malcolm's reach as everything about her yelled class, starting with her Kenneth Cole shoes and her Prada suit. She was in an animated conversation with her dinner mate, an equally sophisticated lady, and she definitely looked too smart to fall for any of Malcolm's stuff.

"Stop dreaming. You can't get that," Calvin joked, and LaShawn couldn't resist snickering.

"The hell I can't," Malcolm responded as he glared at LaShawn. "Malc can get any woman he wants," he bragged.

"Yeah, right!" Calvin scoffed. "She's so far out of your league that you gotta have ten jobs just to sniff her perfume."

"Well, I can be a working mofo." Malcolm laughed, then his tone turned serious. "Wanna bet?" he challenged.

"Would you guys stop! You're being silly. Let's just finish eating," LaShawn softly pleaded. "Besides, it looks like she's having a good time . . . why ruin her dinner?" Then as if to prove LaShawn's point, a round of laughter exploded from the lady's table.

"Oops, my bad. Your fiancée said no." Malcolm smirked, then, "Aw, damn you dropped something." Malcolm made a big show of getting out of his chair and bending at Calvin's feet.

Calvin's eyes widened with confusion as he peered down at his friend. "No, I didn't, maybe Shawn did."

"Yeah, you did . . . your dick!" Malcolm screamed and broke out in hysterical laughter. He picked up the imaginary appendage and threw it at Calvin.

"Naw, quit joking. It ain't like that!" Calvin muttered, frowning. "I'm in!" Calvin answered and LaShawn sucked her teeth so hard that she dislodged a piece of lettuce. She stared angrily at Malcolm. Her hands slid to her lap for her Bible, but then she remembered she'd left it in Calvin's truck. "What are you willing to lose?"

Malcolm considered the question, then grinned slowly and said, "A hundred bucks."

"Bet!"

"A hundred bucks!" LaShawn shrieked. Calvin needed to start saving money for their wedding; so far he hadn't contributed a penny to the fund. She grabbed Calvin's arm. "Calvin, that's too much money. What about our wedding?"

Calvin shrugged her hands off. "It's all right. There's no way possible that Malcolm gonna be able to pull that. You'll see. I just made an extra hundred dollars for your wedding fund."

LaShawn watched in disgust as Malcolm swiped a napkin over his bald head, checked his breath, then sauntered across the restaurant to the lady. Her disgust turned to fascination as the lady smiled and invited him to join her and her friend.

It took him less than ten minutes to find out her name, her profession, her marital status, whether she had kids, and her home and work numbers.

"Man, you got my props. Whassup? How did you do it?" Calvin asked, impressed, then slipped his friend a Benjamin when he returned to the table. LaShawn gulped back her protest.

"Easy, man, it was easy," Malcolm drawled. "You gotta speak their language."

"Word?"

"Yeah, man! Right off I noticed that she was a professional woman, so I had to approach her from that angle. Basically I just told her what she wanted to hear." Calvin smiled. "You know what I'm talking about. With the professional ladies, it's all about your JAC: your job, your abode, and your car. Then you got to put it on hard and tell them that you're tired of dating, that you're looking for a good woman, blah blah blah blah blah," he said and chuckled nastily.

LaShawn shook her head, appalled. She had enough of this, of Malcolm, his uncouth behavior, and most of all how Calvin's behavior changed whenever he and Malcolm were within ten feet of each other. She leaned toward her fiancé and hissed in his ear, "I'm ready to go."

Calvin glared at her, a look not lost on Malcolm. "Come on, Shawn." He glanced at his watch; it was only eleven o'clock. "It's still early, let's hang out for a minute. Besides, how often do I get to hang out with my boy and my fiancée at the same time?" he asked. Then Calvin grinned at her and her heart melted.

"Too often," LaShawn muttered. Fortunately her comment was drowned out by the rap music.

"I'm—not—ready—to—go—yet," Calvin said, emphasizing each word as though LaShawn was hard of hearing.

"Go on, man," Malcolm said, waving them off. LaShawn gave a satisfied smile, which quickly dropped at Malcolm's next words. "We'll hook up later tonight."

She shot a glance at Calvin; he hadn't mentioned that to her. She gritted her teeth and said, "Let's all gather hands and pray for a safe ride home." She bowed her head and reached out for Calvin's and Malcolm's hands.

Malcolm raised his eyebrows at Calvin, who averted his eyes, then reached for his fiancée's hand.

"Why do you have to be so mean?" Calvin asked as soon as they got into his truck. "All Malc was doing was being Malc. I guess Miss Goody Two-shoes is too good to have some fun." He sneered while he spoke, wondering what happened to the lady he had fallen in love with. The one who had always encouraged him to not only shoot for the stars, but to aspire to be one in his own world.

LaShawn flinched. He knew that she hated that nickname. "What's wrong with us? We were having such a good time before Malcolm came. This is like the third argument we had this week. And they were all over stupid stuff."

"Well, I'm not keeping count. But, yeah, you're right, they're all over stupid shit!"

"Calvin!" LaShawn warned.

"What's wrong, because I said 'shit'? Well, shit! Shit! Shit!" he said with satisfaction, tired at having to hold his tongue around her. She's worse than my mother, Calvin fumed to himself. He took his eyes off the road long enough to see LaShawn staring straight ahead with her lips pursed tightly. "Come on, baby, don't be so uptight," he softly pleaded. "It's just a word."

"Yeah, a bad word."

"A bad word? What are you . . . five years old? Come on, Shawn. It's not that serious. It's not like I'm calling you a piece of shit or something."

"It's a vulgar word, regardless of how you use it. And I don't like vulgarity in any shape, manner, or form," she said prissily. "So don't do it in my presence."

Calvin shook his head and didn't respond. The rest of the ride to LaShawn's apartment was made in silence. Being the gentleman that he sometimes was, Calvin escorted LaShawn to her apartment, gave her a chaste peck on the lips, then escaped to an evening with Malcolm.

Chapter 9

"Mom, aren't you ready yet?" C.J. Hopson whined as he barreled into the kitchen, nearly tripping over their dog, Bart. He stopped directly in front of Lauren, just in time to avoid a collision. "I need to be at school early today, they're—"

"They're picking the pitcher for the softball team," Lauren finished. C.J. had reminded her of that fact every day for the last two weeks; she'd be crazy if she'd forgotten. "I know, honey, I didn't forget." She didn't have to look up from her sewing to see C.J. frowning at the endearment, but she couldn't help it. He was her little man, her firstborn. Lauren struggled to push the sewing needle through the thick nylon strap on her daughter's book bag. It had broken yesterday, and she'd warned Debbie over and over again about overstuffing it. But she was hardheaded, just like her father. "Do you have karate practice today? Or soccer?" she asked, shaking her head and suddenly it felt like the room was spinning.

She also had a mind-numbing pounding in her head,

and she felt as though she was going to topple over. She closed her eyes and took deep breaths; it didn't ease the headache, but stopped the dizziness. "I can't keep your and your sister's schedules straight," she said.

C.J. grinned. "I have soccer practice. May I have some more pancakes? Dad isn't even down here yet," he said. He didn't wait for a response before pulling open the oven door for the plate of pancakes that Lauren had warming for her husband.

"C.J., you've already eaten three pancakes, save some for your father," she admonished. She looked up from her sewing to find two pancakes swimming in syrup and a bite missing from each. Lauren opened her mouth to scold him, but bit her tongue instead. At twelve years old C.J. was a husky kid and still growing. The doctor assured her that he was going through an awkward stage, and everything was going to fall into place, just as long as he continued playing sports.

"Lauren!" Cleve shouted from the top of the stairs. "I left my proposal right here," he said, pointing to the table on the landing. "Where is it? I can't tell them that the dog ate it, can I?" he joked.

Lauren sighed and stabbed the needle through the nylon material. Cleve had a short memory. "You sure can't, especially since you're the president of the company. You read it last night in bed, *remember?*"

"That's right!" Cleve said, and he adjusted his suspenders, then retraced his steps to their bedroom. "Thanks," he called over his shoulder. "Lauren?"

"Yes, Cleve?"

"What did you make for breakfast this morning?"

"Pancakes, grits, eggs, and link sausage. The same thing I make every day," she grumbled under her breath.

"Cool, can you fix me a plate and bring it up to me? It'll save me time while I do some work on my laptop."

Lauren's jaw dropped. She was already late for work. "Sure!" she yelled back.

"Lauren!"

"Yes, Cleve!"

"Can you iron my gray pin-striped shirt? I don't like the one I have on. I need something with a little more pizzazz."

"It's already pressed, I picked it up from the cleaners yesterday!" she answered. There were more than a dozen of his dress shirts hanging in the closet, still wrapped in plastic.

"You know I don't like the way they do it. I like the way you do it better, you add that special touch of love to your ironing."

Lauren's hand went to her throbbing head. "Please Lord, give me strength. I'll do it," she weakly agreed.

Her ten-year-old daughter, Debbie, bounced into the kitchen, lost in an oversize sweatshirt that skimmed her meatless thighs and narrow behind. When she saw her book bag in her mother's lap, she jutted her chin at the knapsack as if it was a secondhand castoff. "I'm not going to carry that," she pouted.

"Yes, you are," Lauren calmly stated while keeping an eye on her work.

"No, I'm not!"

"Yes—you—are," Lauren bit out while fixing her daughter with a glare that would even have Hillary Clinton shaking in her pumps.

"No—" Debbie halted at the look her mother gave her.

"Finish your breakfast, then feed the dog," Lauren instructed. "And what are you wearing?" she asked Debbie, who looked like she was dress rehearsing to be a teenage prostitute.

"A sweatshirt," Debbie mumbled, dipping her head, then tugging on the sweatshirt as if she could stretch it to cover her knees.

"What do you have on underneath it?"

"Shorts," Debbie muttered.

"Shorts?" Lauren repeated, incredulously. "Shorts? Girl, you'd better take your butt upstairs right now and put on some *real* clothes."

"Aw, Mom!" Debbie whined. *Everybody* was supposed to wear big sweatshirts. *She* had organized it all yesterday during lunch.

"Debbie, go change! Then feed Bart."

"No way!" Debbie shouted. "It's C.J.'s turn," she wailed, and glared at her older brother. She wasn't afraid of him, he was older but she was taller.

"Nu-uh. I fed him last night."

"Like right. Daddy fed him for you," Debbie argued.

"He helped me out," C.J. said, then stuck his tongue out at his younger sister.

Before Debbie could retaliate, Lauren hissed, "Would you both just shut up!" Her children froze and turned to her in amazement. C.J.'s eyes widened to twice their size and his sister's mouth turned into a grotesque circle. Their mother never, ever raised her voice, not even when C.J. cursed his teacher and was suspended for a whole week from school. Their daddy spanked him so hard that he swore he'd never sit down again and all their mother did was tuck him in bed and caution him about how words are good and bad. But she *didn't* yell at him.

"I'm sorry," Lauren said, bending over the book bag to cut a loose thread. "Why don't *both* of you feed Bart. Debbie, I want you to put on some proper clothes." The pain in her head was banging behind her right eye. Debbie and C.J. both mumbled something that sounded like "sure" and hurried out of the kitchen, each looking back at their mother as if she'd suddenly gone crazy.

She wanted to call her children back and apologize again. She never yelled at the kids, and rarely yelled at all. The book bag and Cleve's breakfast were forgotten as Lauren massaged her temples; the knot of pain shifted over to her forehead, forming a painful band that stretched to both her ears. She went over to the cupboard and pulled out a bottle of aspirin and dropped four in her hand, then chucked them into her mouth and swallowed them dry, the same way she'd been taking them for the past couple of months. The telephone rang and it felt like someone had pulled the band and snapped it against her forehead.

"Hello," she muttered, wondering if a ringing phone was ever used as a torture method for prisoners, because it felt like someone had squeezed her head like a sponge.

"Hey, Lor!"

Lauren smiled, her headache momentarily forgotten; it was her younger sister, Maryann. Her soft Southern drawl hid the fact that she was a phenomenal lawyer. "Hey, Sissy."

"Hey, Miz VP of Public Relations," Maryann teased. "What's going on?"

"Gurl," Lauren started. "It's *already one of those* days, and I'm not even two coffee cups into it," she sighed. "Deb wants to go to school half-naked, C.J. doesn't want to listen, and Cleve is a six-foot-five baby," she finally finished.

"I'm sorry, want me to call back?" Maryann clucked sympathetically, but she had her fingers crossed.

"Nu-uh, what's up?" Lauren asked, glancing at the clock. She was running I'm-going-to-have-to-play-catch-up-with-my-work late.

"Can you watch the kids tonight? I have to meet with a client and Matthew is out of town *again*."

"I *guess*," Lauren said, deflated. She had had her evening all planned out. She was going to spend some time working with C.J. on his Boy Scouts project, finish a newsletter, then head down to her studio and do some painting. She almost felt the brush in her hand and the sensuous movements of her arms in motion. Now, with her niece and nephew staying over, she'd have to abandoned the painting.

"Oh, yeah," Maryann continued as if she just had a sudden revelation, "can you pick them up from school, too?"

"Maryann! That's way on the other side of town," Lauren protested. "They're going to have to wait at least forty-five minutes before I can get them."

"Don't worry about the time," Maryann smoothly interjected. "I've already made arrangements for a teacher to keep an eye on them."

Lauren tucked the phone between her shoulder and neck and reached into the cabinet for the bottle of aspirin, then dropped two more in her mouth. "You've got everything taken care of. You just knew that I was going to do it, huh?" Lauren asked.

Her sarcasm went right over her sister's head. "So you're going to pick them up, right?" she asked.

"Yeah, I'll take care of them, but you'd better pick them up at a decent hour. Or I'm going to deliver them to your doorstep," Lauren threatened.

"Umm," Maryann hedged, "can they spend the night? I don't know when my meeting is going to end, it could go way past midnight."

"Maryann! What kind of meeting are you having? Hell, I'm a vice president at a Fortune 500 company and I've never had a meeting last past six p.m.!" Lauren yelled.

"We have this humongous merger going on and the clients are flying in from the West Coast. Their plane won't land until three o'clock . . ." She trailed off, then suddenly her voice regained its power. "Pleeeeeeze!" Maryann begged. "There's no one else I can call. Pleeeeeeze!" she repeated.

Humph! Her sister was full of it. She knew that the kids could spend the night at her in-laws—but that would've meant that Maryann would actually have to have the kids fed and armed with a clean change of clothing, something that she didn't have to worry about if her sister babysat, because she knew that Lauren would take care of everything.

"You'd better be on your knees," Lauren said half-jokingly.

"I am," Maryann said and held her breath as her sister considered her request.

"Okay, they can spend the night. You owe me—big time!" They talked a little bit more before hanging up. As soon as she clicked off the phone, it rang again.

"I told you I'll do it," Lauren said and laughed into the phone.

"Lauren?"

Oh crap! Lauren frowned; it was her boss, Susan Lords, a.k.a. the Bitch. "I'm sorry, I thought you were someone else," she answered crisply.

"Obviously," Susan replied condescendingly. "Do you plan on coming in today?"

"I am," Lauren answered. "I'm running a little late," she said and chuckled nervously. "The family—"

"I understand," Susan replied, slicing into her excuse. "I really need you here. Last night Ferguson got arrested."

"Ummm," Lauren mumbled. She had always thought he was a little weird. "Let me guess: He got caught with his hand in the cookie jar. What's the rap?"

"It's a big deal. He was arrested for soliciting underage boys."

Shit! "Can't somebody else cover it? As a matter of fact, I have a press release on file from two years ago when Randall got caught smuggling drugs over the border. All we have to do is change the names and situation, then we'll be all set. See, problem solved," she said, then heaved a sigh of release.

As much as she loved her job, there were times when all she wanted to do was take every press release, the company prospectus, and all the crazy employees, and chuck them all into the Atlantic Ocean. As vice president of public relations, she sometimes felt like the world's most underpaid babysistter. Her six-figure salary was hardly enough to make up for all the shit she dealt with daily.

"No . . . that won't do! I want you here. The TV stations have been sniffing around and I bet my momma's ass that they're gonna want a statement. So make sure your makeup looks good."

"Susan," Lauren whimpered, and she didn't care that she sounded like C.J. Her head felt like it was going to explode. She tucked the phone between her shoulder and neck and again reached into the cabinet for the bottle of aspirin, and dropped two more in her mouth.

"I'll see you in an hour," Susan barked, before hanging up the phone.

Chapter 10

Blair stared at the half-empty condom box. She had thrown it on the kitchen table after finding it in Rich's car two hours ago and had been looking at it ever since. She unconsciously rubbed her stomach. What had started as a nervous tickle had snaked its way up and twisted her insides. A bottle of Pepto-Bismol sat in the cupboard, less than six feet away, but she was too upset to get up. Just then Maria sauntered into the kitchen carrying a bag of groceries.

"*Buenas tardes.* What's going on?" she asked, nodding toward the condoms. "Are the kids gonna get a lesson in sex education?" she joked.

Blair shook her head. "No," she replied. "I—um—found them in Rich's car."

"Oh shit!" Maria replied as she started unpacking the food.

"Yeah, oh shit!" Blair repeated sadly. "The car was making funny noises so Rich asked me to take it to the dealer. I didn't know that when they asked me for the maintenance records I'd be finding those in the glove compartment." She pointed toward the condoms as though they were a bomb. "We never, ever use condoms. We're married, for Pete's sake. And then not even before we were married; Rich always said that he liked to feel me. And that's how I ended up with my firstborn. I don't understand what they're doing in Rich's car. Do you think one of his friends left them?" she asked, her voice hopeful.

Blair turned to the lady whom she thought of as an aunt. Their working arrangement spanned nearly a decade and Blair considered Maria a friend more than an employee.

Maria shook her head as she continued putting away the groceries. "Maybe," she offered vaguely.

Blair walked over to the kitchen counter and eyed three dozen cupcakes that she had spent the afternoon baking for her daughter's bake sale. "Yeah, I bet that's it. It was probably Mark in accounting. He always struck me as a little shady. And he's always leering at me, making my skin crawl. Yep, I bet it was Mark," she concluded and the knots in her stomach loosened a little. "Well, if that was the case, why didn't he just throw them away?"

Maria shook her head sadly; Blair just didn't get it. "Maybe he forgot."

Blair wandered around the kitchen. "On our honeymoon, Rich told me that he'd never cheat on me. He'd said that he'd shoot himself first before he'd ever do anything to hurt me. So I know that he won't. Those condoms aren't his," she insisted adamantly. "Do you think I should say something? Oh crap!" she said, frustrated. "Marriage should come with a warning: Only the strong need apply. I just don't want to make a little nothing into a big something."

"It's the little nothings that add up to big somethings," Maria muttered.

"What would you do if you found a box of condoms in Jorge's car?" Blair swiped her finger across the top of a cupcake and stuck a gob of the sweet stuff into her mouth.

The kitchen was silent as Maria stuffed the empty bags into the recycling, sauntered to the table, and settled into a chair. "Well," she started, carefully picking her words. "I wouldn't find them. Jorge would never let himself be in that situation," she said.

"But suppose he did. Just suppose you borrowed Jorge's car and found a half-empty box of condoms in it. What would you do?" Blair pressed.

"Let's just pretend that he was stupid enough to have condoms in his car, and I found them. Remember I told you I once made him cry like a bitch? Well, I'd turn him into a bitch. That thing that the condom covers will be no more," she said darkly and Blair shivered. Maria shrugged at Blair's horrified look. "You asked."

"So you think I should say something?"

"You do whatever you want to do," Maria answered, then strolled off to the living room to do her weekly vacuuming. "But I told you what I'd do," she threw over her shoulder.

Chapter 11

Madison nestled her naked behind into the mattress, then peeked over at her bed partner. His jackhammer-sounding snore told her that he was going to be out for at least a couple of hours. Smiling broadly, she glanced down at her body and blushed; on her right breast was a large hickey. On her partner's taut right butt cheek was a similar one. Last night's game of finding the booty was phenomenal.

"Who said geeks don't have a clue?" she muttered to Eric James, a man she had met last week while strolling through Bloomingdale's. "You got it going on in the bed, it's just too bad you're boring as hell once you open your mouth," she said, and sadly ran a finger over his lush bottom lip. Ironically, it was his tongue she was going to miss the most. "I guess it's time for 'the speech.' "

With that decided, Madison rolled over on her side, then gently nudged him in his ribs. When that didn't work, she patted him on the cheeks. When that failed, she did what her cousins used to do to her when they were younger—she reached over and squeezed his nose shut and clamped his lips shut. Eric woke up sputtering, which quickly turned to deep breathing when he saw a naked Madison turned toward him.

"Good morning, beautiful," he said, his normally high voice had deepened to a very masculine baritone. Before Madison knew what was happening his hands snaked around her waist and he'd flipped her over on her stomach as though she was a pancake.

"Eric," Madison playfully protested. "What are you doing?"

"You," Eric replied as he grabbed a condom packet from his nightstand. He stuck the foil packet between his teeth and ripped it open. Madison shivered. Eric the Lover kept her hot, but unfortunately Eric the Man left her drier than a desert. Eric slipped on the condom before sliding into Madison. She let out a soft groan. "Talk to me," Eric demanded as he grabbed Madison's waist, pulling her up on all fours.

"That feels good," Madison panted.

"I know. Talk legal to me," Eric demanded as he thrust into Madison.

Her eyebrows shot up in surprise and she stopped her movements before looking over her shoulder at Eric. His eyes were clamped shut, his face screwed up in ecstasy as his hips continued to move. He didn't realize that Madison had stopped. "What did you say?"

"Legalese, baby. Say something a lawyer would say," he groaned.

Madison quickly thought back to all the *Law & Order* episodes she had watched. "Witness," she tentatively offered

and her body flushed when Eric's thrusts went deeper. "Affi-
davit," she purred, getting into it.

"Oh, baby," Eric grunted as he quickly flipped Madison
on her back and she flung her legs over his shoulders.
"Keep talking!"

A light sheen of sweat broke out over Madison's body.
"Acquittal, chambers, bench warrant," she rambled as Eric
moved in and out of her. "Oh, Eric. Oh, sweetie!" Madison
groaned as she gripped his muscular arms.

Eric grasped her behind as though it was a basketball.
"Don't stop!"

"Mitigation! Petition! Precedent! Probate—"

"Ah, Madison," Eric croaked before shuddering and
falling on top of her, gasping for air.

She patiently waited until his body stilled, then, "Umm,
you're not done yet."

Eric grinned sheepishly. "I'm sorry, baby, let me wash
up." He sauntered off to the bathroom and returned a few
minutes later and found Madison lying in the middle of the
bed with her legs spread open, giving him a perfect view of
the prize.

"Come on," Madison said and her eyelids fluttered shut
when Eric crawled onto the bed and dipped his head between her legs. She almost catapulted off the mattress when
his tongue breezed over her clit.

"Stay still. I got you," Eric reassured her as he added pressure to her thighs before the tip of his tongue probed gently
into her mound. He plunged deeper when Madison pushed
his head down and her hips began swirling in tiny circles.

"Don't stop," Madison breathed. "Please don't stop," she
begged as she clutched the sheets and her hips began mov-

ing faster. Eric increased the pressure of his tongue on her clit and Madison shouted out as her body convulsed, then lay motionless. "The speech" was forgotten as she drifted off to sleep in his arms.

Sunlight pressed against Madison's eyelids and they reluctantly fluttered open. Her eyes widened when she saw the time, and she almost fell on her face getting out of bed trying to get to the bathroom for a quick shower. "Dammit! I'm gonna be late again," she grumbled.

Madison hurried out of the bathroom, the ends of her braids dancing over her still-damp shoulders. She plopped down on the bed and pulled on her panties.

"Hey, what time is it?" Eric asked while stretching and Madison was struck by how much he looked like a candy apple lollipop against the backdrop of his all-white room. His white comforter, white sheets, white pillows, white rug, and white walls all reminded her of a big glass of milk.

"Did I oversleep?" he asked. He sat up and shook off sleep as easily as he kicked off the covers.

"No, you're fine, I'm the one who's gotta rush. This'll make it my second time this week that I'm late," Madison answered and thought about her agenda for the day. "I won't have time to go home and change," she muttered and fished up her black, wide-legged, cuffed pants off the floor and inspected them. They were the same ones that she wore to work yesterday and to dinner with Eric last night. Eric slipped off the bed and kissed her shoulder before he sat at his desk and booted up his computer, then all she heard was the *clinkety-clank* of his fingers flying across the keyboard.

"Hey, lend me a white shirt," she called over her shoulder; the black top she had worn yesterday definitely wasn't going a second round.

Eric pulled his gaze away from the monitor just long enough to mumble, "Pull one out of the closet."

Madison hurried over to his closet and swung open the doors. She was met with a sea of gray, black, and brown suits, hundreds of white shirts, and dozens of khakis and crew shirts, all color coordinated. His walk-in closet was better organized than most stores. She grabbed a shirt and quickly dressed. "At least everybody *might* think that I had two pairs of black pants," she said observing her reflection.

Eric clicked off his computer, snuck up behind Madison, and wrapped his arms around her waist. "So, what are you doing today after work?" he asked, and placed his chin on her neck.

Madison pressed her lips together and lifted her shoulder, but all that did was make his chin dig deeper into her flesh. When she realized that he wasn't going to move, she pulled out of his embrace and got down on all fours to look for her shoes. "Lauren and I are going to dinner," she said after she found her shoes and slipped them on.

"Can't you do that tomorrow? I want to take you out tonight," he whined, his already high voice increasing to an annoying Pee-wee Herman range.

Madison turned to the mirror. "You have that lawyer thing that you really have to do," she reminded him. "You want to make partner this year, don't you?"

"You're right," he said, circling his arms around her waist while she fussed with her braids.

"Umm, I have to go to the bathroom," she said, wiggling

out of his arms. He was driving her crazy with his constant need to have her near him. He was worse than a damn puppy.

"Sure." Eric laughed and loosened his grip, but he sidled alongside her until she got to the bathroom.

"I *need* to use the toilet," Madison snapped at him.

"Oh, my bad." He laughed again and backed out, but he left the door slightly ajar. Madison immediately slammed it shut. She turned on the sink's faucet full blast and breathed deeply, grateful for the quiet.

"Thank God! That man knows he can smother a body," she muttered, then splashed some water on her face. "It's definitely time for 'The speech.' "

"What would you like me to make you for breakfast?" Eric called through the bathroom door. "Your wish is my command."

"You don't have what I like to eat!"

"I have everything. What do you want?"

Madison peeked at her reflection and grinned devilishly. "Well, I would like an omelet made with egg whites, organic broccoli, carrots, low-fat, lactose-free cheese, and a bean sprout shake. Can you handle that?"

Madison's request was met with silence, then, "No problem, I can get that. There's a Kroger right down the street, it'll only take me twenty minutes," he said just as she opened the bathroom door; she saw that he already had his car keys in his hand.

"Umm, Eric, we need to talk." From the look on her face, Eric sensed that she didn't want to talk about their plans for the weekend.

"Sure. Come on," he said as he led her to the living room, where they settled on the sofa.

"I've been assigned a new project at work that's totally driving me crazy. I can see myself being consumed by it. I just won't have time to see you anymore," she said, then looked sadly down at the floor.

"Whew, I thought you were gonna break up with me. We can see each other on weekends," he replied, relieved. Madison shook her head.

"That won't work. This is a really big project and from what my manager tells me, it'll require a *lot* of my time."

"Wow, you're gonna be on lockdown for sure. No weekends?" Eric asked forlornly.

"No weekends. I heard that there will probably be a lot of traveling involved, as well." Before Eric could ask another question, Madison popped off the couch. "I need to get to work," she said and inched toward the door.

"Cool," Eric said, holding the door open for her. "Can't a brother get a hug?" he asked, then pulled her into his arms. Madison stood stiffly against him. "Dang, girl, don't be shy, give me one that'll last since I'm not gonna see you for a while," he said, tightening his embrace.

Madison pulled out of his arms and blew him a kiss and made her way to her car.

"You're not getting rid of me that easy," Eric said, and smiled. "You're gonna be my lady," he vowed and waved to Madison as she maneuvered her car out of his driveway.

Chapter 12

LaShawn ran a hand over her stomach. She and Calvin were sprawled across his couch like two hippos. "I'm stuffed. Momma likes cooking for you. Did you like the grilled salmon and asparagus?"

Calvin snorted. "It was aw'ight. Why can't she burn some *black* people food? Is it so hard to throw some ribs on the grill, fry up some yard bird, or cook some chitlins?"

LaShawn laughed and gently poked Calvin in his side. "Oh, hush. I saw you dipping in the serving platter more than Daddy. Besides, you know that we're all trying to eat healthier. Look at me, I've lost twenty pounds," she boasted.

"So, you're giving me a chance to peep the body?" Calvin asked, his voice hopeful.

LaShawn let out a frustrated sigh. "Come on, Calvin, don't start, you know how I feel about premarital sex. I want our first time to be special. Our wedding night will be just as God intended."

"I bet He gets hard and gets to sex," Calvin muttered and LaShawn clutched her hands to her heart.

"Calvin, don't you *dare* talk about Him that way! I bet if you went to church sometimes instead of spending your Sundays in bed, you wouldn't be talking like this!"

"Oh, here we go. Now I should be going to church! You want to turn me into one of those dickless, suit-wearing, Bible-quoting men that you used to date. It's not gonna happen!"

"I'm not trying to change you!" LaShawn protested. "Come on, let's both calm down and relax," she said in a soothing tone. Then she cupped his face and lovingly caressed his cheek.

Calvin rested his face against LaShawn's palm and closed his eyes. *She's my rock*, he thought. He opened his eyes and he gazed tenderly at her. "You're right. I'm sorry. I'm tripping," he said sheepishly. "Let's chill," he said, then gave her a chaste kiss on the forehead.

LaShawn's heart melted. This is the Calvin she'd fallen in love with, even-tempered, humble, and sweet. Breaking their eye contact, her eyes wandered over his smooth, cappuccino-colored face and she smiled as though taking a pleasant journey. She leisurely thumbed his thick eyebrows, gently stroked his jaw, then ran her hand sensuously over his goatee. Leaning in, she slowly peppered his face with little kisses.

Calvin groaned softly before reclining on the couch and pulling LaShawn on top of him. LaShawn splayed over him like a blanket. Calvin slipped his hand under her shirt and LaShawn didn't notice it until she felt his hand on her breast. She tensed up faster than a Catholic schoolgirl.

"Calvin!" she screeched and shoved his hand away. "We can't do that. The next thing I know," she pointed to her breasts, "one of these will be out, then the other." She pointed to Calvin's crotch, which had tripled in size within the last two minutes. "Then *that* will be out. It won't be a good situation."

"Shawn!" Calvin protested. "Let me just suck a nipple; hell, I'll be happy if I can just see one."

"Nu-uh, we tried that one time. And we nearly ended up in bed."

"And? What's wrong with that? It's what grown folks do."

"Well, not until we're married. Besides, I thought we were just chilling?" LaShawn gently reminded him. "Let's just lie here and silently count our blessings."

Calvin glared hard at her and LaShawn smiled sweetly in response before snuggling against his rigid body. He turned on the TV and LaShawn immediately opened her mouth to protest, then just as fast closed it. She mentally shrugged before closing her eyes.

LaShawn was drifting off to sleep when she heard keys rattling and metal stabbing metal, as though someone was trying to find the right key to unlock the door. Alarmed, she sleepily peeked at Calvin out of the corner of her eyes. His gaze hadn't shifted from the TV. Suddenly LaShawn heard a triumphant cry as his door was flung open and Rita, Calvin's next-door neighbor, breezed in. LaShawn's jaw dropped into her lap. What the h-e- double hockey sticks was going on here? She has keys to Calvin's apartment? Calvin *just* gave me a key two months ago.

LaShawn snatched herself out of his arms so fast that it looked as though she was blasted out. "Hey, Shawnie!" Rita screeched. LaShawn cringed; she hated that nickname even more than she hated Rita's voice, which sounded like a chicken choking. LaShawn nodded in Rita's direction, but then slid to the other end of the couch and pretended to watch TV as she surreptitiously studied Calvin, who calmly kept his eyes frozen to the TV.

Rita was what her grandma used to call "double-coated ugly"; ugly inside and out. Her beady blue eyes, long nose, thin lips, and frizzy blonde hair reminded LaShawn of a rat.

"Come on in," Calvin called and Rita scurried over to him, grinning all the way.

"Hey, look what I got." She giggled, then held up a small bag of weed. Calvin's eyes widened to the size of headlights, then narrowed to slits as he vigorously motioned toward LaShawn.

He was too late, LaShawn had seen the drugs. "Oh my God! What is *that* doing here? I thought you stopped that," she hissed at him.

"I did," he lied, then snatched the bag out of Rita's hands. Just last week he'd shared a bag with Rita and Malcolm. LaShawn was forgotten as he stuck his nose in the bag and inhaled deeply, his jaw going slack with desire. "Oh shit! This is the good stuff. I'm gonna need a hit . . . or two," he said, nearly drooling.

"Don't do this. Stay focused on your goals, our goals. You've been doing so well." LaShawn was trying to keep her voice even, calm.

"Come on, baby," Calvin pleaded. "I need it to relax. My boss has been riding my ass like it was a roller coaster at Six Flags. I need to destress."

"Butt," LaShawn calmly corrected.

Rita, who was quietly watching the scene, blurted out, "Huh? But what?" Her face twisted in confusion.

"Butt . . . not a-s-s!" LaShawn retorted.

"Yeah, whatever." Rita shrugged and grabbed the bag of weed from Calvin.

"Well, he's been riding my *butt,* and giving me work like he's crazy. I've been working crazy overtime, doing crazy work, and it's all making me crazy. I'm only going to take one puff. I promise," he said, and LaShawn didn't miss how Rita casually strolled into the kitchen and rummaged around until she found a pack of rolling paper.

"Come on!" LaShawn ordered. Rita snickered as LaShawn grabbed Calvin's hand and dragged him into the bedroom. She slammed the door shut and pushed him onto the bed. Calvin's jaw dropped in astonishment. LaShawn *never* acted like this. "I do not want you smoking that stuff!" she shouted as she glared down at him.

On the other side of the wafer-thin door, Rita heard everything as she placed cigarette papers on the coffee table, and gingerly tapped the minced leaves into a sheet before lovingly rolling it into a joint.

Calvin pushed himself off the bed. "Look, all I'm doing is having a little fun. Besides, baby, it's just like having a beer. They both mellow you out." He leaned over to kiss her, but LaShawn angrily turned her face.

"Marijuana is much worse for you than beer. So don't even try it!" Suddenly the pungent smell of weed seeped under the bedroom door and swirled seductively up Calvin's nose. LaShawn watched as Calvin's face filled with longing. "Oh crap!" she uttered, knowing that she was close to losing. She tugged at his face so that they were eye-to-eye.

"Remember what you were like before? All the drugs . . ." LaShawn gave him a minute to absorb what she was talking about.

His eyes grew hard. When she had first met him, he had just gotten out of a drug rehab center. The five years before that had been a blur. But the heady scent of the weed beckoned him; he licked his lips in anticipation. "Just one hit," he begged.

LaShawn reached for his hands. "Think about everything your counselor taught you. Remember he told you that whenever you get the urge to smoke you should visualize the smoke seeping into every pore of your body and infecting them with poison."

"I can handle it," Calvin stubbornly insisted.

LaShawn gripped his hands. "Calvin, use your head. Don't mess up what you got. You've been doing awesome. The sky is the limit, baby, don't fall before you even start soaring. Don't you have a buddy or something to call?"

Calvin vehemently shook his head. "I cut him loose a long time ago. He was as worthless as an Atari game cartridge. I know I can handle it."

"How do you know?" LaShawn asked, exasperated. "How do you know?"

"Because I smoked two joints last week, that's why," Calvin admitted with a smirk.

Shocked, LaShawn dropped his hands. She gave him a hard stare before she pulled open the bedroom door, stalked passed Rita, who by now had smoked half the joint, gathered up her things, and slammed out of Calvin's apartment. She was halfway down the hallway when she heard Rita's raucous laughter.

Chapter 13

Lauren peeked out of her office door, looking to the left, then to the right. "Thank goodness, no Susan." She eased back inside.

Her heart pounded in her chest and her hands shook like butterfly wings as she snapped the blinds closed, dimmed her light, set her phone to voicemail, then turned her radio to her favorite jazz station. She had just a sliver of time before her next meeting and she wanted to use it to regain her sanity and calm her stomach, which lately had been feeling like she swallowed a handful of nails.

Sighing, she slipped her shoes off, then dragged herself over to the couch. Susan had turned her nose up at the piece of furniture when Lauren requisitioned it, saying only wimps owned office sofas, that a real executive would have a trophy case instead.

Curling up on the couch like a baby, she pulled out a pillow and stuck it underneath her head and readjusted it until it was just right. The dim lights and the soft music tugged her into a world where peace ruled, and she giggled deliriously as she floated off into a light sleep. She was snoring softly and well into a full-fledged nap when there were two sharp raps on her door. Lauren jolted upright. She was disoriented, but not so much that she didn't see the door handle turn as she realized she hadn't locked the door. There was only one person in the company who'd walk into someone's office uninvited.

"Shit!" she muttered. "Susan." Lauren bounced off the couch and scrambled for her shoes. Oblivious to the low lights and jazz playing, Susan charged over to Lauren's desk and dropped into the chair. Lauren hastily pulled on her shoes and smoothed down her Dolce & Gabbana skirt while Susan shot her a scathing glare.

"We have a problem!" Susan barked, slapping her feet on top of Lauren's desk.

"Susan, I was—"

"Marcie Brown's father died so she can't make the public relations conference in San Francisco. I need you to represent the company."

"Susan—"

"It's . . ." she glanced down and consulted Lauren's calendar ". . . two days from now, and you'll be gone for four."

"Susan, I can't go . . . my son has karate practice, my daughter has—"

Susan jumped up and hurried across the floor. She turned to Lauren when she reached the doorway. "I want you in my office in five, I'll give you the details." She turned on her heel and stalked out the door so fast that Lauren half expected to see sparks.

On feet that felt like they had been double-dipped in

cement, Lauren hauled herself to her desk and dropped down in her chair, which was still warm with Susan's body heat.

"I can't go to San Francisco," she babbled as sharp pains began shooting through her stomach, as if someone was poking it with a steel rod. Everything that she wanted to say to Susan, but couldn't, poured out. "I have too much work here to do. Who'll do it while I'm gone? And what about my family?" Looking at her calendar she saw that Cleve was scheduled to be in New York. "Crap! Who's gonna watch the kids?" she wondered. "Forget this!" Pushing herself away from the desk she stood up. "I'm going to tell Susan that I can't go. I'm going to tell her that it doesn't make sense for me, a VP, to go halfway across the country to stand at a booth. We should send one of our managers."

Her telephone rang, interrupting her tirade. Lauren eyed it warily before picking it up; it was her secretary, Jennifer. "Julie just called, Susan is waiting for you." Lauren thanked her before hanging up. Julie, Susan's right and left arms, was a Xeroxed version of her boss and expected everyone to jump when she demanded.

"I'm going to tell her that I can't do it. It's as simple as that." Lauren squared her shoulders and marched out the door. She held onto her resolve as she stalked down the hall. It was still going strong as she stepped on the elevator. "She can have one of her ass-kissers go," she said through gritted teeth. "But I'm not going."

Chapter 14

Blair cooked dinner, cleaned up the kitchen, and helped the kids with their homework before she got a chance to ask Rich about the condoms. The house was quiet except for the sound of Jay Leno's voice. Rich was lying next to her in bed, chuckling at a joke the talk show host had made. This was the first time in weeks that he had come home early enough to watch the late show. She didn't want to disturb him, but something made her reach under the bed and pull out the box of condoms and toss it on the bed.

"I found these in your car," she said quietly, watching his reaction.

Rich absent-mindedly glanced down and the smile froze on his face. "You found those in my car? That's impossible. They aren't mine," he quickly denied, then turned his attention back to Jay Leno.

"Rich," Blair pleaded softly and, when he didn't respond, she grabbed the remote and clicked off the TV.

"What the fu—" he muttered, then he saw the remote in

Blair's hand. "Why did you do that?" he asked, turning bewildered eyes on her. "You know I like Jay Leno."

"Because I was talking to you and you weren't listening."

"I was listening. I told you they weren't mine," Rich said. "Now turn the TV back on!" he demanded.

"You may enjoy your TV just as soon as you answer my question," Blair promised nicely.

Rich rolled his eyes and slumped against the pillows.

"How did they get there?" Blair asked.

"I don't know." Rich shrugged. "They're not mine," he stated firmly. "Hey, what's going on here? Don't you trust me?" he asked loudly.

Blair shot a worried glance toward the door. The last thing she needed was for the kids to hear her and Rich argue about condoms. "Keep your voice down! The kids might hear," she hissed.

"They'll hear that their mother doesn't trust their father!" he yelled.

"Why are you acting like this?" she asked, her green eyes wide with puzzlement. "Why can't we have a decent conversation without you shouting?" Blair asked, then clicked the TV on. "Forget I said anything." Blair peeked at Rich's profile while he kept his eyes locked to the glowing screen.

Suddenly Rich announced, "Now I remember how they got there!"

"Do tell," Blair sarcastically muttered.

"Peter, one of the new associates, is getting married. So all the partners got together and took him to a strip club last week." He smiled sheepishly at Blair. "I didn't want to tell you, because I know that you hate for me to go to those places. I didn't touch anyone," he quickly reassured her before she could ask. "But they were a gag gift, just in case *he* wanted to do something at the club."

"But why were they open? And half of them missing?" Blair asked in a suspicious tone.

"I don't know . . . I guess he took some when we weren't looking," Rich answered swiftly, but he saw doubt still swimming in Blair's eyes.

"You're not lying to me, are you?" she asked and was rewarded with one of Rich's dazzling smiles. "I mean, you'd tell me if you're unhappy, wouldn't you?" Her brow furrowed with concern. In response he clicked off the light and TV, then pulled her to him.

"I'm sorry, I didn't mean to yell at you. But what do you expect? Accusing me of cheating. I would never do that to you."

"I'm sorry," Blair whispered.

He cupped her heart-shaped butt, then slipped a hand under her shirt and tickled her flat stomach before he buried his face in her hair. "You're so beautiful," he murmured, grateful that Blair took such good care of herself. His coworkers constantly bitched about how their wives had gained weight and stopped taking care of themselves after they'd had children, but Rich was proud to say that Blair looked even more beautiful now than she did the day they'd met. "Kiss me," Rich demanded and Blair lifted her lips to his and they melted together.

Rich reclined on his back, then pulled Blair on top of him. Her breasts were dangling in front of him like two ripe peaches. He leaned up and feasted on each one as though they were succulent fruit, Blair moaning loudly in response as her hips began slowly rotating against Rich's.

"Mmmm, do you want me, baby?" Rich groaned and Blair nodded. "I can't hear you. What did you say?"

"I want you," Blair whimpered.

"I guess you don't want me 'cause I don't hear you," Rich taunted as he pretended to push Blair off him.

"Ooh, baby, I want you!"

"That's more like it." Rich chuckled. Blair peered at him through heavy-lidded eyes. "Turn around," he ordered and Blair immediately complied. "Get ready to go for a ride," he said before thrusting into her.

He slid his hand around her waist and began teasing her clit; ripples of pleasure ran through her body. The sensation was so overwhelming that Blair sucked in air so fast that she nearly choked.

"Rich," she muttered in a strangled voice. She gripped the covers and threw her head back.

"Let it go, honey," Rich crooned as he leisurely moved inside his wife. He closed his eyes and lost himself in her softness. When he heard her low gasps and he felt her body quiver, he allowed himself his release.

When Blair was snoring softly beside him, Rich snatched up the half-empty box of condoms, slipped out of bed, tiptoed downstairs to the garage, and tucked them under the driver's seat of his car.

Chapter 15

"Mmm," Madison groaned and licked her lips. "This is better than sex." She ran her tongue over her spoon, erasing all traces of chocolate, then returned it to the thick chocolate sundae and pulled out another spoonful. She stuck the calorie-laden spoon in her mouth. "Ooh, ooh God," she moaned when the dessert hit her tongue. Blair laughed.

"Madison, would you like us to leave you alone with that thing?" she teased.

Lauren smiled as she worked on her second piece of hummingbird cake. Next to carrot cake, it was her all-time favorite. Lately, she just couldn't stop eating.

LaShawn had called an emergency meeting at Maxie's, their second-favorite restaurant, to discuss her wedding.

"You know you are *way* too attached to that sundae," LaShawn joked.

"Aw, stop! There ain't nothing wrong with a lady enjoying her food," Madison shot back.

"No, there isn't," Lauren agreed mildly, and Blair smothered a giggle when she saw the teasing glint in Lauren's eyes.

"Thank you." Madison smiled, flinging her braids over her shoulder and turning her nose up at Blair.

"I guess it's been a while since you've had some, huh?" Lauren asked.

"What?" Madison stuttered, narrowing her eyes.

"I mean," Lauren started, "it must've been a while, look at how you're attacking that sundae. You act like it's the last one on earth."

"What's that supposed to mean?" Madison huffed, but carefully studied her dessert as if there was an encrypted message on it, slowly rotating the dish so that she could study it from all angles.

Lauren lifted an eyebrow. "Doesn't that sundae remind you of something, or maybe I should say *some things.*"

"Lauren, stop tripping. I think you've been reading too many public relations magazines. Your brain has turned to mush."

Lauren smirked then said, "Nu-uh. Take a close look at your sundae, what does it remind you of? And be honest."

Madison studied the dessert, then shrugged; she didn't see anything remarkable and she told Lauren so.

"Really? Well, the split bananas remind me of two penises," she said. Her tone was as flat as if she was reporting the weather; that was until she caught Blair's eye and they both burst into laughter.

Madison shook her head, feigning disgust. "You two really need to grow up," she said, then started giggling. "You're right, Lauren, they did remind me of little dicks, but I didn't want to admit it."

"Penis," LaShawn corrected. "Use the word 'penis.' "

"Oops, my bad. Penis," Madison said sarcastically. LaShawn was beginning to get on her nerves. "How was San Francisco?"

"A waste of my time," Lauren huffed. "I had to rearrange my children's lives so that Mommy could spend four days standing at a nine-foot table telling imbeciles about the company's products."

"Dang, it was that bad?"

Lauren nodded. "Hell yeah." LaShawn groaned loudly. Ignoring her, Lauren continued. "It was something our intern could've done. Susan's being a total ass. She wouldn't listen to anything I had to say."

"What did you do to piss her off?" Blair asked and Lauren and Madison looked at her as though she had asked them what color the sky was. "What? I don't know all the subtle nuances or the game playing in corporate America," she said, defending herself.

Lauren gave her friend an apologetic smile before shaking her head. "I did nothing to that lady. She's like the body builder at the gym; y'all know the one. He's wearing the muscle shirt and constantly flexing his muscles."

"Oh," Blair said, suddenly understanding. "So Susan's your body builder?"

"Yes, something like that." Lauren chuckled.

Madison glanced at her watch; it was almost nine o'clock and she still had a forty-minute drive home. "It's getting late. Time for me to go."

"Oh, look at the time," Blair said, "I need to leave, too."

LaShawn and Lauren quickly agreed. Almost simultaneously they twisted around in their chairs for their purses.

"Hold up. I got this," Madison announced, then pulled out her credit card and handed it to a waiter.

Lauren turned to LaShawn. "This was a productive meeting, we made some headway on your wedding plans," she said stifling a yawn.

"Thank y'all so much," LaShawn gushed. "I know my sister is really going to appreciate all this, she's been superbusy with her new job. And I know Calvin is extremely grateful."

"Yeah right," Madison muttered, and Blair gave her arm a quick pinch. "Don't do that, you red-haired—"

Just then their waiter returned to the table, then leaned down and whispered in Madison's ear. "Ms. DuPree, your card has been declined. We'll need to see another one, along with your driver's license."

Madison's eyes widened with shock. "What! My card has been declined? It has a zero balance. Try it again."

The waiter shrugged, then trotted back to the register only to return five minutes later with the same problem.

"Crap! Try this," Madison said and handed him a different piece of plastic. The waiter didn't move. "Oh, you need ID." She handed him her license.

Two minutes later the waiter was back at the table with the receipt. As soon as they all saw the slip of paper, they gave a collective sigh of relief before hugging one another good-bye.

Madison slipped behind the wheel of her car and watched her friends drive off. "Why was my credit card declined?" Madison wondered aloud as she turned the key in the ignition. "That bank is gonna hear from me!"

Chapter 16

"Thank you, Miss Greene!" fifteen little voices chorused and it warmed LaShawn all the way to the tips of her Birkenstock-encased feet. She smiled widely and silently thanked God for her good fortune. Every day she was able to get up and live her passion, teaching kindergarten. From nine o'clock in the morning until two in the afternoon, her life was perfect. A tug at the hem of her smock brought her back to the present. She glanced down and smiled as Terry Walton grinned up at her. Having just lost his two front teeth he spoke with a lisp, but smiled constantly. He was her favorite, not that she would admit it to anyone.

"Miz Greene . . . my daddy's gonna pick me up today and he told me that I'd better be ready." LaShawn's heart unexpectedly jumped and blood rushed to her face at the mention of Terry's father. She glanced at the clock; it was twenty minutes to two, twenty minutes before Terrance Senior showed up.

"Okay everybody . . . let's start cleaning up. It's almost

time to go," she announced as she began walking around the room. "Come on, Towanda, pick those crayons up. They didn't get on the floor by themselves." She caught a flash of movement out of the corner of her eye and she marched over to the aquarium. "Robert, get your hand out of the water." She grabbed Robert's hand and Henry, the fish, plopped back into the water. "Go wash your hands and clean off your desk!" she ordered. Surprisingly, by the time two o'clock came, the room was not only orderly but calm. One by one they all skipped out with their parents or their caregiver.

Once the room was quiet, she sat at her desk to put funny-face stickers on papers and watch Terry play in the corner by himself. It was after three o'clock when she heard footsteps echoing down the hall. She looked up when they stopped in front of her classroom, and her heart flip-flopped as Terrance Walton strolled in. He was what Madison would call luscious. At six-foot-one he was as muscular as a boxer. Dressed casually in slacks and a loose-fitting shirt, he looked finer than any tuxedo-clad man. She quickly scolded herself. Think about your fiancé. But the closer Terrance Walton got, the farther away Calvin was pushed.

"Hey, I'm sorry, thanks a lot for staying late. I meant to call, but time got away from me. Rhonda was supposed to pick him up today, but she had to fly out of town on business," he explained and Terry squealed with joy and jumped into his arms.

"Daddeee!"

"No problem," LaShawn answered, secretly glad that his ex-wife wasn't able to be there. She held up the stack of kindergartners' papers. "See, I have my own briefs to review," she joked. From the couple of times they had talked she had learned that he was a lawyer.

He nudged Terry toward the coat rack. "Go get your coat." As soon as the boy was out of earshot Terrence spoke softly, so much so that LaShawn had to lean in closer to hear him, getting a good whiff of his expensive cologne. "Rhonda is focusing on her career right now, she's trying to make vice president," he said. "I guess Terry doesn't fit into her plans. So instead of having him sit at her mom's house all night while she schmoozes with the big boys, I'm going to take him for a while."

LaShawn turned her lips down in a frown, then asked him if there was anything she could do.

Terrance shook his head. "Naw, you do plenty. All Terry talks about is 'Miss Greene.' He loves your class, especially since you taught him that alphabet song. He sings it day and night. It's driving me crazy," he joked.

"I know exactly what you mean. It should be outlawed, it can definitely work your nerves," LaShawn agreed and they both shared a laugh until Terry returned with his coat and his homework.

"Tell Miss Greene 'bye," Terrance instructed.

" 'Bye, Miz Greene," Terry sang as he and his father strolled out of the classroom. LaShawn waited a heartbeat, then hurried to the door. From there she was able to get the best view of Terrance's butt as he strolled down the hallway.

"Wow!" LaShawn jumped and guiltily turned toward the voice. It belonged to Dolly Moran, one of the school's first grade teachers. "He's a piece of prime rib. Who is that?"

"Oh, nobody special," she answered in a bored voice,

then flicked her hand, dismissing him. "He's just Terry Walton's father."

"What's his story?" Dolly's eyes narrowed with interest. "Is he single, divorced, gay?"

"Divorced. I doubt he's gay."

"Is he seeing anyone?" she asked and LaShawn quickly shrugged. "Well, check it out for me. Let me know if he's free. I would love to be his private tutor. I have a couple of things I can teach him." She smiled wickedly.

Chapter 17

Lauren dropped down onto Madison's couch, slipped her shoes off, and tucked her feet underneath her. Madison's office had a spectacular view of Atlanta's skyline. She cursed herself for not bringing her sketchpad. She hadn't painted anything in months and her fingers itched to capture the scene. "So, you gave your father the money for the abortion?" Lauren asked.

Madison mournfully looked up at her friend. "I helped him get rid of my little brother or sister," she whispered sadly.

Lauren grasped her friend's hand. "Naw, girl, don't let him do this to you. You gave him the money, but you didn't perform the operation. So don't be so hard on yourself."

Madison cocked her head and studied her friend before answering. "Half of me knows you're right, but the other half still feels responsible. And the other half—"

"Wait!" Lauren said. "You have too many halves." She smiled.

"Okay, then change it all to thirds," Madison quipped. "Well, the other third of me is so mad at him. He's a middle-aged wannabe player who's still mooching off his daughter. What the hell is that all about?"

"You let him," Lauren quietly stated. "You've *always* let him."

"I know." Madison groaned. "But I feel like I need to take care of him. If I don't help him out, who will?"

"He's a grown-ass man, he'll get it together."

"I hope so," Madison answered, then, "I always hoped that he'd grow up and be like other fathers. Not Ward Cleaver or Cliff Huxtable or even that Brady Bunch guy. But just a regular father. You know, teach me how to ride a bike and stuff and just hang out," Madison said wistfully. "I want a daddy, not a best friend. Do you think I'm asking too much?"

Lauren shook her head, feeling helpless. It was one thing to console her friend over a broken heart, but this was out of her territory. "No you're not, sweetie," Lauren reassured her.

"I guess he wasn't that bad, he did do some things with me but it wasn't enough. It just wasn't enough," Madison decided sadly. "Anyway," she said brightening, "you know he stayed at my place for two weeks. He and Mosaquiema stunk it all up so bad that I had to have a cleaning service come in and delouse the place after they left. Had my place smelling like a ho house, like a whole ocean of fish up and died in it. It was funky," Madison said, and Lauren burst out laughing.

Lauren playfully fanned her hand in front of her nose. "Now that's funky," she said in giggly agreement. "Whatever happened to your credit card?"

Madison shook her head. "That was so strange. The next day I called the bank and they told me that I sent them a letter telling them to cancel the card."

"Did you?" Lauren asked.

"Do you think I'm crazy? Hell naw, I didn't do that. They're supposed to fax me a copy of the letter. This is too bizarre for me."

"Speaking of bizarre . . . tell me again why you decided to stop seeing Eric," she asked. Madison constantly amused her, the girl was kissing thirty-four and was more commitment phobic than any man she'd ever known.

"Hey, pass me the carton of rice," Madison said, then reached around her friend when she didn't move fast enough. She took her time spooning some onto her plate. "He's too needy. He wants to spend every minute with me," she finally answered.

"Girl, you don't know what you want. You complain when a man doesn't pay you any attention, then bitch when you get too much." Lauren laughed.

"*Humph,* I know what I want," she said, smirking. "I want a big-dicked, tucking-me-into-bed-every-night, loving-me-unconditionally, no-issues-having, spiritually rich man," Madison poured out.

Lauren laughed. "So, that's all you want? You don't want much. I bet you run into men like that all the time. I bet Eric was that and more. You should ask him to marry you."

Madison stopped chewing and gazed at her friend with wide eyes. "Are you totally crazy? Why on earth would I ask Eric to marry me?"

Lauren raised an eyebrow and then said, "Maybe you should; I bet he accepts."

"Puh-leeze. I can't deal with half of Atlanta's fake bougie black folk. I can't imagine hanging out with Eric and his lawyer buddies." She stuck her finger down her throat and mock gagged.

"Is he serious?"

Madison ducked her head, using her braids to shield her face while she played with her lo mein noodles. Lauren sat back and enjoyed the view. She knew that this was one of Madison's stalling techniques, so she let her take her time. "I don't know, we had only been seeing each other for a couple weeks," she finally answered.

"Talk to him," Lauren said softly.

"I can't. I told you I gave him 'The speech.' " Madison answered and Lauren laughed out loud.

"Which one this time? The 'I'm going home to take care of my father'? Or the 'I'm going to be traveling a lot for my job.' Or my favorite: 'I've decided to be celibate.' "

"None of those. I told him that I'm starting a new project at work. And I won't have time to see him."

"Uh-ha. Why can't you just tell them the truth? That you have commitment issues bigger than the United States and you'll never resolve them."

"I don't have *commitment issues.* I just haven't found the right man yet. Everybody isn't as lucky as you. We all can't get a Cleve." Madison huffed, then studied her friend. From the moment she walked into her office, she noticed that something was off about her. She leaned in closer for a better look. "Are you okay?" she asked.

"Yeah, why?" Lauren asked.

"Well," Madison shifted in her seat, "your right eye's been twitching ever since you sat down."

Lauren's mouth dropped with disbelief. "Is not!"

"Girl, your eye looks like a damn camera and you're snapping pictures with it," Madison said and Lauren shook her head. "Look in the mirror."

"I will." Lauren pulled out her compact and saw that Madison was right. She looked like someone was giving her electric shots. She watched her eye jump to its own beat and how the skin around it immediately followed, like it was playing follow the leader. "Madison!" she yelled, then softened her voice. "What's happening to me?"

Madison shook her head, just as confused as her friend. "I don't know. You doing okay?"

"I'm fine," Lauren said. "I'm healthy," she continued, not mentioning the headaches that blurred her thinking or the stomachaches that had her clutching her sides or the constant desire for sleep.

"Maybe you and Cleve should take a vacation," Madison gently suggested. A coworker of hers had the same problem. First it started with a nervous shake of his hands, then the tick started in his right eye, then the left. The last straw was when his head and shoulder began meeting every couple minutes and he had to be sent out on leave. She didn't want that to happen to her friend.

Lauren shook her head. "I'm fine," she said, a little sharper than she intended.

"Excuse me!" Madison huffed.

"I'm sorry," Lauren apologized. "My head's been bothering me." When Madison raised her eyebrows, she quickly explained. "They've only been teensy-weensy headaches."

"*Headaches!*" Madison remembered the pills Lauren had popped during their night out.

"Yeah, only a couple," Lauren admitted, a little scared by Madison's reaction. She made it seem like she had an aneurysm that was getting ready to burst at any minute.

"I think you'd better see a doctor."

"I don't have time," Lauren protested and glanced down at her watch. "Oh my gosh! I'm already late. I have a PIM meeting," she said, and began clearing away Madison's table.

"Don't worry about it," she said and nudged her friend toward the door. "What's PIM anyway? I never heard of that."

"It's Parents for Instilling Morals," she said breathlessly at the threshold.

"They rope you into everything, huh?"

"I guess," Lauren said, smiling. "See ya." She hugged her friend.

"You better go see a doctor," Madison said, pulling away.

"I will."

"Promise?"

"I promise," Lauren lied as she hurried down the hall to the elevator. Suddenly without any warning the hallway spun precariously around and her lunch sprang up to the back of her throat. Blindly, she reached out for the wall and clung to it until the world righted itself. Beads of perspiration dotted her face, and she stood frozen until the elevator doors swooshed open. I'm fine, she said harshly to herself, then marched into the elevator, where she slumped against the wall. Just as the doors closed, she crumbled to the floor.

Chapter 18

"Sweetie, you take such good care of me," Blair whispered before kissing Rich on the corner of his mouth, which tasted salty from the shrimp dipped in butter that he'd just eaten. "I had a good time today. I can't wait to tell the girls about it," she gushed, and held up her freshly manicured hands to admire the seashell pink color. It looked dull against her flushed body, which was glowing brighter than the candle flickering in the middle of their table.

Rich's lips curved up into an indulgent smile. He loved seeing her happy. "How was the spa?"

"Oh honey! The facial, the mud bath, the pedicure, the manicure, and the massage, everything was all so wonderful! Gosh, I can't think of when I had a better time," she said, giving him a one-hundred-watt smile. Right out of the blue, Rich had surprised her with a gift certificate for a day at the spa. She was still stunned by his generosity, not by the cost, even though the three-hundred-dollar price tag did make her jaw drop, but by the thoughtfulness of the gift.

Months ago she had mentioned how much she wanted to have a day of self-indulgence. Rich rarely listened to anything she said.

"And," Blair continued, looking up at her husband, "the kids loved the zoo." She giggled and squeezed his thigh. Playing with the kids and wrestling with them the way he did today turned her on. Seeing him in the glow of soft candlelight was an even bigger turn-on, his black hair shining healthfully and his dark eyes sparkling.

Rich leaned toward his wife and cocked his head in a way that reminded her of Colin Farrell. "I love—" His mouth dropped open so wide that she could count each and every one of his teeth if she was so inclined. His head inched slowly around as if it was a tracking device that had honed in on its target. Blair raised an eyebrow at her husband and turned to see what captivated him; the object of his interest was halfway across the restaurant.

She was a petite lady, with blond bouncing hair. She was squeezed into the requisite black dress so short that it barely covered her bottom; the piece of material looked more like a two-dollar T-shirt. But it was her walk that drew attention to her. She was like a bitch in heat, prancing around and switching her ass so that every male within a two-mile radius could pick up her scent.

Blair cut her eyes at Rich. He wore a dazed look, as if he had been drugged; she wanted to slap him. "Do you need a napkin to wipe up that drool?" she coolly asked, and realized she might as well have been talking to herself because Rich was stuck in the zone, the bitch zone. Irritation bubbled up her spine and threatened to erupt. "Do you know her?" Blair snapped.

"Um . . . no," Rich stuttered. "Not at all," he reassured her as he quickly composed himself. Seconds later he was the Rich Blair she knew. "Some women will do anything to get male attention," Rich scoffed. "But not you," he said smoothly. "You're a natural beauty. You look so beautiful tonight," he said as his gaze ran appreciatively over his wife. The emerald green dress that she was wearing clung to her curves. "I love you," he said and then leaned down and tenderly brushed his lips against Blair's. "Come on, let's walk over to the theater. It'll be good to get there early."

Rich rested his hand on the curve of Blair's behind as they strolled out of the restaurant and over to the theater.

"I'm loving the seats," Blair gushed. "Honey, this is so wonderful. We haven't been to the theater in ages. Everybody looks so nice dressed up," she said, eyeing the crowd as though she was watching TV. "Hey, isn't that the lady we saw at the restaurant? What are the odds of her showing up at the Fox Theatre the same time we did?" Blair said, pointing to the same blond lady Rich couldn't keep his eyes off. She and her date were sitting three rows in front of them.

"I don't believe that's the same person," Rich said, and pointedly stared at his program. "Oh look, my company is a corporate sponsor. I can't believe they spent ten thousand dollars just to have their name listed on a piece of paper," he said, shaking his head.

"You sure that isn't the same lady?" Blair insisted. "Look at her. She keeps turning around to look at us. I'd make a bet that she's the same person. All she has to do is stand up. That'll prove everything," she said, nodding her head.

"I think she keeps looking at you because you're so beautiful. She's just jealous," Rich said, then gave Blair a passionate kiss.

"You're too sweet. Do you think the kids are behaving themselves?" she asked. "Maybe I should call home to see."

"Honey, you worry too much. Maria has everything under control. I'm sure that the girls are asleep by now, and your son is playing video games. Besides," he added, "if you leave now you're going to miss the opening scene. You don't want to do that, I hear it's a doozy."

"Um, okay," Blair acquiesced and laced her fingers through her husband's.

"Sit back and relax," Rich instructed and gave her hand a comforting squeeze.

Three hours later Rich and Blair were strolling through their front door.

"See, they're okay," Rich gently chastised. It was like Rich said, the girls were asleep and Rich Jr. was playing video games. Maria was in the kitchen enjoying a cup of tea and left when Blair and Rich got settled.

"I know. I worry too much," Blair said sleepily.

"Even about me? You worry about big ole me?" Rich teased. He had taken off his suit and slipped under the covers naked and Blair noticed the tented blanket.

"Do you think she was pretty?" Blair asked. She had already showered, blow-dried her hair, and changed into a sheer negligee, but she couldn't shake the image of the lady in the restaurant. The evening gown was zipped up in its vinyl bag, and hanging in the closet ready for the next event. Now she sat at her vanity looking in the mirror while brushing her hair. She tilted her head and switched the brush to her left hand and resumed her counting—one hundred strokes, every night.

"Is who pretty?" Rich asked, flipping through a financial magazine. He had picked it up when he saw Blair head for her vanity. Experience told him that he had at least another fifteen minutes before she'd come to bed.

Blair brushed harder and faster. "The lady who spent the entire evening staring at us."

Rich sighed and tossed the magazine on the bed. "She didn't spend the *whole* evening looking at us."

"Just about. It just seems odd, you know?" Blair said, glancing over her shoulder.

"Forget about it. You know what's odd?"

"What?"

"That you're way over there and I'm lying here horny as hell."

"Oh Rich," Blair giggled. "You're Italian, you're supposed to be horny. I'd be worried if you weren't."

"Come on. Your hair can wait. I want you now."

Blair chuckled before placing her brush on the counter and strolled over to the bed, giving Rich a chance to get an eyeful. She slid beneath the covers and Rich immediately rolled on top of her.

"Want the lights on or off?"

"Leave them on, all the better for me to see you," Blair teased as she stroked her husband's face. "Thank you so much for today, I truly enjoyed it." She sighed before pulling Rich's lips toward hers and slipping her tongue in his mouth. Rich gently suckled it, and Blair moaned lightly as her hands roamed down and cupped Rich's behind. It was firm and deliciously rounded.

Her fingers floated over his backside, and Blair knew that he enjoyed the sensation because he slowly rotated his pelvis against hers. "I'm going to take a trip downtown," Blair sang and Rich groaned with appreciation, then made a move to roll off her. "No, stay where you are," Blair ordered. "Just lift up a little." Rich did as instructed and she slithered down to his thighs, then gently kissed his birthmark; it was the color of a graham cracker and shaped like a fuzzy star.

She continued kissing it until the skin around it turned a delicate pink. Blair sighed happily before scooting up a smidgen and sensuously sliding her mouth across his penis, teasing with her lips until she opened her mouth and invited him into its warmth.

"Oh God!" Rich shuddered.

Blair giggled as she reached up and softly caressed his shaft, from his sack to his tip; she didn't stop until he was so hard it felt like he could break down a door with it. All the while his hips were moving with her hand.

"That feels good, baby," Rich moaned. "Suck me," he begged.

"What do you want me to do?" Blair teased as she reached down and cupped his sack.

"I want for you to suck me! Lick me!" Rich ordered.

"Lick you? Suck you? Whatever for?" Blair taunted.

"Do it!" Rich ordered.

"Say please."

"Please," Rich answered in a strangled voice. Blair grinned as she leaned up and teasingly licked and flicked at his penis before taking him in her mouth. As her lips closed around his hard member he gasped and her body flushed with desire. Reaching up, she cupped his behind and gently guided him deeper in her mouth. "Aw, baby," he groaned, then he froze and grabbed Blair by the shoulders and pulled her up and entered her in one motion.

She gasped as her hips bucked up and her legs encircled his waist. She wrapped her arms around his neck and held on for dear life.

Afterward, Blair fell asleep nestled in Rich's arms, the blond lady forgotten.

Chapter 19

Madison stirred her café au lait as she waited. Maxie's was crowded and her gaze periodically darted toward the door. Her father had called the night before, begging her to meet him. She glanced down at her purse; it was stuffed with five hundred dollars in cash. Whenever her father visited it always cost her.

It was seven o'clock when her father ambled into the restaurant, thirty minutes late. Madison shook her head; some men just can't let go of their youth, and her father was one of them. Today his sixty-year-old body was covered in an Enyce sweatsuit complete with the matching skullcap. He was also iced to the max; both pinky fingers boasted diamond rings, two-carat studs dangled from both earlobes, and a huge, gold, diamond-encrusted cross swung from his neck. Madison almost sneered, but caught herself. *Here he is looking like a BET music video reject and he couldn't afford his girlfriend's abortion.*

"Hey, Daddy," she smiled, before getting up and hugging him.

"What kind of bougie place is this?" He frowned as he squinted at the menu. He refused to get reading glasses. "What's 'focaccia, brochette, bow tie, feta cheese', and don't let me get started on the drinks, 'cappuccino, mocha latte, macchiato, and espresso.' What happened to a regular cup of coffee and a ham on white?" he grumbled. Madison sighed and pulled the menu from his hand and studied it.

"Here it is," she said, pointing to an item. "Just tell them you want white bread with this. And here's the regular coffee."

He peered at the item. "I don't know why they didn't just put that down," he griped and Madison was beginning to think that the golden arches would've been a better choice.

"So, what's up?" Madison asked, as she took a sip of her drink.

"I'm not going to be around forever," he began.

Madison's heart jumped into her throat. No matter how trifling her father was and how little of a role he played in her life, she loved him and would miss him if something terrible happened to him.

"You're not *dying?* Are you?" she whispered fearfully.

Her father laughed, a big, booming laugh that was healthy and full of life. "Aw, hell naw! Nowhere near it, girl. I have enough juice in me to last ten lifetimes. Just ask Moe . . . I put it on her so good last night that she begged me to stop. And I didn't use Viagra, either. It was all natural," he boasted loudly. Madison dropped her head in her hand, embarrassed.

"So, why the meeting?" she asked. Suddenly he started fidgeting; he adjusted his skullcap, his necklace, and the cuffs of his sweatshirt. His hand was inching to his right ear when Madison called out. "Daddeeee?"

"I don't know how to say this," he muttered and Madison studied him. His eyes were lit with fear.

"Daddy?" She reached across the table and covered his hand. "Just tell me. It's not that bad. After all, I am your daughter. I'm tough. I can take it," she said bravely, although she felt a little weak.

"You know that I haven't always been the father I should've been to you," he started and Madison nodded. "I know that I haven't always been there for you. Hell, I missed half your childhood and just about as much of your teen years. Don't even ask me where I was during your twenties. But no matter where I was, you were always on my mind."

"I know, Daddy," Madison said automatically; she never imagined her father thinking of anyone other than himself.

"I'm so proud of you. You've helped me out of some jams—" His voice thickened and Madison patiently waited while he composed himself. It didn't take long. "I just wish your mother was alive," he said quietly, then went silent. Madison was quiet as her father gathered his thoughts. "I'm just gonna say it." He paused, then looked at her face; it was the picture of calm, but underneath fear was fighting to come out. "Are you ready?" he asked and Madison nodded. "Okay, well, I'm just gonna say it. I'm gonna put it out there for everybody to see, I'm gonna—"

"Daddeeee!" Madison shrieked. "Just say it!"

"I'm not your real father," he confessed, ducking his head.

"What?" Madison sputtered. "What did you just say?"

"I'm not your biological father," her father repeated.

"I don't understand. What do you mean, you're not my real father?" Madison asked, shell-shocked. She slumped in her chair. He was the only father she knew. Pictures of him on the special occasions that he decided to show up at flashed in her head like a slide show.

"Well," he said as he sighed. "It's kind of hard to explain. You know, I married your mother when you were one year old?"

Madison nodded. She knew that she was already born when her parents had married. She attributed it to poor planning on their part.

Her father's face tightened, then said, "Your biological father was sent to prison right after you were born."

"My biological father?" Madison muttered in disbelief, then swayed in her seat.

"Are you okay?" Lucius rose to help her.

Madison pressed her hands into the chair to steady herself. "I'm fine," she whispered. They were silent, then, "This could all be a big mistake. How do you know you aren't my father?"

"I'm not," Lucius said quietly.

Madison rested her hands on the table and leaned toward Lucius, staring him in the face. "But how do you know?" she pressed.

"I know," he insisted.

"How do you know? Did you take a paternity test?"

"I didn't need to take a test."

"Well, see, there you go. There's a chance you might be my father. We should go down and take a test. I have money, see," she said, her voice almost maniacal as she reached into her purse.

"Stop!" Lucius hissed. "Listen to me."

"What?"

"I'm not your father," Lucius said gently.

"You're lying!" Madison shrieked, then hopped out of her chair and charged at her father. He caught her hands as she sobbed. "You're lying," she whimpered against his chest. "Why didn't Momma tell me?"

He shrugged, then awkwardly patted her on the back. "Ashamed, I guess. You know how your mother was. Straight-laced to the T."

"Where is he now? My . . . father?" She gulped, barely able to get the word out.

"Oh, he's been dead for over thirty years. He didn't last long in prison. He was there three months before he got himself killed. You okay?" The whites of Madison's eyes had turned an alarming shade of pink.

"I'm fine," Madison whispered before easing back into her own chair. I guess that explains why I don't look like him, Madison absentmindedly thought. "Why tell me now?" she asked.

He shrugged. "It's been bothering me. I felt that you needed to know."

"It's been *bothering* you?!" she yelled. "So it's okay to come in and fuck up people's lives just because something's *bothering* you?" she practically spat.

"Calm down! I didn't want you to find out from some-one else," he said, a little scared. He had never seen her this mad. "Besides, I hate secrets," he confessed.

Madison tugged napkins out of the dispenser and

dabbed at her face. "What the hell is really going on, Da—" It didn't seem right to call him that anymore. She bit her tongue and stared at him.

He held his hands out. "Everything's all good, baby, I wanted you to know."

"What I don't understand is why? Why tell me? We could've gone on the same way we've been going. You the absentee father who can't handle his shit and me the loyal, stupid daughter who's walking behind you with the pooper scooper, cleaning up after you."

Her father shook his head.

"I need to go," Madison announced, standing up, then plopping back down in her seat. "The check, I need the check," she said, dazed.

"Please call me," he pleaded. Madison looked into his eyes and saw the man who had sang her "Happy Birthday" on her fourth birthday, the man who had taught her how to make a mean fried bologna sandwich, and the man who had given her her first Barbie doll.

"I will," she promised softly. "Are you still my—" *daddy?* she wanted to ask, but the word clung to her lips, and no matter how hard she sputtered, it wouldn't come out. Instead, she fumbled with a few dollars, slapped them on the table, got up, and fled out the door.

Chapter 20

LaShawn and Calvin walked around Target, or Tarjay as Madison called it. It was Saturday afternoon and the store was filled with full-time mommies with sugar-high children and part-time daddies with their part-time kiddies. LaShawn and Calvin were already an hour deep into registering for their wedding gifts.

"Come on, Calvin, we're almost done," LaShawn said in a soothing voice, as though she was talking to one of her kindergartners. "We have just a teensy-weensy bit left," she said and felt a little bad about the white lie. They had a *lot* left to do. What had started off so promising turned uglier than a rain-soaked Tammy Faye Baker.

That morning Calvin had massaged her feet and made her a pitcher of sweet tea before driving her to Target. Looking at him now, with his mouth curled down and furrowed brow, LaShawn didn't see a trace of the man who just two hours ago squeezed fresh lemons for her tea.

"Why do I have to be here?" he sulked. "Why couldn't

you bring one of your girls?" LaShawn flicked a glance in his direction, but kept silent. He had been in a bad mood ever since she suggested that they not add a PlayStation 2 to their gift registry.

"Because, this is *our* wedding," LaShawn reminded him. "Do you like these towels?" she asked as she picked up a plush watermelon-colored towel and stuck it in Calvin's face.

"It's aw'ight," he mumbled and turned his head away, bored with the whole day. He glanced down at his watch and grimaced; it was getting late. Rita and Malcolm were planning to stop by with some weed. He and LaShawn never talked about what he did after she had stormed out of of his apartment, but Calvin knew better than to mention Rita or Malcolm to his fiancée. "I don't know a damn thing about towels," he grumbled, then slouched against a display counter.

"I think they're nice . . . and I'm going to register us for four," LaShawn said and to prove her point she quickly scanned the item. "There," she said, satisfied, and placed it back on the shelf. "But we can't have the bathtowels and not have the matching washcloths and hand towels, can we?" she asked sweetly as she reached for the matching items.

"Where do you plan on putting all this stuff? It's not like there's room in either of our apartments."

"Oh, didn't I tell you?" LaShawn asked, pulling herself away from the bathroom accessories long enough to peek back at him. "We have an appointment with a realtor next weekend. She's going to show us houses. Let me know if you want to see the houses before we do the drive-bys and we can pull them up on the Internet."

"Houses? Houses!" Calvin shouted, incredulous. This was the first he heard about buying a house and he said as much.

"Calvin," she whispered, then looked nervously around. Fortunately, they were the only ones in the aisle. "Calm down. I wanted to surprise you. We're not buying one on Saturday, we're just looking . . . then when we see one we both like, then we buy." She laughed softly as she reached out to stroke Calvin's hand, but he snatched it away from her.

"I know how it works. Whaddya think, I'm stupid? Why didn't you tell me about the house thing before now?" Calvin asked angrily.

"Calvin." LaShawn let out an exasperated sigh. "It's not a *house thing*. You know we'd talked about buying a house. I was just trying to move things along. I know that you're busy at work. I didn't want to bother you," LaShawn apologized.

"If you want to buy a house, then dammit, bother me!"

"I'm sorry," LaShawn repeated.

"Aw, fuck! This is too much, I'm going to the electronics department to play some video games," Calvin mumbled. "And hurry up, I've got things to do," he flung at her over his shoulder.

"Calvin! Don't go . . ." But she was talking to herself. "Calvin!" she yelled, not caring if anyone heard her, but he kept walking. "I was just trying to help," she muttered to herself. She was staring listlessly at the towels when she heard a squeaky voice.

"Hey, it's Miz Greene!" She felt a tug on her pants and looked down to see Terry smiling up at her. She looked up and right into Terrance's eyes. Her normal pleasantries jumbled in the back of her throat, and it took two good throat-clearing coughs before anything came out.

"Hey," she stuttered. "I didn't know you lived on this side of town."

"I don't . . . his mother does," Terrance answered, as he sneakily checked her out. She looked a lot better without her teacher uniform; he hadn't recognized her until Terry said something. He liked the way her jeans hugged her thick legs and the way her hair skimmed her shoulders. "I'd just picked him up when I remembered that I needed to get a new shower curtain for his bathroom," he said, then whispered loudly, "The last one had monsters."

"It did, Daddy, it really did!" Terry insisted. "I saw them. They jumped right out of the water and chased me," he said solemnly.

"Really. What did you do?" LaShawn asked. She loved hearing children's stories.

"I did this, kiii-ay!" he shouted and executed a karate move. "Then I did this, aiii-yuh!" he yelled, twirling around.

"Did you get them?" LaShawn asked wide-eyed.

Terry nodded. "But they keep coming back," he said ruefully.

LaShawn and Terrance smiled at each other. Then Terrance said, "We'll get something with footballs or basketballs on it." He stepped over to the shower curtains and pulled out three, each with different designs, and held them up for Terry. "Hey, look at these! We have basketballs, footballs, and soccer balls, all kinds of balls. Which one would you like?"

Terry carefully considered each curtain, then pointed to the brightly colored one decorated with basketballs.

"Oh, what a surprise," LaShawn teased and playfully rolled her eyes. Terrance held his hands up.

"Nu-uh, he picked it out all on his own. All I did was give my boy options," he said, laughing. "What are you doing?" he asked, spying the scanner in her hand.

"Oh, I'm registering . . . I'm getting married," she said, then almost guiltily held out her left hand.

"Nice," Terrance answered, and caught himself from peering too hard at it; he needed a microscope just to see a sparkle.

"Thanks!" LaShawn blushed.

"So, how does this thing work?" Terrance asked.

"Oh, it's easy. And I've had a lot of practice. Here, I'll show you," she offered and she expertly scanned several items.

"Hey, watch it now, that might be a little dangerous," he joked as he stuck his hand in his belt loops and pretended to shoot at LaShawn. "Hey, pawdner, that's way cool," he drawled.

"Yeah, way cool!" Terry mimicked.

"That's the worst John Wayne impression I've ever heard," LaShawn announced, but she was laughing so hard that she could barely force the words out.

"Hey, a brother can try." Terrance shrugged, smiling. "You mind if we hang out with you for a while?" he asked, not wanting to leave her quite yet.

"Not at all, I'd love the company."

Calvin was forgotten as the trio moved toward housewares. LaShawn was having so much fun with Terrance and Terry that registering for her wedding gifts went ten times faster than it did with Calvin. The trio buzzed around the store with the familiarity of a family, and before she knew it she was done.

Calvin headed back to where he'd left LaShawn. "What the fuck is this?" Calvin stopped in his tracks, then scurried behind a store display. Craning his neck, he peeked at LaShawn, who was standing a few feet away. "Who's that dude LaShawn cheesing at?" His blood boiled at how freely LaShawn gave away her smiles. A veil of red dropped over his eyes when LaShawn got on her tiptoes and wrapped her arms around Terrance's neck. "Ain't this some shit? Little Miss Church Girl hugging on another man. Whassup with that?" He silently watched the small group as his lips turned into a hate-filled smile.

Chapter 21

Blair set the blow-dryer on her vanity top and shook her mane of red hair, then smiled at her reflection. "You're looking good for a broad in her thirties," she crowed as she slowly made a three-hundred-sixty-degree turn in front of the mirror. Besides a few stretch marks and ten extra pounds, she pretty much looked the same way she did when she walked down the wedding aisle to Rich. She gave herself a saucy wink, pulled her hair up in a ponytail, and put on her sneakers before sailing through the house, then down the driveway to her mailbox.

She gave an airy wave to her neighbor, Mrs. Cohen, who was kneeling next to a flat of flowers ready to be planted. Blair glanced back at her professionally manicured yard and felt a twinge of guilt; unlike her neighbor she didn't have a green thumb.

At the mailbox Blair pulled out the stack of mail and absent-mindedly thumbed through it.

"Bill, bill, party invite, wedding invite, bill, junk—oh!"

Blair's hand stopped in midair. At the bottom of the stack lay a blood-red envelope; women's intuition told her that it wasn't a party invitation. Narrowing her eyes, she held the envelope up to the sun. In a blink she noted the flowery writing, the musky perfume, and an emptiness where the return address should be.

Taking a deep breath, she slid a manicured nail under the envelope's flap and the words plummeted her, stunning her into despair.

Blair,

   I'm so deliciously head over heels in love with Rich, I mean we're both crazy in love with each other, he's told me so many many times. For the past year he has been my reason to wake up in the morning, my reason to smile, and my reason to live.

   I didn't want to let you know this way, but I wanted to get it out in the open . . . we're all adults, aren't we? If you don't believe a word of this, look at the pictures. Also ask him about the conference he attended in April. San Francisco is sooo beautiful that time of year.

   P.S. I want Rich to be with me forever, and I plan on making that happen.

The pieces of mail slipped from her hands and fluttered to the ground. But what didn't escape her grasp was a picture of her husband and the blonde from the restaurant. She was sitting on top of her husband like he was Mount Everest and she had just conquered him. They were lying on a bed in front of a mirrored wall and one of them was cocky enough to take a picture of their reflection. It was blurry, as though they were under water, but clear enough for Blair to make out the lady's face and Rich's.

"This can't be happening," she said and moaned loud enough for Mrs. Cohen to look over and ask her if everything was okay. Blair gave her a loose smile, numbly picked up her mail, and staggered into the house.

Maria had the day off and Blair listlessly stumbled through her chores, including picking up the children from school and cooking dinner. Later that evening when Rich sauntered through the front door, he found Blair curled up in an oversize chair in the living room waiting for him. Fortunately, the children were upstairs out of hearing distance.

"Hey, babe," he boomed, smiling down at her.

Blair stared malevolently from the chair. If her eyes were lasers, he'd be dead. "Is it true?" she yelled.

"Is what true?" Rich's brow furrowed as he walked to the kitchen and poured himself a glass of juice, then made his way back to the living room.

"This!" Blair shouted, throwing the letter and picture at him. They both watched the papers slide off his chest and drop to the floor, lying between them.

Rich glanced down at the mess on the floor and did a double take, moving his head so fast that he nearly cracked his neck in two. He snatched them up with his forefinger and thumb as if they were contaminated. While he was studying them, Blair was scrutinizing him. She watched as he processed the evidence. "Baby," he began, "that's not me. It's a doctored picture."

"Fuck you!" she yelled, then gasped; she had never

cursed at him before, it sounded odd out there, jabbing away at them like a dull sword.

"Fuck me?" he repeated, and a smile tugged at his lips; she had never spoken to him like that. It was a turn-on.

"Yeah, fuck, fuck, fuck you!" she said, liking how the word felt on her lips. And the power she felt uttering it. She hopped out of the chair, stood toe-to-toe with Rich, and punctuated each word with a jab to his chest.

"Blair, listen," he implored, and with one hand he grabbed both of her wrists and stopped her poking. "All this isn't true, somebody is obviously trying to cause trouble. Do you think that I'd do anything to hurt you?" he asked. Rich felt her shrug against him. "Here, look at me," he instructed and tilted her face up to him. "Look in my eyes and see how much I love you."

Like a novice detective, Blair frantically searched his eyes for any sign of deceit or mistruth, but she only saw confusion and love.

"I don't know," she whimpered. Her voice trembled and her resolve was weakening. She wanted to believe Rich. "But the pictures . . . what about the pictures and the condoms?" she begged him and he quickly attempted to extinguish her worries.

"*Pshaw*, I told you the condoms weren't mine, they're—" It took Rich only a breath to remember the name he told Blair. "—Peter's. And the picture," he continued. "The picture is so fake, any amateur photographer can tell you. Here, let me show you. See, look right here, if this was a real picture, there should be a shadow right here, and what's up with her body, it looks way bigger than mine, it doesn't look natural. I don't know how you didn't see it before. This was all done on a computer. They can take anybody's face and pop it right on anybody's body, and just like that, you have incriminating evidence."

Blair snatched the picture out of his hand and studied it. "It's the lady from the restaurant, the one that had you panting like an overheated Saint Bernard."

"No—it's—not," Rich stuttered, flustered. Blood rushed to his face, turning it a strawberry red. "Let me see that," he demanded, then scrutinized the picture. "It's not her," he calmly decided.

"It is, too," Blair challenged.

"No, it's not, see." He held the picture out for her. "The only thing these two women have in common is that they're both blondes."

The woman's face was a fuzzy composite in Blair's head. She vaguely remembered what she looked like. The glimpses that she did get of her were now a blur. Blair looked at the picture for the millionth time and admitted to herself that he did make sense, but still . . .

"I'd never do anything to hurt you," Rich soothed, running his hand over her hair, which always reminded him of a fiery sunset.

Blair moved her head to his rhythmic caress; she was like a cat being comforted by its master. "I don't know," she whispered helplessly.

"You don't know what, honey?" Rich asked, as he sat down in the oversize chair and pulled Blair onto his lap.

"I don't know if this is true," she wailed against his chest.

"It's not," he reassured her firmly.

"It's not?" Blair asked, looking into the eyes of the father of her children, her husband, her best friend and lover.

Rich shook his head. "No."

"Well, why would anyone do this?" she asked, dabbing at her eyes with the edge of his shirt.

"Some people are freakin' idiots. They get their rocks off by fucking up people's lives. Go figure," he said, and shrugged.

"So you didn't do it?" Blair asked.

Rich laughed and Blair pressed her body against his, finding comfort in the way it moved next to hers. "I didn't do a thing," he said. "Kiss me," he instructed. Blair's lips met her husband's and it felt like the life was being breathed back into her. "I want you," he whispered in her ear and Blair giggled. Everything was going to be okay.

"I want you, too," she murmured and reached down to stroke his bulge.

"Let's do it right here."

"Here?"

"Mmmm, right here."

"What about the kids?"

"They're upstairs. And if we're real quiet, they won't hear a thing."

"I'll be real quiet," Blair promised, looking solemnly at him.

"I know you will, baby," Rich muttered. "I don't know how you ever thought that about me," he mused. "You're my life, you know that, don't you?" He said it with so much conviction that any doubt that she had quickly vanished, along with her top, jeans, and her underwear.

"There's something to be said about making love in the living room," Blair mumbled, as Rich's mouth clamped to her nipple and tongued the pink bud as if it were an ice-cream cone. "Oh gawd, your mouth feels so good!" she shrieked and Rich quickly covered her mouth with his, smothering her screams. "Rich," Blair gasped, pulling away from his mouth. "I want to make *you* feel good."

Rich went slackjawed when Blair slid to the floor and knelt between his legs and tugged off his shoes, his pants, and his boxer shorts. He moaned and his legs automatically opened wider when she softly grasped him and pumped her hand up and down, from his tip to his base. Then her mouth closed in over his penis and he groaned softly.

The ringing from the phone cut through Rich's moans.

"Don't get that. I love it when you suck me," Rich panted.

"I need to," Blair protested. "It might be something important," she said, then picked it up.

She listened quietly while the female caller recited every one of her husband's business trips, what he wore to each, and the most damaging information, the birthmark that decorated the inside of his right thigh.

"Who is it, babe?" Rich asked lazily. He couldn't wait for Blair, so he decided to pleasure himself. He stroked himself with a familiarity that only he had mastered.

"It's your bitch!" she hissed, whacking him across the head with the phone.

Chapter 22

Madison grabbed a bottle of wine and a glass, tucked her photograph album under her arm, and walked slowly to the living room.

"I think that I'm gonna need you tonight," she said, smiling grimly at the wine bottle as she uncorked it, then filled the wineglass. It wasn't until after she gulped down some wine that she found the strength to open the album. "Here we go," she whispered shakily.

Madison opened the album to a picture of her mother lovingly beaming down at her while cradling her in her arms. Madison slowly traced her mother's face; tears slipped down her cheeks. "I miss you so much," Madison choked out. "I truly do!" Madison ran her hand across her face before flipping the page. Lucius grinned up at her. Madison pulled the picture out of the protective plastic, her eyes narrowed to slits as she studied it.

The picture was taken at a picnic, and her mother, aunt, and cousins were in the background. "If you were my real daddy, would you have been around more?" Madison asked the picture.

Madison set the photo on her coffee table, then turned the pages until she got to the end of the album. The last picture showed Madison in her cap and gown proudly waving her MBA degree. Her mother and Lucius stood nearby.

"Momma, why didn't you tell me? I would've understood," Madison said. "I thought we were—oh no!"

Madison watched openmouthed as her plate glass window exploded into a million pieces. A rock fell at her feet. Madison threw the album to the side before she dropped to the floor. "Ohmigod, what the fuck is going on?" she wondered as she crawled over to her phone and quickly punched in 911.

"Someone just threw a rock through my window," she whispered into the phone.

"What's your name and where are you calling from?" a monotone voice asked.

"Someone's trying to hurt me," Madison whimpered after she'd answered the request for information.

"Is he in the house?"

Madison fearfully looked around her living room. "No. Please send someone," Madison tearfully pleaded.

"Are you the owner of the house?"

"Yes!" Madison hissed. "Are you going to send someone?"

"We'll send a car right out. Please stay in the house and be ready to identify yourself when the police arrive."

Madison clicked off the phone and quickly called Lauren, but got her voicemail. She frantically punched in LaShawn's number, but got her voicemail, as well. "Crap!"

Madison fumed as she almost threw down the phone. "Who am I gonna call now?" An image popped in front of Madison. The phone was slick with her sweat and she gripped it as though it was her lifeline as she carefully hit the buttons.

Madison nearly cried with relief when she heard his voice. "Eric?"

"Who's this?"

"Madison . . . Madison DuPree," she blurted.

"Hi, beautiful, what's up?" he asked, alarmed by her voice.

"I need your help. Someone threw a rock through my window and I'm scared. I don't want to be here by myself," she said, her words coming out in one panic-filled gush.

"Word? Somebody broke your window? I thought you lived in a nice neighborhood."

"I thought so, too. I guess I was wrong," Madison answered miserably.

"Do you want to come over here?"

"I need to stay here. The police are on their way, can you—?"

"I'll be right there," Eric softly promised.

"Hurry up," Madison begged. Thirty minutes later Eric was at her doorstep.

"I really appreciate you letting me spend the night," Madison said, giving Eric a grateful look. The night before, he had stayed with her while the police took the report. He had pulled out her vacuum and cleaned up the trillion slivers of glass, then somehow managed to find a piece of plywood, which he used to cover the gaping hole. "You really don't have to do this," Madison argued weakly, but a smile tugged at her mouth as Eric walked into the guest bedroom carrying a tray spilling over with McDonald's takeout.

"It's not a problem. Here, eat," he urged, settling the food in front of her, then stretching out on the bed before grabbing a breakfast sandwich. "I hope this is okay. After the last time . . ."

Madison blushed. Her last breakfast request was so bananas that she was surprised he even did attempt to feed her. "It's perfect. How did you know I fiend for McDonald's breakfast?" Madison asked around a mouthful of egg and sausage.

"Just a hunch," Eric said, shrugging. "Have you thought about who might've broken your window?"

Madison shook her head. "And I really thought about it. I know for a fact that I haven't pissed anybody off. I think it was some kids fooling around. They got scared and ran," Madison concluded.

"What time is the glass man coming today?"

Madison glanced over at the alarm clock. "Not until three."

"We still have time," Eric said.

"Oh no . . . you don't have to be there. You may leave as soon as you drop me off. You've been so wonderful . . . coming over, cleaning up, letting me stay over at your place. I truly appreciate it. I'll be okay."

"I know that. But I want to be there, okay?"

Madison nodded. "Sure," she said grinning.

"Are you all done?" Eric asked; the only thing left on the tray were greasy food wrappers. The girl ate more than a quarterback and a defensive lineman combined.

"I am," Madison said, then stretched. "I need to take a

shower. I'll be right back." She hopped off the bed and hurried to the bathroom. At the door she turned back and glanced at Eric. "Thanks again for all your help," she said sincerely before going into the bathroom and firmly shutting the door after her.

Eric threw away the wrappers, then made his way back upstairs to the bathroom. He softly knocked on the door. "Do you need anything?" he called.

"Soap!" Madison yelled. "The little bit that's here is hardly enough to clean my butt."

Eric laughed. "Hold on! I'll get you some!" he shouted, then in lower tones, "Got to have that pretty little ass of yours clean." He sauntered over to his linen closet, snatched up a bar of soap, then retraced his steps back to the bathroom. "Here's your soap," he said through the door.

"Well, bring it in," she encouraged and waited for him.

Eric tentatively pushed the door and it swung open. Steam smacked him in the face as Madison pulled back the shower curtain. His breath caught in the back of his throat at the sight of her body. Cascading water caressed her, licked her high breasts, tickled her flat stomach, and kissed the spot where her legs met. "Madison," he hissed as the soap slipped from his hand. Lust washed across Madison's face as Eric peeled off his clothes. He paused at the edge of the tub before giving her a questioning look. She gave a small nod of approval and he stepped in.

A delicious shiver of excitement shot through her when Eric's hardness brushed against her leg. They locked eyes, Eric's wide and determined and Madison's heavy-lidded and relaxed.

Eric's hands tangled in her braids as he pulled her face toward his and hungrily smothered her mouth. His tongue pushed past her lips and was eagerly met by Madison's. "I missed you so much," he murmured. In a frenzy he ran his hands up and down her body like a blind man seeing for the first time. Eric kissed her hard on the lips, then bowed his head and mouthed one nipple, then the other one.

"Turn around, baby," Eric instructed and a dazed Madison easily complied. "I wanna kiss that beautiful ass of yours." Madison hugged the tiles as Eric's hands stroked her behind. Her legs wobbled when Eric started nibbling on her butt as though it was a piece of chocolate. He kept at it until Madison whimpered lightly.

Eric made a sound that was between a sharp intake of breath and a sigh as he knelt down and stuck his head between her legs and tenderly kissed her spot. "Perfect," he uttered as his tongue slipped over her delicate folds.

"Eric," Madison moaned in a voice that was just as shaky as her legs. She leaned back against the warm tiles as her thighs tightened around his head.

"Sit down here," Eric said, patting the edge of the tub, and Madison straddled the porcelain, one foot braced against the wall and the other on the tile. Eric eased between her legs and his mouth zeroed onto her button. Two tongue flicks later Madison exploded. Eric gathered her up in his arms and trailed his finger up her arm, then blew softly in her ear. "I can make you feel like this every day of the week," he promised and Madison's body went stiff before she hopped up.

"I gotta go!" she said, grabbing a towel and rushing into the bedroom, where she plucked up her clothes and threw them on.

"Hold up! Where are you going? I thought you wanted me with you when the repairman came," he said. He had his pants half on and Madison had to force herself not to laugh at him.

"I got it," Madison assured him. She snatched up her purse, then practically ran to the front door. Eric was right behind her.

"You wanna stay over tonight?" he asked eagerly while zipping up his pants.

"I'll be fine."

"What happens if the kids come back?"

"They shouldn't, but if they do, there's a good chance that they'll get caught. The police said that they'll do an extra patrol of the neighborhood." Madison stood at her car. "Thanks again for your help. I don't know what I would've done if you hadn't been home," she said and gave his arm a quick squeeze.

Eric nervously cleared his throat. "I really liked what happened . . . in the shower," he hastily explained.

Madison blew out a stream of air, then said, "Umm . . . that should not have happened."

"I enjoyed making you feel good. And I'll do it any time you want."

Madison smiled at the prospect. She was still tingling, but she ruefully shook her head. "Naw, Eric, it's not gonna work. My schedule . . ." she offered with a soft shrug.

"Oh, I see," Eric said. But Madison knew he didn't. "Well,

you'd better get going, you don't want to miss the repair-man." He opened Madison's car door and she slid in. A blink later and she was halfway down the driveway.

Madison tapped on her brakes and came to a sudden stop. She glanced in her rearview mirror; Eric was still standing in the same spot she had left him. "He really likes me. Maybe Lauren was right. I should give him a chance," she mused.

Chapter 23

"Stop making a fuss," LaShawn scolded Madison.

"I don't wanna be here," Madison whined for the hundredth time. "Tell me again why I'm sitting in this oversize doll house?" she asked as she thumbed through a well-worn bridal magazine. All the models grinned big, toothy smiles as though they had found nirvana. So far, she and LaShawn had trekked through three malls, hand-picked their way through two garage sales, and waded through tulle and ruffles at half a dozen bridal boutiques, all for the perfect cake topper.

"It's not a doll house, it's a boutique, specifically a *bridal* boutique. And you're here because no one else could make it," LaShawn answered as she fingered through miniature figurines and flowers.

"What happened to your fiancé? Shouldn't he be here?" Madison asked, but she knew the answer to the question.

LaShawn shook her head. "I don't want to overwhelm my baby. But believe it or not, he's been helping me with the wedding stuff," she answered, then her lips turned into a secret smile that Madison immediately noticed.

"Ooh, what's that look for?"

"What look?" LaShawn asked innocently as she dipped her head and stared intently at a porcelain dove.

"That look that says: I wanna jump his bones," Madison joked, then her eyes widened and she smacked her hand over her mouth. "Girl," she drawled, "you gave him some, didn't you? Calvin finally got past the golden gates. Hallelujah! I bet you're stress-free now, aren't you? Sex does that for you," she whispered conspiratorially.

"No! No! No!" LaShawn yelled so loudly that the shopkeeper started heading in their direction, but turned away when LaShawn waved her off. "Calvin and I didn't do anything, so get your mind out of the gutter, missy," she said in a prissy voice, then she softened her tone. "May I ask you something?" she asked nervously and Madison nodded. LaShawn took a deep breath and plunged on. "Have you ever been attracted to more than one man at the same time?"

Madison's eyes widened and suddenly she hooted as comprehension dawned. "Oh my God! Miss Goody Two-shoes got *two* men. It's always the quiet ones."

"Keep your voice down. I don't have two men," LaShawn hissed. Embarrassed, she looked over her shoulder and was grateful when there wasn't anyone within earshot. She didn't want anyone to think she was *that* kind of girl. "Come here," she demanded as she grabbed Madison's hand and pulled her down a deserted aisle where dusty party favors littered the shelves. "You'd better not tell anybody what I'm about to tell you."

Madison's skin tingled. She loved gossip and this

sounded like it could be juicier than Morris Chestnut's butt. "I won't," Madison promised.

"I know you, Madison. Promise me."

"Aw, geesh. I promise," Madison solemnly vowed. "Whassup?"

"I have this student whose father picks him up every day. Well, anyway, I ran into them at Target and they ended up helping me register for my wedding gifts."

"Calvin wasn't helping you with that, either?" Madison asked incredulously.

"He was there . . . at first, but he got mad and I sent him away to play videos. Anyway, when I was walking around the store with Terrance, that's his name, it was as though—" She clamped her mouth shut and gave Madison an embarrassed look.

"It was as though you two were registering for gifts for your wedding?" Madison softly prodded.

LaShawn nodded. "It was so perfect, there were no arguments, I didn't have to watch what I said, it was so peaceful. And it felt right, like we're supposed to be together. I love Terry, that's his son," she hurriedly explained before Madison could ask.

"What are you going to do?" Madison asked.

LaShawn shook her head. "Nothing," she said. "I love Calvin and I've accepted his ring, so . . ."

"You don't have to go through with it."

"Oh, yeah I do. I can't do that to Calvin. He'd be so hurt and embarrassed."

Madison rolled her eyes, but didn't say anything. Something told her that Calvin would be okay. But out loud she said, "But you and Terrance are vibing."

"True. But I can't break off my engagement just because I'm *vibing* with someone who isn't my fiancé."

"People have done it for less. Listen." Madison rested her hand on LaShawn's shoulder. "No one will be mad at you if you decide not to get married. Not your family and not your girls. We all just want you to be happy."

"I'm happy and I know that I'm making the best decision," LaShawn said, smiling.

"Well, you do whatever you want. I want you to know that, whatever you decide, I got your back and I know that Lauren and Blair do, too. Let's go find you a cake topper," Madison said, suddenly energized.

"This is it," LaShawn breathed an hour later. "It's perfect. Deliciously perfect," she crowed and reverently studied the topper; it was hand-blown glass—a man and woman with their arms entwined, the man gazing adoringly down at the female.

"Fabu! Now we can go," Madison muttered. LaShawn floated to the register. As the cashier was boxing up the cake top, Madison leaned into LaShawn. "You don't have to do this," Madison gently reminded her. "The invitations haven't even gone out yet."

"But they will," LaShawn said confidently as she handed the clerk her credit card. "Are you coming to the invitation-stuffing party?"

"Do I have a choice?" Madison grumbled and LaShawn grinned and shook her head as she and Madison traipsed out of the store.

In one hand LaShawn had the topper and in the other she held a bag of Chinese food. Humming softly to herself, she strolled down the hall to Calvin's apartment. At the door she rapped her knuckles against the metal, and when her knocks weren't answered she slipped her key into Calvin's lock.

The door swung open to a dark living room. LaShawn tiptoed in and flicked on the living room lights. She winced and almost clicked them off. Everywhere she looked was evidence of Calvin's sloppiness. Lakes of junk littered the floor. Plates with dried food glued to them were scattered among dirty clothes, including his soiled underwear. "Ewww, gross! This is definitely gonna change when we get married, I'ma have to give boyfriend a crash course in housekeeping," she muttered, then her ears perked up.

Muffled sounds were coming from the bedroom. "He must've left his TV on," she said as she picked her way through the living room to the source of the noise. She flicked on the light and froze in her tracks, too shocked to go any farther. Less then ten feet away from her was Calvin. He was butt naked, spread-eagle on the bed, his hands and feet securely tied to the bedposts, his eyes screwed shut, and he was jabbering like a fool as his hips bucked up. On top of him, riding him like he was a mechanical bull, was Rita.

The Chinese food and her precious cake topper fell from her hands and she let out a screech so loud that it could've been heard two floors down. Calvin's eyes snapped open and his mouth widened to a large O. Rita flipped off Calvin and, with as much dignity as a lady who had been busted cheating with another woman's man could muster, hobbled around the bedroom plucking up her clothes. "I didn't want to do anything," she babbled. "He made me." As soon as she gathered up her clothes, she stopped in front of LaShawn. "You know you're my girl, don't you?"

"Get the fuck away from me!" LaShawn hissed, her voice deadly. "Get the fuck out of my sight! Get the fuck out of here!" she shouted. LaShawn was too incensed to notice that vulgarity flowed out of her mouth like rotten sewage. When Rita didn't move, LaShawn raised her right hand to slap her. Rita's pale skin, flushed with sex, suddenly went deathly white with fear. While keeping her eyes on LaShawn she backed out of the bedroom, into the living room, and out into the hallway. She didn't turn around until she was safely in her own apartment.

LaShawn whirled on Calvin. This was her first time ever seeing him naked. Despite her anger, she had to look, she wanted an eyeful. Stepping closer to the bed, she peered down at him. Calvin shrunk against the bed. His sinewy body was covered with tattoos, she counted ten alone on his chest, arms, and legs; she would hate to see what his back looked like. His lightly muscled arms and legs shook with fear. Her gaze traveled to where his legs met and she studied the spot with interest. A couple of minutes ago it was hard enough to poke somebody's eye out, now it lay limply against his thigh, shriveled up to the size of a peanut. She snorted in disgust.

"Why, Calvin?" she asked, then the tears came, a sea of them rolling down her face. Then came the pain, waves and waves of it; she clutched her stomach and fell to her knees and howled. She cried for her naïveté, the wedding that wasn't going to happen, and losing the love of her life. In the snap of two fingers, her life had changed.

LaShawn wailed until her stomach hurt and her eyes felt as though someone had scrubbed sand into them. She shakily got to her feet and glared down at Calvin.

"Tell me why you had to do this? I gave you everything. I took real good care of you. Tell me why."

Calvin tugged at his restraints, then said, "Because of you. It was your fault."

"My fault!" LaShawn screeched. "How was Rita sliding on you like you were a fireman's pole my fault?"

"Because you wouldn't give me any," Calvin said softly and LaShawn's mouth dropped in shock. "That's right, I did it because I wasn't sexually satisfied," he finished, then jutted his chin out.

LaShawn blindly reached down and snatched up the first thing her hand touched, then torpedoed it at Calvin, grinning coldly when the shoe slapped him in the ribs. "Don't you use that excuse. Don't you fucking dare," LaShawn hissed. "When you signed on with me, you knew what the deal was. You knew that I practiced abstinence and I wanted to do so until our wedding night. So that's a sorry excuse. Coming from a sorry man."

"Whatever," Calvin muttered, his side still stinging from the shoe. "Only thing I know is that if we were doing it like normal couples, I wouldn't have to be with skanks like Rita."

"Skanks? How many *other* women have you slept with, Calvin?" LaShawn asked, then braced herself for his response.

"Rita was the only one," he lied.

"I don't believe a word you're saying." LaShawn almost spat as her gaze swept over his body, then something registered that hadn't before. Her eyes widened with fear. His penis was bare. "You didn't use protection? You were going to come to me on our wedding night with other women's shit on your dick? That's fucked-up, Calvin!"

He averted his eyes as she gave his deflated penis a contemptuous glance.

"And you know what? I didn't miss a fucking thing! 'Bye, Calvin," she said sadly. She gave him one last look before stepping over the Chinese food and her broken cake topper and walking through his living room. She picked up her purse, removed his key from her ring, and left it on the coffee table. Without a backward glance, she walked out of his apartment.

Hearing the door slam brought Calvin back to life. "Shawn!" he called out, as he struggled against his restraints. "Shawn! Heeelp me!"

Chapter 24

Lauren was perched on the side of the examining table, her feet dangling over the edge. She couldn't stop fidgeting with the paper cover-ups. The indignity of it all wasn't the fact that no matter how hard she tried to adjust the cover up her butt still peeked out, but that it was tinted a light purple, as though it would make the appointment feel more like a costume party instead of what it really was.

She angrily swatted at the paper. She didn't understand why she had to undress. She told the nurse that all she wanted was a rash checked out, but the nurse still made her take off her clothes. That's how Dr. Patel found her, fussing with her paper gown and her butt pressed into the cold leather.

After asking her some preliminary questions, Dr. Patel set down his chart and began his examination. "Now, let's take a look to see what we have here. How long have you had these hives?" the doctor asked, but he wasn't looking at her. He was hunched over her, tiptoeing his fingers over the rash. The miniscule bumps made a mask on her upper body; they started at her hairline, covered her shoulders, and ended right underneath her breastbone, where her boobs rubbed against them, which had irritated them even more. They were angry, little red splotches on her skin that itched incessantly.

After she had passed out in the elevator, Cleve forced her to make an appointment with the doctor. And for two days after that Cleve had constantly reminded her how lucky she was that one of the building maintenance men had found her and not some pervert.

Lauren shrugged and nervously dangled her feet. "A couple weeks, I guess," she answered, then paused, remembering what she had to do today. "Is this going to take long? I need to pick my daughter up from school, my son from his computer class, my husband's clothes from the dry cleaner, drop the dog off at the vet, stop by the grocery store to pick up refreshments for my PTA meeting tonight, then finish a twenty-page proposal for a new product my company is launching," she babbled, and suddenly her eye started twitching and Dr. Patel's eyebrows shot up as if he had discovered something new.

"See that?" he said, and pointed to her jumping eyelid. "See that? What's all this?"

"What? What's all what?" Lauren asked, her gaze slipping away from the doctor's as she pretended not to know what he was talking about.

"I saw a twitch," he said, his voice almost accusatory.

Lauren gently messaged her eye. "Nu-uh," she denied, then, "only a little one," she reluctantly admitted and pulled her hand away when she no longer felt the spasms.

"This isn't good, young lady. Now tell me what's wrong," he asked sympathetically while he pulled a chair up to the examining table and the story poured out. He had been her doctor for two years now, a lifetime in the HMO system.

Dr. Patel learned about how she constantly crammed thirty hours of activities into a twenty-four-hour day. Her words tripped over one another as her pain flowed from her.

"If you keep this schedule up, you're going to end up in the hospital," Dr. Patel said gently. "Take my word for it. Nothing good comes from carrying a burden that's too heavy for you."

Lauren vigorously shook her head. "Who's going to take care of my family? Nobody else can do it," she huffed and imagined Cleve doing half the things that she did and she smiled. The poor man could barely get dressed without coming to her for instructions.

Dr. Patel gave her a conspiratorial smile as if they shared an inside joke. "I know exactly what a wife and mother do, my wife has been one forever. And I'll tell you the same thing I told her. Take a vacation, and try to figure out how you can cut back on some of your responsibilities; otherwise, I'm going to keep seeing you." He pointed to her face. "These hives and twitching eye are just a warning sign, soon you'll be suffering from ulcers, problems with sleeping, low sex drive, all because of stress. Take care of it now. I'll prescribe this cream for you, which will take care of the hives, but you'll need to reevaluate your lifestyle," he finished.

Lauren crossed her arms in front of her chest and dropped them when it felt like the paper was going to tear. "I take a half-hour lunch every day," she lied; that only happened once or twice a week.

"Wow! You give yourself a whole two and a half hours out of a forty-hour work week. Isn't that generous of you," he drawled.

"It's enough," Lauren argued.

"It's enough?" Dr. Patel repeated incredulously. "That's hardly enough to keep a flea relaxed. You're going to run yourself down, then who's going to be there for your family—and *you?*"

Lauren left the doctor's office armed with a prescription for cortisone and his words echoing in her head.

Chapter 25

"Who's this? Who's this?" LeeAnn repeated into the phone, and she was answered by slippery wet sobs. "I'm gonna hang up if you don't tell me who this is," she threatened.

"Lee—Ann," Blair wailed, hiccupping as she tried to catch her breath. "It's me."

LeeAnn furrowed her yolk-colored eyebrows and pulled the phone away from her ear, staring hard at the receiver as if it could tell her who was on the other end.

"It's me . . . Blair," she finally choked out.

"Blair? What's wrong? You sound like somebody died."

Blair hobbled into the guest bedroom and closed the door. "A part of me did," she whispered. "I don't know where to start," she said, gulping back tears.

"Start what?" Her sister was beginning to scare her. "Tell me what's going on with you!" LeeAnn demanded, then fell quiet as Blair told her about her and Rich's argument. "No way, you're crazy," LeeAnn protested. "Rich kisses the ground you walk on." She rummaged around a drawer until she found a cigarette. She lit it up and inhaled deeply, sucking the smoke deep into her lungs and instantly relaxed as the nicotine flowed through her vessels.

Blair shook her head. "That's what I thought, too, but they were fake kisses," she said sadly.

"Tell me exactly what happened." Blair was the pretty, smart one, who had found her knight in shining armor. He got herself out of the hellhole and into a castle.

Blair settled on the bed and glanced around the room. She was glad that she had decorated it in her favorite colors. It was going to be where she slept from now on, since Rich refused to leave. "There's this waitress," Blair slowly started, picking her words like an apple picker would fruit, carefully and with a purpose. "She works in the restaurant across the street from his office. It's funny, all this time I always worried if he had eaten a nutritious lunch. Little did I know that he *ate* his lunch," she said bitterly.

"Oh, Blair!" LeeAnn cried, then stubbed the cigarette into an overflowing ashtray. "He's just like all the other men."

"Mmmm," she said absentmindedly, but she kept talking. "It's been going on for a year."

"Did he fess up?" LeeAnn demanded.

"Hell no! No, he didn't confess to a damn thing. He denied it until the truth smacked his ass. She sent a letter, then called. "

"She called you?" LeeAnn asked. This was something right off a talk show. "She *called* your house looking to start something? That bitch!"

"And she sounded like she was still in high school."

"I'm so sorry. What are you gonna do?"

"I don't know," Blair moaned; her perfect world had turned into a horrible nightmare.

"You're not going to leave him, are you?" she rushed on before Blair could continue. "I mean, men cheat all the time. Hell, look at Charlie. He cheated on me so many times that I've stopped counting. Men are like dogs, just don't give him any treats anytime soon and he'll come back to you with his tongue wagging, " LeeAnn finished firmly.

"Little that's done you," Blair muttered, but louder she said, "I don't know what to do."

"Please don't leave him," LeeAnn begged. "You remember how it was . . . when we were little?"

Blair sighed. An image of the trailer home she and her family grew up in jumped into her head. The trailer park had more poor white trash in it than it had trailers. On warm nights people would sleep outside with their pets; just thinking about it made her stomach roll. The idea of living that way again scared her. And if she could help it, it would never happen. "It was bad. But we're not little anymore."

"You have three kids, and you've never worked," LeeAnn argued, pointing out a truth that Blair didn't want to admit to herself.

"I have no idea what I'm going to do, but I tell you, whatever it is, Rich is gonna regret screwing around behind my back," she vowed.

Chapter 26

Blair rushed into yoga class, threw her workout bag in the corner, and ignored the frowns and groans thrown in her direction for disrupting the class as she squeezed in between Lauren and Madison; LaShawn was at the front of the class. She gave her friends a diluted smile, then eased into position. Closing her eyes, she lifted her right foot and placed it so high on the inside of her left thigh that it grazed her crotch. She steadied herself and forced herself to focus.

She opened her eyes and studied her class members, trying to figure out which one had the perfect marriage. Probably a quarter of them, Blair surmised.

Sixty minutes filtered away to just a memory, signaling the end of the class. The four friends showered and changed, then walked over to Leonard's. Leonard and Thomaseena were both off; Blaine, the assistant manager, escorted them to their table.

Madison slowly chewed her grilled chicken as she stole covert glances at Lauren. Lauren had been quiet all evening, as if she had something on her mind. "What's wrong with you? You're not your usual perky self," Madison joked.

"Thanks," Lauren said sarcastically, then softened her tone. "You're right. I'm stretched to the max. I'm suffering from the 'disease to please,' " she said glumly.

"Isn't that an Oprah phrase?" Madison asked. "Oprah knows she can twist some words together. She needs to come out with a book."

"Well, whatever," Lauren said, dismissing Madison's rambling. "But yeah to your first question, I don't know how to say no," she said.

"It's such a simple word," Madison teased. "Just say it. Come on, I'll help you."

Lauren shook her head at her friend. "You need help. Anyway, my doctor said that I need rest, *big-time rest,*" she finished. She didn't tell them about the hives, headaches, or the fainting spell.

"What kind of rest? Hiding-up-in-your-room rest? Laying-on-the-couch rest? Or running-out-of-the-country rest?"

Lauren chopped up a meatball, then said, "Hell, all of the above!" she joked. "I really need to do something," she said, glancing down at her watch, her mouth turned down at the corners, worrying about all the things she needed to do.

"Why are you watching the clock? Need to be somewhere?" Blair asked, after Lauren flicked her wrist for the third time that evening.

"Maryann needs me to pick up her medicine," she answered automatically as if the request was normal, then she lowered her fork. "Look at me," she said, locking eyes with each friend before moving on until she had three pairs of eyes glued on her. "Look at me," she repeated. "Even when I realize what my problem is, I can't stop it. I just keep going, and going . . ."

"Like that little bunny," Madison cut in and everybody laughed. She reached for Lauren's hand. "Now that you realize this, what are you gonna do? If you keep on like this, life is gonna kick your ass."

LaShawn sniffed. "Madison, I don't know why you always have to be so vulgar." Surprised, Madison looked over in her direction; she had forgotten she was there. She had been quiet for most of the evening.

"It's already kicking my ass," Lauren admitted and ignored LaShawn, who disapprovingly smacked her teeth. "I'm going crazy. I've been snapping at my kids, pulling my hair out over my job and . . ." She gulped deeply, then said, "Cleve and I haven't made love in months," she revealed, and she suddenly felt free, as though the secret had been a heavy ball weighing her down.

Her friends began babbling at once.

"God bless you."

"I didn't know."

"Dang, girl, no sex for months? How can you live?" All eyes turned to Madison. "What?" she shrugged.

"I've been pushing him away so much that I think he might be having an affair," Lauren declared, ashamed. "It's not like he's getting any at home."

"Hell, a man could be getting it at home and still cheat," Blair whispered and the way she said it made everyone stop eating and look in her direction.

"Blair? What's wrong, girl?" Lauren asked. She couldn't imagine anything wrong with Blair's marriage; she lived such a charmed life. But when she saw her friend's face red-den and her eyes become glassy, she knew she was wrong.

Blair choked back her tears as the story poured out of her, every sizzling detail.

"Oh gosh," Madison moaned, sick to her stomach. Rich and Blair gave her hope that there was such a thing as a truly happy marriage. "What's going to happen to you two?"

"I don't know. We're just kind of limping along. He's tip-toeing around the house, waiting for me to say something, but we're kind of taking it day by day," she said, thinking about her children. She didn't want to do anything that would take them away from their father. "At least we have a wedding to look forward to." Blair sniffed, then grabbed LaShawn's hand.

"No y'all don't," LaShawn muttered. Lauren, Blair, and Madison all looked at one another, not sure if they heard correctly.

"What?" they all asked at the same time.

"I'm not getting married," LaShawn admitted, and the tears that she had been holding back all evening spilled forth. "We're not getting married," she repeated, in a tear-soaked voice.

"Oh baby," Blair crooned as she took LaShawn's trem-bling body into her arms. Madison and Lauren sat help-lessly as LaShawn silently cried into Blair's shoulder. Once she was done, she escaped to the ladies' room. When she re-turned, her face was puffy and her eyes were almost swollen shut, but that didn't stop her from telling them what hap-pened. Her voice was raspy from all the crying.

"I knew that brother wasn't any good. There was some-thing about his eyes, all shifty and shit," Madison said.

LaShawn nodded in response. "Yeah, he sent dozens of roses to my apartment. I got so many that I had to give some to my neighbors. One time he showed up right before school, trying to talk to me. I had to call security to escort his butt out. At least he hasn't shown up at my apartment," she said.

"And you haven't spoken to him since?" Lauren asked and LaShawn shook her head. Lauren was proud; her friend had more backbone than she had given her credit for.

"It was hard . . . not calling," LaShawn said. "You know we used to talk to each other at least three times a day. I feel lost," she said forlornly. "I want some type of closure, but I guess sometimes it's not possible."

"Don't worry about closure, you got it, baby. It smacked you in the face, when he decided to screw his neighbor," Madison retorted. "Can't get much more closure than that." The group agreed and everybody gazed sadly at one another for a moment.

"My daddy isn't my daddy," Madison admitted in a soft voice.

"What?"

Madison nodded. "My father is some guy who was killed in prison. Now I'm over thirty, with no husband, no kids, and no daddy." She started to cry and Blair passed her a handful of tissues. They waited until Madison composed herself.

"Are you going to look for his family?" LaShawn asked.

"I don't know." Madison sniffed. "I haven't thought that far ahead. I just keep wondering, how could my mother keep this secret from me? I mean, what would've happened if I had gotten sick and needed some type of blood transfusion?"

"You've never seen your birth certificate?" LaShawn hesitantly asked.

Madison nodded her head. "I did, but the father's name was missing. And when I asked Mom about it she said that Lucius never got a chance to sign it. And of course I believed her. Lucius was always a half-assed parent. I was so stupid."

"No you weren't, you trusted your mother. Nobody can fault you for that. Is there a family member you can ask? Doesn't your mother have a sister?" Blair asked.

"Yeah, Aunt Pearl. Maybe I'll give her a call. Thanks," Madison said. "And then there was the broken window, the credit card thing, and last week my car was keyed. Somebody's trying to drive me crazy."

"Whose boyfriend did you steal?" LaShawn asked dryly.

"Nobody's. I'm not dating anyone. I'm taking a break from men," Madison admitted. Then Lauren stood up.

Blair raised an arched eyebrow. "Where are you going?" she asked.

"To see if dogs are talking because the world must be going crazy if Madison DuPree is giving up men."

Everybody laughed. "Sit your silly behind down," Madison said. "I want to figure out what I want in a man. That's all."

"Aren't we the bunch," Lauren said, chuckling. "Pitiful, just plain pitiful. Our lives are a big mess."

"You know what the sad part is?" Madison asked the group.

"What?" Lauren, LaShawn, and Blair asked at the same time.

"That none of us has confided in the others," Madison whispered sadly.

"Shame. That's why I didn't," Blair admitted. "You all thought I had the perfect marriage. *Hell,* I thought I had the perfect marriage, now we all know that isn't true," Blair said as she pushed down a sob. "I guess I was trying to wrap my mind around the whole situation before I told you guys."

"It wasn't until I went to the doctor that I realized how sick I really was," Lauren said quietly. "It's so hard for me to admit when I need help. Y'all know that I'm a superwoman, but I think it's about time that I gave up my cape."

"Well, I just didn't want to burden anyone with my problems," LaShawn chimed in and the group quickly pooh-poohed her.

"And I was one confused cookie. I mean, how can I tell y'all about my—father, um, I mean Lucius, when I don't even understand it all myself," Madison said.

"We're here for you, honey," Blair reassured her.

"Let's promise each other one thing," Lauren said.

"What?" LaShawn asked.

"That we never, ever keep secrets from one another. This is crazy. Here we are, as close as sisters, and we didn't even come to one another. Well, let's not let this happen again." They all nodded in agreement.

"It would be so nice to get away from it all. A place where we can forget about our problems and chill," Lauren mused.

"We can always drive down to Savannah and stay at a bed-and-breakfast," LaShawn offered.

Blair shook her head. "No, too boring. We'll have too

much time on our hands to think about our problems. Any other ideas?"

"I know," Madison exclaimed, with sudden inspiration. "Let's take a cruise," she said, and looked around at her friends for consensus.

"I do need to relax," Lauren said. "Otherwise, a man with a big net is gonna come get me," she joked. "And I'm gonna take the time off. Susan had better not say a damn thing."

"I definitely need some fun and some time to think," Madison chimed in, thinking about her chaotic life.

"A cruise would be nice," LaShawn admitted. "It would be good to get away from everything. My momma calls me up every day just to make sure I'm okay. I don't want to tell her how I'm really feeling, but she's making things worse for me. Sounding all pitiful. Sometimes I don't want to answer the phone. But I know if I don't she'll just show up at my apartment."

"And I need to think about what to do," Blair said thoughtfully. Her lips slid up into a tentative smile, and suddenly life didn't seem so gray. "Who's going to coordinate this?"

"I will," LaShawn said, and pulled a travel brochure out of her bag. "I just happen to have this," she said to the astonished looks from her friends. "I was looking for honeymoon ideas. It wasn't like Calvin was going to man up and do it." She spread open the brochure and studied the schedules. "There's a fourteen-day cruise leaving for the Caribbean this Saturday. It's going to Puerto Rico, St. Martin, St. John, St. Thomas, and the Bahamas."

"It's kind of soon," Lauren and Blair mumbled simultaneously, then caught each other's eye and giggled.

"So what kind of activities do they have?" Blair asked.

"Everything!" LaShawn answered as she ran a finger over the listing of activities. "We can snorkel, swim with the stingrays, take a glass-bottom boat tour, and gamble," she recited, then, "and a whole bunch of other stuff. And there's always shopping." She laughed. "I think it'll be fun. Don't y'all?"

Madison pressed her lips together, envisioning her dream vacation swirling out of her reach. "If we stop to think about it, we'll never do it," she pressed. "Look, it was meant to be. We all agreed on a cruise, then LaShawn whips out a cruise schedule. It's as if *He* wants us to go."

"Let's do it," Blair whispered, thinking about Rich's reaction; he'd be pissed. To hell with him! She smiled wickedly at her thoughts.

"Yeah!" Lauren and Madison agreed.

"It's a go, then," LaShawn said, pulling out her cellphone. "I'm going to make the reservations right now," she said and called her travel agent. She wanted, no *needed*, to get away from everything. "Hey, y'all, the agent says that a huge Atlanta singles group will be on the ship. They're practically taking it over," LaShawn informed them. "Still want to go?" she eyed her friends.

"Well . . ." Blair hedged. A *singles* cruise. . . ."

"Go ahead," Madison and Lauren said at the same time.

LaShawn sent up a silent prayer of thanks and coordinated the trip. In less than twenty minutes they were all booked on a two-week Caribbean cruise.

Chapter 27

The women were so satisfied with the turn of events that they all ordered desserts. They were enjoying the sweet treats when Madison yelled, "Let's have a contest!"

Lauren quirked an eyebrow at Madison. "What kind of contest?"

Madison pretended to consider the question, but she already knew what she wanted. "Let's see who can have the most sex!"

"Madison!" Lauren practically shouted. "You just said you were giving up men."

"I know, but I changed my mind," Madison quipped.

"That fast?" LaShawn asked. "You change your mind more times than Whitney Houston changes wigs," she joked.

Lauren glanced up at the ceiling. "Lord, please help our little lost soul."

"I don't know," Blair said, but her eyes gleamed with interest.

Madison turned to LaShawn. "You don't have to partici-pate," she quickly reassured her.

"Maybe I want to," LaShawn answered, then jutted out her chin.

"What?" Madison asked. "Oh my." Madison laughed, fan-ning herself. "Miss Goody Two-shoes gonna get down and dirty?" The group laughed too, but all eyes turned to LaShawn, who just two minutes ago was a born-again virgin.

LaShawn blushed. "I'm not saying that I'll *do* anything, but just in case the situation comes up . . ." she said grin-ning at her friends. "And I'm not going to do anything with anybody unless I'm absolutely sure that he's a good guy."

Madison snorted. "Good guy? An oxymoron."

"Besides, abstinence wasn't working. I've ended up with more duds than I can count. I think it's time that I try some-thing different," LaShawn said.

"Now you're talking." Madison laughed.

"Let's just pretend that we do have this contest," LaShawn started. "How will we know who won and, most importantly, who'll be the judge?" All eyes turned to Lauren.

"Nu-uh," she said, holding up her hands. "I don't want to be sucked into your crap. Count me out."

"Come on, Lor," Madison whined. "You're the only one of us who won't be on a dick hunt. You can be objective."

"No!" Lauren said firmly.

"Please," Blair and LaShawn begged simultaneously.

"No!" Lauren said while shaking her head.

"I'll buy you a drink," Madison promised.

"No!"

"I'll buy you a new bathing suit," Blair offered.

"Hell no! The last thing I need is a new bathing suit."

"I'll walk your dog for a month," LaShawn offered.

Lauren shook her head. "That's what kids are for."

"I'll buy you a new sketchpad," Madison offered and she bit back a smile when she saw the glimmer of interest in Lauren's eyes. Aha! She went in for the kill. "And a set of watercolors," she offered nonchalantly.

"Oh hell. Make it oil paints and I'll do it," Lauren acquiesced and a cheer went up.

"So, are we having any rules?" Blair asked.

"Nope," Madison said, shaking her head. "No rules. You can do whatever you want to get whomever in bed with you."

"But how will we know who wins?" LaShawn asked. "Not that I plan on winning," she quickly added and Madison smirked.

"Well . . . what about the one who used the most condoms?"

"I am not counting used condoms," Lauren blanched and Madison looked at her in amazement; she didn't know that someone with her complexion could actually pale. "Count me out!"

"No, no, no," Madison answered. "You won't have to count used condoms. We'll collect the condom wrappers. So whoever has the most wrappers at the end of the trip wins."

"What does the winner get?" Blair asked.

"The best fucks of their life," Madison roared. "To the future 'Slut of the Caribbean.' " Madison held up her glass and toasted.

Chapter 28

"Where are you going?" Rich rushed into the bedroom. He had come home to find Ariel in tears with Caitlyn and Richard helplessly standing by. Between sobs and broken voices, he pieced the story together well enough to learn that Blair was in their bedroom packing her clothes.

Blair brushed past him. "Do you really care?" she shot at him while dropping clothes into her suitcase.

"Of course I do. You're not leaving me, are you?" he asked quietly. His lips were drawn into a grim line.

Blair rounded on him. "Would that make you happy?"

"No, it wouldn't," Rich answered contritely. "I would be happy if you talked to me. We can't go on like this, living like strangers. It's been weeks since we've had a decent conversation. I miss you," Rich said, reaching out to touch her hand.

"Get your hand off me," Blair hissed. "You didn't miss me while you were pounding an imprint of your mistress's ass into her mattress."

Rich ran a hand through his glossy hair. "I told you that

was a mistake. I would like for us to forget everything and move forward."

"Move forward?" Blair repeated, incredulity ringing in her question. "We're talking about your infidelity, not playing a game of Monopoly." She moved to her lingerie drawer and intentionally plucked out her sexiest pairs of underwear and nonchalantly tossed them into the suitcase. She could feel Rich's eyes on her as she flitted to the closet.

"I'm going to ask you again . . . where are you going?"

"I'm taking a cruise," she answered flatly.

"A cruise?" Rich repeated. His face went blank, then suddenly emotion spilled into his face and his lips curled into a smile. "That's a good idea. That's exactly what we need. I can move some things around and—"

"You're not going," Blair deadpanned and resisted the urge to chant "na na na na na" when his face dropped faster than a Miss USA contestant's hairdo caught in the rain.

"Who are you going with?" Rich asked quietly.

It was on the tip of her tongue to say a man's name, but instead she said, "The girls."

"The girls? I don't believe you. Just like that." He snapped his fingers. "You and your friends booked a cruise. That's bullshit. You're going with a man; who is it?"

Blair let out a frustrated stream of air. "There is no man. I'm really going with Lauren, LaShawn, and Madison. Just because lies easily fall from your lips doesn't mean that everybody is doing it."

"But you are coming back, right?"

"No, I'm going to abandon my kids," she shot back. "And don't worry, you'll get fed. Maria's going to stay here until I get back."

"When will that be?" Rich asked between clenched lips.

"A couple of weeks."

"I don't want you to go."

"You gave up any right to question my comings and goings when you slept with that bitch!"

"I'm not seeing her anymore," he said quietly.

"How many were there?" Blair asked, still throwing clothes in her suitcase. When she didn't get an answer, she faced Rich. Shamefaced, he averted his eyes. "Oh my God," Blair breathed, her eyes wide. "She wasn't the first . . . God dammit! You bastard!"

"Let's not talk about this. All you'll end up doing is making yourself more upset."

"How many?" Blair hissed.

"Blair," Rich pleaded.

"How *many?*" Blair repeated.

"She was the only one," Rich answered.

"You're such a bad liar. Tell me how many," Blair demanded.

Resignation crossed Rich's face. "Three, four, maybe . . . five. I guess."

"You guess?" Blair thought she might be ill. "People guess how many gumballs are in a bowl, people guess the weather, and people might even try to guess my age. But dammit, Rich, people do not *guess* the number of lovers they've had," Blair retorted. "You know what?" she asked sweetly.

"What?"

"I bet you come up with an exact figure, because you're gonna have a lot of time to think about it!" she said as she closed the top of her suitcase.

Chapter 29

Madison pulled up in front of her Aunt Pearl's house. The once-middle-class neighborhood had declined to lower middle class. Many homes were unkempt, with peeling paint, cracked windows, and graffiti-marred doors.

Madison got out of her car and walked up the steps toward a two-story, pale yellow house with white shutters. She placed a hand over her heart, which felt like it was going to break right through her chest it was beating so fast. She inhaled deeply before ringing the doorbell. Before her hand dropped to her side, the door flung open and Madison was face-to-face with her mother's sister.

"Hey, Maddy, come on in," Aunt Pearl said, grabbing Madison's hand and pulling her into the house. "You haven't been to visit me in ages, girl. How're you doing? Come on back to the kitchen and sit down."

"I'm fine, Auntie," Madison said. "Can I get a hug?" she asked.

"Oh, girl, where are my manners? Of course you may

have a hug. Come here." She opened her arms and Madison clutched her aunt as though she was a life preserver.

Madison gave her a quick squeeze before she stepped out of her aunt's arms and sat down. "Thanks, Auntie, I needed that."

"So how's your big corporate job?" Aunt Pearl asked as she moved around the kitchen, stirring food in pots and pulling bowls out of the refrigerator.

"Crazy. Man, they are working a sister like crazy. They're definitely getting their money out of me." Madison laughed. "What's been going on with you?"

"Same old stuff, nothing new. You know nothing changes around here," she answered.

Madison nervously cleared her throat, then softly said, "Auntie, my daddy, I mean Lucius, told me the truth."

Pearl stiffened, then turned around to face her niece. "Oh, Lord, I wondered how long he was going to keep the secret. I'll give it to him, he lasted longer than I thought he would."

"So it's true?" Madison asked in a flat tone.

"I'm afraid so," Pearl confirmed. She walked over to the kitchen table and sat down. "Don't be mad at your mother. She did what she thought was best for you. Things were different back then. Unwed mothers were frowned on. Not like today where single women are dropping babies as though they're laying eggs."

"I understand all that," Madison said. "But why couldn't she tell me? Why hide the truth from *me*?"

"She was ashamed. See, your biological daddy, Leroy Mead, was as cool as an ice cube, and he could sweet-talk any girl out of her panties. Now, your momma didn't give in to him as quickly as the other girls did. She made him jump through hoops. She did all the right things, and he courted her properly."

"What happened?" Madison asked.

"Well, like I said, Leroy was a sweet talker. He was tired of the game and wanted to get married. So one summer night he talked his way right into your momma's underwear. He had asked her to marry him, so it was okay for them to do it."

"They were engaged?"

Pearl shook her head. "Not really, he had given her some plastic, bubble-gum-machine-looking ring. By the time she found out she was pregnant with you, Leroy had been arrested for running numbers. Three months after that he was killed in prison."

"Why would Lucius marry her knowing that she was carrying another man's baby? That's too much of a selfless act for Lucius."

Pearl chuckled. "It was. But he loved you like you were his own."

"Yeah, when he was around," Madison muttered.

"And if he hadn't told you, you'd never have been the wiser."

"I know," Madison moaned. "But I am so mad at Mom, not because she got pregnant, but because she didn't trust me enough to tell me the truth."

Pearl reached over and grabbed Madison's hands. "Look at me, baby," she instructed. Madison reluctantly met her eyes. "She wanted to, she really did. But she didn't want you to know how stupid she was."

"She wasn't stupid," Madison said as tears streamed down her face. "And I wouldn't've hated her. How could I? She was my best friend." Madison began to sob and Pearl got up from her seat and held her niece until her tears subsided to a trickle.

"You're gonna be okay," Pearl assured her as she handed Madison a handkerchief.

"Thank you," Madison said, dabbing at her eyes and blowing her nose.

"Why don't you stay for dinner?" Pearl said, her voice warm and inviting.

"Oh, I can't," Madison said. "I need to get home and pack. I'm leaving tomorrow for a two-week Caribbean cruise."

"That sounds so exciting. Well, go on, but don't you forget where I live."

"I won't," Madison promised as she made her way to the front door. Before she walked outside she turned to her aunt, gave her a hug, and said, "I need to find Lucius."

Pearl's brow furrowed. "What are you gonna tell him, baby?" she asked.

Madison shrugged. "I'm not sure. I'll know when I see him."

Chapter 30

"This time tomorrow, I'll be chilling on a cruise ship," LaShawn sang as she threw motion sickness medicine in her suitcase, then clicked it shut. "Hallelujah. It'll be wonderful to get away. Especially after everything that's happened," she muttered to herself. "Oh well, that's all in the past," she said brightly. Then she looked longingly at her bed, her body flushed and her mound beginning to tingle. "Mmm, you're calling my name," she said.

She sauntered over to the mirror and slowly unbuttoned her blouse, she bared one shoulder, saucily rolled it before exposing the second shoulder. She gave a little shake and her shirt dropped to her feet in a puddle of silk. Her pants were next; grasping the elastic waistband of her sweatpants and underwear she tugged them off, then toed them away. She absentmindedly glanced at her unclothed body before crawling on top of her covers.

With the confidence of a lady familiar with what gets her excited, she gently ran her hands over her body and her lips formed a small O every time her hand grazed one of her hot spots.

LaShawn cupped her breasts, cradling them as though they were nuggets of gold. "I've missed you babies," she cooed as she gently kneaded them, panting softly as her nipples grew as hard as bits of topaz.

One hand lingered over a breast while the other hand eased past her stomach and slid between her legs. A moan that sounded like ecstasy mixed with awe escaped her as her finger skipped past her full lips.

"Awwww, God!" she whimpered as she slowly fingered herself and her hips slowly inched upward to meet her hand.

"Don't you want to share, Shawn?"

LaShawn's eyes flew open, and they grew even wider when she saw Calvin standing over her, looking at her as though she had three eyes and ten arms. Her hips stilled. "How did you get in here?" she stuttered, her mouth dry as her cotton sheets.

He dangled a key. "You gave this to me. Remember?" he asked.

She did. As soon as he had given her an engagement ring she had given him the key; the relationship swap-a-roo. Shit.

His eyes swept over her body, still dewy from her touch. "So this is why you kept your legs locked up tighter than a maximum-security prison. You were doing yourself," he said with a snicker. "Damn! Malcolm said you were a tight ass. But I told him that you were a good church girl. I guess we were both wrong."

"What are you doing here?" LaShawn asked as she attempted to cover her body with a blanket.

Calvin slipped off his shoes, then slid into bed with LaShawn. "You know this is my first time in your bed," he joked before testing the mattress.

"And your last!" LaShawn sputtered.

"Funny," Calvin muttered, then gently cupped her face and said, "I want for us to get back together."

LaShawn blinked a couple times, unsure if she heard him correctly. "I'm sorry, what did you say?"

"You heard me. I want you back. We can go back to the way it was and you can have the wedding of your dreams."

LaShawn's eyes narrowed as she cocked her head to the side. "Are you crazy? You come up in my home, after what you did to me, asking me if we can get back together? How crazy does that sound to you?" She pulled away from him quickly.

"It's not crazy. I miss you . . . and, I love you," he whispered, looking like the man she had fallen in love with and LaShawn's heart immediately melted.

"You do?" she softly asked.

Calvin nodded. "Being with Rita made me realize how much you mean to me."

LaShawn's heart hardened. "So being with a druggie opened your eyes? Get out of my bed and get out of my home!"

"I don't know why you're acting like you didn't do anything. I wasn't the one running around Target with another man." He sneered when LaShawn flushed. "Yeah, you thought I didn't know about that. But I saw you and ole boy running around the store like it was y'all's wedding and not ours."

"Yeah, I ran around the store with him. After you

stomped away like one of my kindergartners. I want you to leave!" LaShawn ordered.

"Leave?" Calvin snorted, then snatched the cover away. "And miss all this?" he asked. "I'm gonna get what's mine," he said as he began unbuttoning his shirt.

"What are you doing?" LaShawn screeched, not liking the look in Calvin's eyes.

"Something that I should've done way before now. But I was trying to be a man, respecting your feelings and everything. That's over now," he said, laughing harshly as he unzipped his jeans and slid out of them.

LaShawn's eyes stretched at the tent in front of his boxers.

"Just go, Calvin," she pleaded. "If you leave now, everything will be cool."

"Oh, everything is gonna be okay," he said in a soothing voice as he pulled down his boxers and then kicked them and his jeans away. His shirt quickly followed. "I have something that works better than your hand." He pulled her into his arms. LaShawn went mannequin-still, hoping that he'd leave her alone. Instead Calvin began groping her, his hands squeezing her body roughly.

"Please stop!" she begged, and began pummeling his back with her fists. He easily shrugged off her blows.

"You want this. Your fingers can only do so much," he breathed as he pinned her arms against him. "I got the big stick, baby."

LaShawn reached between his legs and grabbed his balls and was rewarded with a loud scream. "Get off me!" she said coldly.

"I can't move," Calvin squeaked, sounding like Michael Jackson.

"Yeah, you can!" LaShawn hissed, then twisted the spongy balls. Calvin yelped. He drew his hand back, prepared to smack her.

"Go ahead and hit me," she taunted. "And by the time I'm done with you, you won't be able to tell your dick from your pinky finger. So try me!" she dared, then squeezed tighter and Calvin howled with pain as his hand fell to his side. "Move!"

With LaShawn's hand between his legs, he hobbled out of her bedroom, through the living room, and toward the front door.

"Get out!" LaShawn barked.

"What about my clothes?" Calvin asked.

"What about them?" she asked coldly. "Are you going to leave or will I have to call the police?"

Chapter 31

"Are you going to be okay?" Lauren asked Cleve for the millionth time as she folded her clothing and placed it into her suitcase. She had made charts of the children's schedules, composed lists of important phone numbers, and stocked the freezer with enough food to last a month.

"I'll be fine," Cleve reassured her. "You go and have a good time."

"Oh, I forgot to tell you!" Lauren exclaimed. "C.J. has a dentist appointment next week, and on Saturday Debbie has a sleepover at Meaghan's. Both phone numbers are—"

"On the list," Cleve finished for her. He chuckled, then pushed the suitcase off the bed. Before Lauren could yell, he fell onto the bed and pulled her on top of him. Lauren snuggled against his hard body. "Relax, baby," he soothed. "Your black king got everything under control. The only thing I want you worrying about is whether to order a strawberry or banana daiquiri."

"I'm not sure if I can do that," she murmured. "I've always been a Type A personality."

"You can and you will," Cleve demanded. "Remember what the doctor told you."

"I'll try," Lauren said, then, "Susan almost had a heart attack when I told her I was going on vacation."

"Did you tell her to shove it up her ass?" Cleve asked; he despised Susan. He felt Lauren shake her head.

"But I threatened to quit if she didn't give me the time off. It's not like I don't have it coming to me." She thought of her two months of vacation that was gathering dust. "I'm going to miss you," she said suddenly.

"I'm going to miss you, too," Cleve said. "Has that rash cleared up yet?" he asked as he hooked his finger on her shirt, then peered inside. "I can't see," he complained.

"Stop!" Lauren demanded, and pushed Cleve's hand away. She knew that her hives were the last thing on his mind. And what he had in mind didn't spark any interest in her. She was worn-out.

As soon as she told Susan she was taking a vacation Susan had started working her as though she was an illegal alien. Susan had pushed up the due date on the annual report, had her oversee two different conferences, and asked her to lay the groundwork for the executive's video bios. Half of what Susan wanted didn't get done and it joined a three-inch pile of work filling her in-box.

Lauren sighed. All she wanted to do was find the nearest pool and sit beside it. She looked intently into her husband's eyes. "Baby," Lauren started, "I'm so exhausted I can barely keep my eyes open. It's taken all my strength just to pack."

"I understand," Cleve murmured as his hands roamed over her back.

"Cleve," Lauren warned.

"What?" Cleve asked innocently as his hands wandered to the waistband of her sweatpants. Before she could protest he slipped his hands in and cupped Lauren's behind. He grinned when he discovered she wasn't wearing any panties.

"Honey, stop!" Lauren protested.

"Just trying to relax you," he answered as he gently turned Lauren onto her back and pulled off her sweatpants.

"Cleve, I really need to finish packing."

"But the doctor told you to relax. And I'm trying to relax you."

Lauren struggled to sit up. "No. All you're doing is trying to get yours."

Cleve pulled back and looked at his wife, as comprehension filled his brown eyes. "You hate me, don't you?"

Lauren shot up off the bed. "No! That's not true. I don't hate you." She reached out to grab his hands. "Baby, I'm just tired. I don't have anything to give you right now."

Cleve opened his mouth to protest, but then he saw exhaustion ringing his wife's eyes, giving her bags big enough to carry the Atlanta Falcons, and tightening her mouth until it looked like she had tasted something sour. He opened his arms. "Come on. I know what'll make you feel better."

"Cleve. I don't have the energy—"

"Just trust me, okay?" He grinned.

Chapter 32

The first thing Madison noticed when she opened the door to her and Blair's stateroom was the large arrangement of roses and toddler-size teddy bear on the credenza.

"I can roll like this anytime," Madison said, looking over Blair's shoulder and ogling the gifts. "This is a classy cruise line," she said, admiring the cabin; it was bigger than she had imagined. Two full-size beds dominated the room, each with matching dressers and vanities and their own private balcony beyond a sliding glass door.

Madison dumped her luggage on the bed closest to her and made a beeline toward the gifts. "I wonder who's sending us a bon voyage gift," she said, giggling. She plucked up the gift card and her face dropped like an undercooked soufflé. "It's from Eric. He's so sweet." Madison grinned.

"You like him, don't you?"

Madison shook her head. "I like him as a friend. I thought I wanted more with him, but I can't see us together.

I almost told him," she mused, thinking about the last time she saw Eric. "He's so nice, he let me stay at his place after somebody broke my front window. And remember the stuff going on with my credit card?" Blair nodded. "Name mixup. Another Madison DuPree canceled her card," Madison explained.

"They didn't check the Social Security number?"

"One would think they would, but they didn't. It's all straightened out. Anyway, the window thing happened a couple weeks ago. Eric was my knight in shining armor," Madison gushed.

"Did you give him thank-you sex?" Blair asked and Madison averted her eyes before sheepishly nodding.

"It just happened," she said. Then, "No, it didn't just happen," Madison amended. "After everything that happened with my father and the broken window, I needed some human connection. Man, I can still feel his—"

"Madison!" Blair interrupted, her face flushed. "Too much information. Now, let's focus." Blair sighed and placed her suitcase on the other bed. "So you seduced him?" she asked as she quickly commandeered the dresser she wanted.

Madison considered her question. "I guess you could say that," she decided. "But I can tell you that he wasn't complaining."

"I bet," Blair said sarcastically.

"So what did Rich say when you told him you were going on vacation?" Madison asked.

Blair flopped down on the bed and propped her head in her hands. "He accused me of running off with another man," Blair said, chuckling bitterly. "Can you believe that?

He's the cheater—not me. I honestly don't know how we got to this point. I don't know how we became so disconnected." She stared absentmindedly at her coral-painted toenails, trying not to give in to the tears that tickled her nose and teased her eyelids.

Madison saw Blair's nose redden and her cheeks turn the color of strawberries and knew that tears were close. She hurried over and knelt in front of her friend. "It'll be okay," she soothed. "Have you thought about what you're gonna do after the trip?"

"No." Blair sniffled. "I'm just taking it on a day-by-day basis. Some days I want to do a Lorena Bobbitt on him, and other times I just want to take him into my arms and forget that any of this actually happened."

"I'm sure you'll come up with the right decision," Madison said. "If you do decide to leave him with one less appendage, make sure you use something sharp. There's nothing worse than trying to cut something with a dull knife, you'd be sawing for days," Madison joked and Blair laughed. "Good, you're smiling again. For the next fourteen days, think fun . . . hell, think about our contest. Now, go clean up! We have men to catch."

"Thanks. I needed that," Blair said, giving Madison a hug before she sauntered into the bathroom. Five minutes later she popped out, her eyes sparkling. "Let the games begin," Blair sang as she and Madison headed for the door.

Chapter 33

"Are you okay with the room?" LaShawn asked timidly. It wasn't what she had reserved.

"It's fine. It really is," Lauren lied. The cabin was a tampon box on water. If it were any smaller they'd be walking on top of each other.

"I'm so sorry," LaShawn apologized for the hundredth time. "I called the purser and I was told that the ship was full, so they're gonna credit my account for the full price of the room."

"That's wonderful, girl. Mo' money for you." Lauren laughed, then abruptly stopped when she saw LaShawn's face, which looked like she was one minute away from a total meltdown. "What's wrong?"

"Do you think I pushed him to it?" LaShawn murmured.

Lauren didn't have to ask. "Come on, sit down." Lauren settled on one of the twin beds and LaShawn on the other. Lauren gently tested the mattress, not knowing how she was going to sleep on it, as it was no bigger than a slice of bacon and harder than a rock. "Calvin was like a lion. And you know lions, all they do is hunt and eat. It was in his nature to act the way he did."

"But if I would've gone to bed with him, he wouldn't have done what he did. I mean, he would've been satisfied. Don't you think?" she asked, looking imploringly at Lauren.

"Unless you have a crystal ball you have no way of knowing that," Lauren answered firmly. "But let's just suppose you went to bed with him . . . would that have made you feel better?"

LaShawn shrugged. "I don't know, but maybe I'd still have him."

"No, I don't think so. Calvin is a man who will never appreciate what he has. You could've danced around in a g-string for him and he would not have even uttered a thanks."

"Calvin wasn't like that," LaShawn answered, defending her ex-fiancé.

Lauren shook her head. "Where was Calvin when you needed someone to bring you home after you had your surgery? Where was Calvin when you had your eyes dilated and you needed someone to drive for you? Where was Calvin when your car was out of commission for a week and you needed a taxi service?"

"I know, I know," LaShawn said. "You're right."

"The man wasn't any good for you. I give it to you, girl, you tried your hardest. More so than I would've if I had been you. But you can't turn a pig into a prince. It's not gonna happen. And as for not sleeping with him, you did the right thing. Save it for the right person. Not just anyone should be allowed to open that precious gift."

"He almost did," LaShawn said softly.

"So Madison was right, you were getting a little hot in the panties." Lauren laughed.

LaShawn shook her head. "I mean," she started, nervously licking her lips. "I mean . . . he almost *took* it."

The grin fell from Lauren's face. "You mean he . . ."

"Yeah, he almost raped me," LaShawn finished for her.

"Oh baby!" Lauren gasped. "When did this happen?"

"Last night," LaShawn whispered as she bowed her head.

"What happened?"

"He caught me—" LaShawn clamped her mouth, then cleared her throat. "He snuck into my apartment while I was in the shower."

"That asshole!" Lauren spat. "He tried to rape you in the shower?"

"No, he waited until I was finished and was in my bedroom—" The thought of what could have happened the night before left her speechless. Tears raced down her face as though trying to reach a finish line.

Lauren reached over and pulled LaShawn against her. "Oh, let it out," Lauren soothed, rocking LaShawn against her chest. "You're safe here. He can't get you. Just cry." Lauren held her until she could no longer feel LaShawn's body trembling against hers.

"He got on top of me," she half spoke, half hiccupped, her lips curled into a grimace at the memory. "Then somehow he pinned my arms so that I couldn't move," she recited as though in a trance. "And he was about to rape me when—thank you, Jesus—I got one hand free. Then I grabbed his balls and squeezed them like they were grapes," she said, a shiver of fear running through her body. "My ex-fiancé wanted to rape me!" LaShawn wailed. "I should've given it to him when he wanted it."

"So you think his almost raping you was *your* fault?"

"I do," LaShawn said.

"Here I am thinking you were talking about his cheating on you. How stupid am I?" Lauren asked as she thumped her forehead with the heel of her hand.

"You didn't know what I was talking about."

"But it's not your fault. No way is his behavior your fault. He made the conscious decision to sneak into your home and try to rape you. The only thing you're guilty of is falling in love with an asshole."

"But what does that say about my judgment?" LaShawn asked, worrying her bottom lip. "I was going to marry a rapist! It's almost like I was asking for it." She reached for her Bible, but realized it was in her purse.

"No woman deserves to have her body brutalized. And I know from the very center of my soul that you didn't ask for it!" Lauren vehemently replied.

"I was naked when he came in," LaShawn murmured, her eyes downcast.

"Did you tell him you wanted to fuck?" Lauren fired at her and LaShawn shook her head. "Did you tell him that you wanted to make love?"

"No," LaShawn whispered.

"Did you tell him that you wanted to see that little twig he calls a dick?" LaShawn giggled, but shook her head no. "So even after all that, you still feel that you asked for it?"

LaShawn thought about what Lauren said, then, "You are so right. Thank you so much." LaShawn leaned over and gave Lauren a tight hug. Then she stepped over to the porthole and opened it. She nonchalantly slipped off her engagement ring and was about to toss it out to the ocean when Lauren saw her.

"Wait!" Lauren shrieked. "Are you crazy? What are you doing?"

"I don't want any more memories of him," LaShawn answered, her face rigid with determination. "I don't even know why I was still wearing this."

"Damn, girl, burn all his pictures, erase his number from your cellphone, but don't be stupid." With that, she pulled LaShawn's arm back into the room and slammed the window shut. "Besides, you paid for that ring."

Chapter 34

Madison made her way down the corridor and up to the sun deck. After she and the girls checked out the men and watched the Miami shoreline as it dissolved into the water, she left them to run down to her room and change into her lime green bikini, the one with the bottom that cupped her butt, making it look like a ripe Granny Smith apple. Everywhere she looked there was one fine brother after another, and she knew her bikini would draw their attention.

She had men on her mind when she turned the corner and collided with a flesh-covered cement wall. She swayed unsteadily as if the ship had hit rough waters. The pile of magazines that she had planned on reading fell from her hands. "Excuse me," she murmured, flustered as she bent down to pick up her reading material.

"No problem," the wall drawled.

Madison looked up, expecting to see a three-hundred-pound animal, but instead she smiled brighter than a hundred-million-dollar lottery winner. Dreadlocks swam around a honey-hued face, and silver eyes glinted mischievously at her.

"Let me get that," the man said, as he bent down and scooped up her magazines. "I'm Trey," he said, introducing himself.

Madison's eyes traveled upward. Six-two, two hundred ten pounds, muscles popping out like he's the Hulk. Damn, he's phat phine. "I'm Madison. Thanks for picking up my magazines," she said and waited while he arranged the magazines into a neat pile.

"It's the least I can do, since I knocked them out your hand." He smiled and his cheekbones lifted and hollowed out two perfect dimples. Madison inhaled sharply and leaned into him. She was close enough to smell his cologne, a light, fruity scent that made her wish he were a peach she could bite.

"Oh, don't worry about it. It was partly my fault. I really should watch where I'm walking. I didn't bruise you or anything, did I?" Madison flirted.

"I'm not sure, wanna check?" Trey asked and gave her a wink.

Madison shook her head. "Another time," she said as her gaze slowly ran the length of his body.

"Is that a promise?"

"Is that the Atlantic Ocean out there?"

"Bet. Just say when and where."

" 'Bye," she said. "Thanks again," she called out as he walked away.

Madison sat down on a chaise lounge and settled into her favorite position, with her right leg outstretched and the left one bent. She slouched in the chair just enough so that it took an inch off her waistline. It was a position that took years for her to perfect, experimenting with dozens to find one that was the most successful for getting male attention.

Madison picked up a magazine, then slipped her sunglasses on and just as she did so, she noticed Trey by the pool. He was sitting on the edge, his head bowed, as if thinking. He had pulled his hair into a huge ponytail and it rested against his back like a satiated snake.

Madison smiled to herself and was about to call him over, but stopped when a model-type lady, wearing nothing more than two eye patches and a string for a bikini, parked herself next to him.

I bet he likes that type, Madison silently huffed and snatched up the first magazine that her hand touched. She adjusted it on her lap, pushed her sunglasses on her nose, turned a few pages, and promptly fell asleep. She lay akimbo on the chaise, in her lime green bikini, her sunglasses askew, and her mouth open wide enough for a fish to hop in.

Trey happened to glance at her and, seeing her asleep, excused himself from his new friend. Her lip gloss-slick lips slid into an easy smile, but pinched into a pout when she saw him go over to Madison and tap her on her shoulder.

"Wh-a-a-a-t?" Madison groaned and tucked her head under her arms, then drifted back to sleep. Trey tugged at her braids. Madison pulled her arms away and looked up into Trey's silver eyes and her clit jumped to attention; that jolted her awake. "Hey," she murmured, knuckling her eyes.

Trey grinned; even disoriented she looked cute. "You dropped your magazines again."

"Thanks," she said, then tried to be discreet about wiping the drool from the corner of her mouth, but Trey caught her.

"Don't worry, I didn't see that river you were leaking. And even if I did, I wouldn't tell anybody," he teased, and whistled while he looked off into the ocean, pretending not to see her as she ran her hand over her mouth a second time for good measure.

Madison did a quick rearranging of her bikini top. It was a good thing that he woke her; another hour or so and something critical would've gotten burned, and it would not have been pretty. After a couple of seconds of giving Madison some time to get herself together, Trey slid into the chaise next to hers.

"You enjoying the cruise so far?" he asked.

"It's off the chain!" Madison said. "There are so many fine men," Madison flirted.

"As well as beautiful women," Trey tossed back. "I've got the finest one sitting right next to me," he said and graced her with a dimple-laced smile.

"What time do you usually go to bed?" Madison asked.

Trey's brows furrowed with puzzlement, but he answered the question. "Normally around eleven . . . but I know that it's going to be a lot later on the cruise. Why?"

"I just wanted to know what time I needed to be at your cabin door," Madison answered.

"Is that right? What do you plan on doing in my room?"

"Any and everything I want to," Madison drawled while watching for his reaction.

"Really? So I don't have a say in this?"

"Do you want one?"

Trey shook his head. "Hell naw!"

Chapter 35

LaShawn stepped on the treadmill and adjusted the speed to a leisurely pace. She was surprised to find the cruise ship's gym fully equipped with cardio and weight-lifting equipment. She had invited the girls to join her, but when they turned her down faster than an anorexic rejects a chocolate candy bar, she was secretly glad. As much as she loved them, she needed a break.

The sounds around her simmered to a soft buzz as she focused on moving one foot in front of the other. The view will certainly make my exercise time go faster, she thought. The treadmill was in front of a large window that overlooked the ocean.

Her eyes locked on the water as she walked five miles. Forty minutes later, she felt as though she had been dunked in the water she had been admiring. Her hair was plastered to her head, sweat poured off her face, and her T-shirt clung to her like a damp shadow. She was halfway across the gym when she heard:

"Miss Greene, I mean, LaShawn."

She whipped around toward the sound of the voice. Her mind went blank with shock and her feet felt like they were glued to the floor; no matter how much she wanted to walk to him she couldn't. Suddenly aware of how she looked, she pulled up the hem of her T-shirt and patted her face as he made his way to her.

Standing in front of her wearing nothing but a pair of sweatpants and sneakers was Terrance.

"Terrance," LaShawn stuttered. "What are you doing here?" she asked, then blushed when she realized how rude that sounded. She quickly softened it with, "I mean, this is a surprise! I didn't except to see you here . . . on the ship."

Terrance grinned. "My frat brothers are having a reunion. What are *you* doing here?" She was about to answer him when a group of people sliced between them. "Hey, let's get out the way before we're run over," he joked, then wrapped his arm over her shoulder and guided her to a quiet corner. Terrance let his arm drop to his side, but LaShawn still felt the heat of it. She was so flustered that she had forgotten Terrance's question and had to be reminded of it.

"My girls and I decided that we needed a vacation, so here we are enjoying the sun and drinks with umbrellas in them," she answered casually, unable to take her eyes off his chest.

"How about having one of those umbrella drinks with me?" Terrance asked and LaShawn's hand flew to her hair, then to her face. The sweat had dried, leaving her face dry and tight, and she knew without looking in a mirror that her hair looked like she had stuck her finger in an electric socket.

"I, um, look terrible," LaShawn stuttered.

"And I smell bad," Terrance joked. "Why don't we both clean up and I'll meet you on the Lido deck in about an hour. Is that cool?"

LaShawn nodded and hurried off to her room. She was on the Lido deck in thirty minutes. Dating Calvin had taught her to move at warp speed, since he hated to be kept waiting.

She was sitting at a table, enjoying the ocean breeze, when Terrance showed up. She still couldn't believe he was on the ship.

"It's peaceful, isn't it?" he asked as he settled into a chair across from her. LaShawn noticed that he had changed into a muscle-squeezing T-shirt and thigh-hugging nylon sweat-pants.

"Beautiful, too," LaShawn murmured. She liked the tight-T-shirt-wearing Terrance a lot better than the buttoned-up one.

"Not as beautiful as the lady sitting across from me," Terrance said and LaShawn blushed. No one had called her beautiful before, not even Calvin. "I'm sorry, no disrespect to your fiancé. It's just that when I see something beautiful I have to comment on it."

"I'm not getting married," LaShawn blurted out.

"Sorry to hear that," Terrance said, unsuccessfully trying to suppress a smile.

"I can see that you're all broken up about it," LaShawn teased.

"I am. Tell me what happened. Only thing I can say is that he must have been a fool to have let you go."

LaShawn silently agreed before she filled Terrance in,

giving him the CliffsNotes version. When she finished, Terrance couldn't help but give her engagement ring a pointed stare.

"Believe me, it's off," LaShawn said, catching the direction of his glance. "I haven't decided what I want to do with the ring. A couple of my friends think I should have it made into a pendant, but I don't know." She shrugged. Just then the waiter showed up and took their drink order.

"I guess I have to take your word for it, don't I?" Terrance asked. "But look at it as a blessing that you didn't get married. The only good thing I got from my marriage was Terry."

"That can't be true," LaShawn said.

"Like hell. The lady I married was manipulative. She played more games than a wannabe gold digger. I can't stand women who use men as their personal toys. Unfortunately, those are the types I tend to meet. But not you. You're real, and I've always been attracted to you," he admitted.

"Me?" LaShawn squeaked.

Terrance nodded. LaShawn was a natural beauty, unlike his ex-wife, who was on a first-name basis with the MAC consultant. "I think you're sexy as hell," he whispered.

Dazed, LaShawn didn't notice the four-letter word. "You think I'm sexy?" she asked.

"Yeah, there's something about you . . . an innocence," he said, studying her.

"Thank you," LaShawn said softly.

Just then the waiter showed up with their umbrella-laden drinks.

"A couple of my boys plan on going into Puerto Rico to do some parasailing tomorrow. Wanna hang out with us?"

"Darn it! I can't. I made plans with my girls."

Terrance leaned in closer and gently brushed her hand and she shivered. "What about dinner then?"

"I'd love to," she uttered.

"Sounds like a plan."

Chapter 36

The sketchpad fell from Lauren's hands as she drifted off into a deep sleep. An hour later she awoke feeling refreshed. She grinned lazily and stretched, reaching for the sun.

"This is so luscious," she said and beamed as she watched couples stroll by. For the first time in ages, she was able to do what she wanted without having someone screaming at her for attention, without having someone pulling at her for something, and without someone thinking of her as their personal assistant. For the first time in months her head felt as light as a cloud.

Lauren laughed and wiggled her toes as she thought about Cleve's going-away present. He had lit some candles, warmed some oil, turned on some classic Prince, and massaged her so good that for an hour her stress was a memory.

Several of the passengers were talking on their cellphones and she got a sudden yearning to talk to Cleve.

"This will probably be my last chance before we get too

far out," she said, then reached down for her purse and fished out her phone.

"Hey baby," she whispered seductively.

"Lauren?" Cleve asked, surprised, as his hand stilled on the kids' dinner, a can of spaghetti. He hadn't heard this much sexiness in her voice in a long time.

"It's me," she said, chuckling. "How's everything?"

"Fine," he answered, still shocked at the sound of her voice.

"How're the kids?"

"They're fine, they miss you. They should be getting dropped off any minute," Cleve answered while emptying the can's contents into a pot.

"Cleve—?"

"Lor?"

They both laughed nervously.

"You're my heart, you know that, don't you?" she asked seriously, the playfulness gone from her voice. Her hand gripped the telephone.

"I know, baby," Cleve whispered.

"I'm so sorry about everything. My snapping at you and then being stingy in bed. Nobody tells you that you don't earn any medals for being Superwoman."

"You got my vote and a handful of gold medals," Cleve answered.

"Thanks," she sighed, relieved. Then she said, "I've been thinking about going part time."

"You sure?" Cleve asked, surprised. After being a wife and mother, her job was her life preserver, it kept her buoyed in the sea of life.

"While I was sketching this morning, everything became

so much clearer to me. I was drowning, baby. Besides, I can't do both. I *refuse* to do both. My family is too important to me. *You're* too important to me. I want to be a wife and mother more than I want to be a vice president."

"I'm loving the sound of that," Cleve said, and Lauren heard the smile in his voice. "So when are you going to tell Susan?"

Lauren grimaced. "The ship has Internet access and I was going to send her an e-mail, but I changed my mind. As much as I dread it, I think that I should tell her in person."

"You think she's going to agree to your terms?"

"Nope. She's gonna fight it the same way Mike Tyson fights civility, but hopefully she'll come around . . . if not, I'll leave. It's as simple as that," Lauren stated forcibly.

"Look at my baby getting tough," Cleve said proudly.

"Damn straight. How's everything *really* going at home? I know I just left, but how are the kids? And—"

"You're on vacation," Cleve said firmly.

"I know." Lauren sighed. "But I—"

"Baby, let it go," Cleve demanded. "Remember what the doctor told you."

"It's gone," Lauren stated reluctantly. "On to a new subject. So how are *you* really doing?" she asked, her voice deepening sexily.

"Really?"

"Mmm," she purred.

"I'm fine," Cleve said. He leaned against the kitchen counter and grinned into the phone, loving the flow of the conversation.

"You are that, yes indeed," she flirted. "I miss you," she whispered.

"What do you miss about me?" Cleve asked.

"I miss your dirty socks in the middle of the floor," she teased.

"Really?"

"Mmm. I miss your snoring."

"I don't snore," Cleve said, pretending to be offended.

"Trust me, you do. I already miss knowing that you're not gonna be lying next to me for the next fourteen days."

"I didn't think you'll miss that," Cleve said quietly, thinking back to their last attempt at lovemaking. He didn't want to spoil the mood, but she had hurt him.

"I do, I'm sorry, baby," she whispered.

"You're forgiven. Tell me what else you miss."

Lauren laughed softly. "You know this call is expensive, I'm way over my minutes."

"Don't worry about it, I can afford it." He glanced quickly at the kitchen door before readjusting himself; he was getting hard. "What else do you miss?" he repeated.

"We're moving in dangerous water and I'm not talking about the ship. I have people walking all around me," she said, watching the passengers ambling by.

"Whisper it to me," Cleve begged.

"I miss your kisses," she purred.

"What do you miss about my kisses?"

"I miss the way they glide over me."

"My kisses glide?"

"Yeah. They glide over my face."

"Where else?" Cleve panted.

"My neck," she whispered.

"Where else?"

"My boobies." She giggled.

"God, I love your boobies." He groaned. "Where else?"

"My stomach."

Cleve moved to the kitchen's island, which concealed his bottom half from view, then stuck his hands in his pants and slowly began stroking himself. "God, baby, where else?"

"My pussy."

"Lauren, stop it!" he ordered, then, "No, tell me again." He moaned softly as he stroked himself, he was harder and bigger than he had been in a long time.

She smiled; hearing his groans she knew what he was doing. "My pussy. Your tongue slipping and sliding all over my big, hot clit."

Cleve felt himself spurting all over his hand. "Aw God!" he shouted.

Lauren closed her eyes and pictured Cleve's face, his eyes scrunched shut and his mouth open wide. "Oh God, I wish you were inside me. I miss you," Lauren said.

"Miss you, too. Baby?"

"Um."

Cleve washed his hands. "You having a good time?"

"Yeah."

"Are there a lot of men?"

Lauren smothered a giggle. "There's a *lot* of them and they're all over the place."

"Don't forget that you're married," Cleve growled into the phone.

"You're silly." Lauren giggled. "I'd better go now."

"Love you," Cleve said quietly.

"Love you more."

Chapter 37

Lauren, LaShawn, Madison, and Blair strutted into the dining room, looking as if they were on a Paris runway. They made their way over to their tables and found one of the seats occupied by an attractive older woman.

"Hi, I'm Rose," she announced and Lauren immediately thought of Patti LaBelle; with Rose's warm brown skin and bright smile, she could easily be mistaken for the famous singer. "You ladies worked it across the room, and I said to myself, I sure hope those young ladies will be stuck with me," she joked. "I didn't want to be stuck with some old geezer who'd spend the whole dinner telling me about his bowel movements."

"She's funny. I'm gonna sit next to her!" Madison exclaimed, and plopped down next to Rose.

"Thank you, baby. I'm glad that somebody wants to be with me," she said sadly. Over dinner, she told them how she and her lover of five years had planned this trip together, right down to the color of her thong, but then he had had other plans. At the last minute he left her for another woman.

"I can't believe that," Lauren huffed. After spending less than an hour with Rose, she found it hard to believe that anybody would leave her, much less do anything that would break her heart.

"I can," Madison threw out. "All men are after the asses," she said and snickered.

Rose gave her a high five. "Thank you, girl. You're right about that."

"And you were together for five years?" Blair asked.

"Yeah, five wonderful years," Rose answered, still sadly. "It was sooo good."

"Why did he leave?" Madison asked.

"Because some rich woman with big money switched her ass in front of him, and like all dogs, he bit."

"I know what that's like," Blair lamented. "I know exactly what you're talking about. My husband couldn't keep it in his pants."

Rose gave a sympathetic cluck, then said to the group, "Men are like thongs—no matter what size you get, they're always a pain in the ass," and laughed loudly. "So tell me, what are you ladies doing here? I see two wedding rings and one engagement ring and no men in sight. What's going on?"

"Well, you know my story," Blair answered. "Next!" She motioned to Madison.

She patiently waited until the waiter placed their drinks on the table and walked away. "We're here to fuck as many men as possible," Madison answered crudely but succinctly.

Rose froze in the middle of lifting her wineglass, suspended as though posing for a picture, then a raunchy laugh sputtered out from her lips. "Madison, I can tell we're gonna be fast friends," Rose gasped between tears.

Chapter 38

Blair perched on the barstool and rested her chin in her hand as she glanced at the people parading by. Everywhere she looked there were families. They all came out in the late afternoon like mosquitoes on a hot summer night. There was a family sitting across from her on a couch; the man was holding a newborn, while her toddler poked at her calf, begging for attention, and through it all her husband gazed adoringly at her as if she created the Earth.

Blair smiled bitterly. "Good luck, lady. Hopefully, you'll have better luck than I did," she muttered.

They were all supposed to meet at the pool, but at the last minute Lauren, LaShawn, and Madison decided to go to the spa. But she wanted some time to herself. "Give me a Long Island iced tea," she grumbled to the bartender. Blair was blind to the charm of his sultry dark eyes, long curly black hair, and olive-stained skin.

"That's not a drink for a cruise," he softly chided. "You need something frothy with a piece of fruit, something that'll look nice with your red hair," he said, gazing at her. His eyes glossed over her hair, danced over her eyes and nose, and skidded to a stop at her mouth. Blair self-consciously licked her lips and the bartender rewarded her with a wink before turning away. He filled the blender with ice cubes, strawberries, and other ingredients with lightning speed.

While he was mixing her drink, Blair's hand stole to her hair and she tentatively touched a bouncy curl that caressed her shoulder. The beautician in the ship's salon insisted on letting her hair dry naturally, something that Joey, her regular hairdresser, would never allow her to do, because—according to him anyway—she'd look common. But today her hair had dried into thick, luscious curls. "You like my hair?" she asked shyly.

The bartender bobbed his head up and down. "It's hot! It reminds me of . . ." He tilted his head, stuck a finger to his chin, and thoughtfully studied Blair as if she was an exquisite piece of art. "It reminds me of hot molten lava, bubbling over your shoulders," he said poetically and passed Blair a frosted glass brimming with a juicy red drink with the promised fruit sticking out. She handed him her card for payment and he waved it away. "It's on the house."

"I can't let you do that. You'll get into trouble," Blair protested, but not too hard, since drinks were expensive.

"No, I won't," he insisted. "Every day my boss comes to me and says, 'Antonio, make sure you give a beautiful lady a free drink today.' " He winked at Blair before continuing, "And that's what I'm doing."

"Thank you," Blair said graciously. She brought the straw to her lips and cautiously took a sip of her drink, and that sip was quickly followed by a second, and a third, then a fourth. It *was* better than a Long Island iced tea.

"Enjoying your cruise?" he asked. He had grabbed a container full of lemons and began quartering them in preparation for the dinnertime crowd.

Blair could barely keep her eyes off his hands. When he picked up a lemon he didn't just hold it, he cradled it, then with the gentlest touch he squeezed it softly before placing it on the cutting board and slicing it.

"I am," Blair answered, tearing her eyes away from his hands. "This is my first cruise, and I love it. Do you like working on the ship?" Blair murmured, and reddened. She had just pictured Antonio's hands moving over her body and cradling her breasts.

Antonio shrugged, and went back to quartering lemons. "It's okay. I could have a worse job. Back home, my cousin, Marco, spends his days following donkeys around with a shovel. I can't do that. I'm trying to get him a job on the ship bussing tables. Now me," he pointed to his chest, "I took a semester off from school to see the world. I'm the first person in my family to go to college," he said proudly.

"Congratulations! So where are you from?" she asked.

"Italy," he said, and he jabbed himself in the chest with his forefinger.

Another Italian! "I'm Blair, from Atlanta." I'm an over-thirty, married woman with three children, out in the middle of the ocean with one helluva sexy man.

"Blair from Atlanta, where's your husband? Every time I see you, you're by yourself. If you were Antonio's woman, you'd have to kick me away from you," he said.

"You've seen me before?" She looked at him, amazed and

flattered at the same time; nobody had *looked* at her since college, well, not that she was aware of. She tried to suppress a delicious giggle, but it bubbled out, giving away how she felt.

"Yeah, sunning up on the deck," Antonio confirmed. "If I was your husband I wouldn't let a beautiful lady like yourself go out alone, I'd be at your side forever," he flirted. Antonio pursed his lips together and blew a low, sultry whistle that hit the spot between her legs, causing a rush of excitement to run through her.

"My husband isn't here," Blair said in a shaky voice. She quickly took a gulp of her drink.

"Oh," was all he said before he was called away by a group of new customers, and Blair watched him flirt with the females while at the same time showing the men the utmost respect. By the time they walked away he was sticking twenty dollars in tips in his back pocket.

"I bet your girlfriend gets really jealous at all the women who throw themselves at you every night, huh? What do you do when a lady wants more than just a drink?" she boldly asked. What are you doing, Blair?

"Maria, my girlfriend, she's back home, waiting for me. But Maria and I have an understanding. 'Whatever happens on the ship, stays on the ship,' I think that's how it goes. My friend Jerome told me that; he and his girlfriend have the same type of understanding. Anyway, pretty lady, are you going to the party tonight on deck?"

"Only if you promise to be there," she answered coyly and looked him boldly in the eyes.

Chapter 39

"This is so luscious," Lauren said before taking a deep breath.

"That's freedom you're smelling," Madison joked. "For the next twelve days we're free to do whatever the hell we want."

"Amen!" Blair chimed. "But this is really beautiful. I'm so glad we came," she said, looking around one of the largest islands in the eastern Caribbean. The boat had docked in San Juan, Puerto Rico.

"So what do y'all want to do?" Lauren asked as she glanced down at her watch. "We're gonna be here all day."

"Let's go to Old San Juan," Blair said. "I've read that they have magnificent buildings and exquisite boutiques."

"Well . . ." Madison started; that didn't sound too exciting.

"Come with us sightseeing and we'll do something fun later."

"Okay," Madison agreed.

*   *   *

"Good choice," Lauren complimented Blair. "Old San Juan is breathtaking." She pointed to a building across the street from them. "Is that a casino?"

"Yep, it looks like it. They're popular over here. It's a booming business," Blair answered.

"Old San Juan got it going on. Check out the cobblestones," Lauren said, pointing down at the ground. The blue stones made her think she was walking on water.

"Oh, those are *adoquines,* stones that the Spanish brought to the country," Blair responded.

"Somebody's been doing her homework," LaShawn teased.

"I had a little time last night to do some reading. Old San Juan was as far as I got, so don't ask me anything else about Puerto Rico. It sure is busy, isn't it," she said, turning her attention to the crowd.

"It is," Lauren answered as she sidestepped several people who had crossed her path. "It looks like everybody on the ship decided to tour Old San Juan." The meager streets were stuffed with tourists. "So what else did you learn?"

Blair grinned. "You're testing me? Well, I can tell you what little bit I know. Here goes . . . Old San Juan has over four hundred sixteenth- and seventeenth-century restored Spanish buildings. It has tons of plazas, there's the Plaza de San José, Plaza del Quinto, and Plaza Colón, to name a few."

"Impressive," Lauren said. "Why don't we check out some boutiques?" They all nodded, then made a beeline to the closest store.

Two hours later and half a dozen shopping bags between

them, they found themselves back on the cobblestone street. "What's next?"

LaShawn whipped out a tourist guide. "We can go to a baseball game."

"Aw, hell naw," Madison groaned. "We don't even watch the Braves play. What else you got?"

"Just a suggestion," LaShawn bristled. "What about a horseback ride through the countryside?"

Lauren pursed her lips with interest. "That's a possibility. What else?"

Suddenly they heard, "Hola!"

The girls were so engrossed in the scenery and trying to figure out what to do that they didn't notice the attractive Puerto Rican man who had sauntered up to them. At a little over six feet tall and one hundred and seventy five pounds, he was all muscle. His tank top showed off biceps the size of cantaloupes and his shorts gave them all the perfect view of calves that were rippled with muscle. His glossy black hair was highlighted with blond streaks. But it was his eyes that none of them were able to look away from. They were light blue with flecks of gray and surrounded by eyelashes so long and black that they looked fake.

"*Túeresfina!*" His remarkable eyes zeroed in on Madison.

"Hola!" the ladies chorused.

"What did he say?" she asked, excited.

"He called you fine," Blair answered.

"Ooh." Madison giggled. "*Gracias.*"

"How did you know what he said?" LaShawn asked Blair.

"Maria," Blair answered. "I'm nearly bilingual," she joked.

Madison couldn't take her eyes off the man. "Tell him

he's fine, too," she instructed Blair. Blair did and the man grinned. "Now ask him his name."

"Como se llama usted?"

"Me llamo Miguel, y usted?"

"Mellamo Blair. Mi amiga se llama Madison."

"Hi, Madison," he drawled in a heavily accented voice and nodded to them all.

"Oh, he makes my name sounds so sexy. And he's so gorgeous." Madison was quiet for a second, then said, "Do all the contestants have to be passengers on the ship or can they be any old body?" Madison asked, her eyes never leaving Miguel's face. She already had it memorized; his blue eyes, long nose, and kissable full lips. "I want him," she breathed.

Miguel winked, as if he understood her.

"Madison!" Lauren almost shrieked. "You're out of control!"

"I thought we were supposed to have fun?"

"Fun, yes, but you're not supposed to be fucking your way through the Caribbean!"

"That's the main objective of our game, remember? The Slut of the Caribbean," Madison reminded her.

Lauren let out an exasperated stream of air. "I know exactly what you ladies—and I'm using the term loosely—are doing. But Madison, you can't just screw anybody, it's just nasty," Lauren said, frustrated.

"Where would you do it?" Blair asked. "You can't go to a hotel, that could be dangerous. And you definitely can't go to his house, that would be crazy. As gorgeous as he is." Blair shot Miguel a look. "And he is gorgeous, but he's a stranger, and for all we know he could be a murderer."

"You're right," Madison said regrettably, then, "Maybe—"

"No maybes! Tell him 'bye!" Lauren demanded.

"Lauren!"

"Tell him!"

"*Adiós.*" Blair waved to Miguel, and Madison, Lauren, and LaShawn mirrored her actions and walked off. Miguel watched Madison and her friends through narrowed eyes as they merged into the crowd of people.

"Are we gonna have to send you back to the ship?" Lauren asked Madison.

"I wasn't going to do anything," she said, thinking of Trey. If anybody was going to be a constestant, it was going to be him.

"Yeah, right!" LaShawn retorted.

"I wasn't," Madison insisted. "I was only joking, I knew he couldn't understand English. Okay, okay, he was beautiful and I guess I was tempted just a little bit," she admitted.

"Just behave yourself," Lauren advised. Then, "Is it too early to eat?"

"No. It's about lunchtime," LaShawn answered. They strolled down the street until they found a restaurant that had a line of people wrapped around it.

"Wow! This place is crowded. You guys sure you want to eat here?" LaShawn asked, eying the long line.

"That means it must be good," Lauren answered. "Let's get in line." Forty minutes later they were seated and had given the waitress their orders.

"Oh, this hit the spot," Madison moaned. "I didn't realize I was so hungry. Anybody want a taste of my fried chicken?"

Blair shook her head. "I'm working on this steak."

"Me, too," LaShawn chimed in. "My steak is delicious! How's your sandwich, Blair?"

"Yummy! And I can't get enough of the sangria," she said as she reached for the pitcher and refilled her glass.

A half an hour later they all were slouched back in their chairs, relaxed.

"I almost made a mistake," Madison announced.

"We know. You were going to play find the booty with Miguel," Lauren said.

"Not that. I almost told Eric that I wanted a relationship."

Lauren's eyebrows shot up. "Really? Why didn't you? He's a good guy."

Madison shrugged. "He's not the right man for me," she said, repeating what she had told Blair earlier. For the second time that day, Trey's face popped in her head.

"You'll find the right man," Blair reassured her.

"I know."

"Okay, since no one wants to go horseback riding or to a baseball game, why don't we go to the Bacardi rum plant," Blair said.

"A rum plant?" LaShawn asked, wrinkling up her nose. "Are y'all sure that's what you want to do?"

"Yep!" her friends chorused.

After the tour of the plant they finished off their visit to Puerto Rico with more shopping at the malls and visiting the local shops for some authentic pieces of art. They were dragging themselves back to the ship when they heard Madison's name being called. Madison turned and saw Miguel hurrying toward them.

"You're on your way back?"

"You speak English?" Madison asked and Miguel winked at her. The blood suddenly rushed to her face, heating it, then just as fast it plunged to her feet. "You understood everything I said."

Miguel nodded. "I did. Now tell me how I can be a contestant in your game?"

Chapter 40

"There's the man who's gonna give momma the trophy," Blair said, nodding toward Antonio. He was sitting alone in the corner nursing a drink and Blair couldn't help notice how he stroked the glass as if it was a lady's body. A shot of desire ran through her. "He's going to help me win the Slut Award or I'm going to break my pelvis trying," she joked.

Blair, Madison, Lauren, and LaShawn were each stretched out on their chaise lounges, enjoying the warm sea breeze caressing their bodies.

"What?" Lauren sputtered, pulling herself out of sleep. She napped more than a properly sexed newlywed.

Madison jutted her chin at Antonio. "So when is this gonna happen?"

Blair grinned mischievously. "I don't know . . . pretty soon, definitely sooner than later," she answered. "Do you guys think I'm bad? You know, for thinking about cheating on my husband?" Blair whispered nervously. "I'll be breaking our wedding vows."

"Hell, not only did Rich break them, but he shredded them and tossed them out into the street like they were a pair of his dirty drawers," Madison said, practically snorting. "So don't you feel bad about anything! Go get that man and put something on him that'll have him talking in tongues," Madison urged Blair.

"Give me a minute," Blair said. "I need to work up my nerve. It's been forever since I've been with another man. It's not like I can walk up to him and tell him that I want to jump into bed with him."

"Why not?" Madison demanded. "I do it all the time."

"Well, we all don't live in Slutville," LaShawn joked and Madison rolled her eyes.

"It's a fun place . . . maybe you should hop on a bus and come on over," Madison quipped. "The party never stops over here."

"And I bet you're the mayor," Lauren teased.

"Go back to sleep," Madison said and pretended to toss her drink at Lauren.

Lauren pushed herself up and turned toward Madison. "I'm up. I didn't mean that in a bad way," Lauren quickly explained. "What I meant is that you're always having a good time in or out of the bed. And you didn't get caught up in the mommy thing; Madison is about Madison and nobody will *ever* come before you."

"That makes me sound so awful," Madison protested. "Doesn't it?" she asked LaShawn and Blair.

"Girl, listen to what I'm saying, I admire you," Lauren admitted, and she nodded when Madison looked at her in amazement. "That's right, I *admire* you," she repeated, enunciating each word. "I can't see you losing yourself when you get married . . . like I did," she said, and smiled. She didn't look like her usual vivacious self; shadows crossed her face, gauzing its usual glow, and every line and wrinkle made themselves known. "I kept telling myself that I loved helping people, that I loved working in corporate America. I had the title, the big money, and the expense account. But all I was doing was living the life of the walking dead."

"Wow! That's deep," Madison said. "I didn't know you felt that way. You *always* kept your shit tight. I was so jealous of *you*. You had the family, a good *black* man, two beautiful kids, and nothing bothered you."

"Welcome to the world of the walking dead. You see, we perfected the Superwoman image. Well, no more—this lady is hanging up her cape."

"Amen!" the group chorused.

Trey sauntered up behind Madison and leaned down close to her ear. He was so close that he could've caressed her earlobe with his tongue if he'd wanted. "Hey, Madison," he whispered.

Goose pimples raised on her arms and her heart beat against her bikini top. She didn't have to turn around to see the speaker, she'd recognize his voice and scent anywhere. Madison tilted her head so that their mouths almost touched. "Hey," she said softly and blushed when she felt her friends' eyes on her.

"I was walking by and saw you. Just wanted to say hi," he said, his warm breath teasing her mouth.

"Well, hi." Madison grinned. Lauren watched the interaction and smiled to herself. Is this the one? she thought.

"I'll see you later," Trey said as he strolled off.

"Yeah. You'll see me later," Madison said dreamily. She couldn't rip her eyes away from Trey as he made his way across the deck.

"Damn, he was hot. *Who* was that?" Blair asked as her eyes zeroed in on Trey's broad shoulders. "Is he one of the contestants? If not, I'll take him."

"Like hell," Madison sputtered. "He's mine. You just focus on that one," she said, nodding curtly toward Antonio.

"If you change your mind . . ."

"I'm not changing my mind," Madison answered and Lauren grinned. She had seen something in Madison's eyes that she'd never seen before.

They people-watched for a little while, then Lauren turned to Madison and said, "How're you feeling about your father? I know you've been thinking about him, it's all over your face. You've been trying to hide it . . . but I know you, girl. You've been moping around like somebody stole your best bag of human hair."

"I'm not," Madison protested, then Lauren fixed her with a glare. "I've been feeling a little better since Trey. But I don't know what to do about my father . . . I didn't get a chance to talk to him before I left. All these years I was so mad at him for playing ghost, but now I kinda admire him. I mean, he took care of another man's baby. Not too many men would do that. And on top of that I feel empty," Madison confessed. "It's like nothing can fill me up, not food, not shopping and . . . not even . . . sex," she admitted in a soft voice, then ducked her head.

"I thought you loved sex," LaShawn asked, astonished. "Madison, you're the personification of sex, how can you hate it so much?"

Frustrated, Madison rolled her eyes. "I *don't* hate it. There are times when I'm not satisfied. It's like when it's over and I'm lying there next to him . . . I'm like, is that it? It's like he got the ice-cream sundae with a cherry on top and all I got was a scoop of vanilla ice cream."

"Ooh, that's not good at all," Blair said, laughing.

"*Anyway,* let's forget about the sex part of it for right now," Lauren said. "I think you need to focus on why you feel empty. And no one can fill up that space except you," she said and Madison nodded. "Now," she continued, "the sex part is something different. You're jumping in bed so fast with these guys that you aren't giving yourself the time to get to know them." Madison settled back in her chair and thought about what Lauren said. After meditating on it, Madison agreed.

"So how's the sex between you and Trey?" LaShawn asked and Lauren and Blair gaped at her. "Madison doesn't *own* the sex topic," LaShawn huffed, then arched her eyebrows at her friend. "Well?"

"I don't know. We haven't done anything yet," she admitted, then sat back in the chair wearing a lopsided grin. "But he does this thing with his tongue, he—"

"Too much information," Lauren said, cutting her off. LaShawn, who was sitting on the edge of her seat, entranced, shot her a dirty look. "Well, it was," she shrugged.

"What do y'all think is going on with Rich?" Blair asked.

"He's just going through his own thang. You know how men do, they're all like women anyway. I wouldn't be surprised to wake up one morning and have Matt Lauer and Katie Couric announce that men have a period, too, you know, because they do start acting crazy during certain times of the month. Do y'all hear me?" Lauren asked, and it was over, any bit of decorum that was left had evaporated. It was as if she had pulled a cork on a champagne bottle, laughter spurted out all over, drowning them with its freshness. The four friends were almost on the floor laughing and close to tears. LaShawn was laughing so hard that she could barely get her question out.

"Even Cleve?" she gasped, holding her stomach.

"Even Cleve," Lauren concurred dryly, and that started a fresh laughing jag.

Blair slid into the conversation. "I know why Rich had an affair," she said quietly, and laughed mirthlessly; she had said it so softly that she thought that they hadn't heard her, but they did and they all looked at her expectantly.

" 'Cause he's an asshole?" Madison asked.

Blair smiled sadly and shook her head. "Because I'm a nobody."

"That's not true," Lauren pooh-poohed. "You're not a nobody."

"He's a jerk," Madison retorted. "You're gorgeous. I wish I had red hair like yours."

"And you're smart," LaShawn added.

"In *his* world I'm a nobody. In *his* world everybody's smart, beautiful, and sophisticated," she said. "And then he comes home . . . to me. The housewife, whose most stimulating conversation was whether she sent his clothes to the dry cleaner or washed them using the delicate cycle."

"He was stupid to do what he did," Lauren said. "And you're not listening to us. We think you're all those things, smart, beautiful, and, let me add for the record, sophisticated."

"Thanks, girls. I'm so glad I have you all in my life. I

don't know what I would've done without you," she said, a grateful look in her eyes. "All this has been an eye opener," Blair admitted. "It made me realize that I need a passion other than my family."

"Like what?" LaShawn asked.

Blair shrugged. "Dunno. Maybe I'll go back to school. I never finished my degree. I got pregnant with Richard my first year in college and had to drop out."

"Let us know. We'll help you in any way we can," Lauren said, reassuring her.

"Maybe it was the sex. Was it good?" Madison asked.

"Gurl," Lauren warned, rolling the word over her tongue until it sounded like a drum roll for a beheading.

Blair grinned. "Yes! We were great together, and it only got better. The last couple of years he left me breathless."

"Guilt," Madison muttered.

"Guilt?" LaShawn and Blair uttered at the same time.

"Guilt," Madison confirmed. "Rich isn't dumb. Check it out, he was screwing Blair and a lady on the side. And if he dropped off with you," she glanced at Blair, "he knew you'd probably start asking questions. So he kicked it up a notch."

"And what a notch it was," Blair said, smiling. "Just thinking about sex is getting me horny. It's time to hustle over to Antonio," she said, slipping off the chaise. "Watch this," Blair said sotto voce to her friends. She smiled slyly as she adjusted the top of her tangerine-colored bikini before pulling her shoulders back and pushing her breasts out like two extra-large grapefruits. She fixed her eyes on her target and sashayed over to Antonio.

"Do you think she's gonna do anything?" LaShawn asked, entranced.

"Well," Lauren contemplated as she picked up her drink. She was secretly glad that Blair was taking control of her life and making her own rules since she'd been living by someone else's for too long. "What has she got to lose?" she asked under her breath.

"Nuthin'," LaShawn answered.

"Exactly," Lauren said, nodding. "Let her get her groove back. And the best thing for her is that little boy with the tight ass."

"Girl, you are so bad," Madison said, giggling. Sometimes Lauren said things that were so uncharacteristic of her that instead of shocking Madison, it amused her. She gave Antonio a second look: His ass *was* tight.

LaShawn, Madison, and Lauren watched in amazement as Blair whispered something in his ear and led him away. They could almost see the sex rising off them.

"Damn!" Madison said, admiring Blair. "My new idol."

"To Blair," LaShawn held up her glass in a salute to her friend.

"Go, Red," Lauren said, laughing.

Chapter 41

Lauren looked over the railing of the ferry into the water. "I'm not sure about this," she groaned and gave her friends a nervous smile. The small ferryboat trudged through the water like a nine-month-pregnant lady, toward Little Bay Beach, St. Martin, where they were going to snorkel.

"It'll be fun!" Blair promised.

"Have you been snorkeling before?" Lauren asked and Blair shook her head. "So how can you make that statement?" Her hands were clammy and a light sheen covered her face, and it wasn't from the hot sun.

"Hey, lighten up. It *will* be fun," Madison cajoled. "Besides, we all got to wear our cute swimsuits," she joked. "And we look *damn* good!" They did and most of the men on the boat couldn't take their eyes off them.

LaShawn reached for Lauren's hands and gave them a light squeeze. "Are you okay?" she asked; Lauren's hands felt like cold liver.

Lauren gave LaShawn a jerky nod. She was able to hold

it together all the way up to when they were given their equipment and were instructed to get into the water.

"I can't do this," she said, terrified, and backed away from the water. Everybody else had their equipment on and was frolicking in the water like dolphins.

"What's the matter?" LaShawn asked, concern for her friend etched over her face.

Lauren shrugged. "Don't know. It doesn't seem natural . . . breathing through that little pipe. Y'all go on. I'll wait for you on the beach." She gestured toward a shady tree. "I'll be right over there when you get back."

"Well, we really don't have to go," Madison said as she pulled on her flippers. "We can sit on the beach with you so that you don't have to be alone."

Lauren smacked her teeth. "Yeah, right. I can see that you really want to stay, Miss I-Can't-Wait-to-Get-into-the-Water. Go on!" she ordered. Smiling, the three struggled into their gear then hurried off, till Lauren wasn't able to tell their pipes from any of the other dozens out there. "Ten more days of fun in the sun," Lauren muttered, then trudged over to a tree and plopped down and a few minutes later her eyelids began to droop.

"So you're not a snorkeler, either?"

"Oh!" Lauren started, her eyes fluttering open. Through bleary eyes she looked up to see a bare-chested Boris Kodjoe standing over her. She knuckled her eyes and the veil of sleep fell away, clearing her vision, an action that she immediately regretted. The image sharpened to show the man standing over her wasn't the movie star, but a likely candidate for his double.

She breathlessly scanned his face, taking in his chiseled

cheekbones, his ginger-colored eyes framed by impossibly long eyelashes, and his succulent lips. Her eyes skidded down his café-au-lait-colored skin to his wide chest, his flat stomach, and thick muscular legs. "I'm not," Lauren responded, embarrassed by her thoughts. What the hell is wrong with me? she asked herself. To hide her growing confusion she pretended to find a more comfortable spot to rest against on the tree. "I don't like all that water on my face," she admitted.

She looked up to find his luscious lips curled up in a grin. "I understand," he chuckled, then dropped down next to her. "It just seems—"

"Unnatural," they both uttered at the same time. After a surprised silence they both laughed. Lauren unconsciously held her breath as she watched his stomach muscles contract and constrict with each breath. "I—um—don't remember seeing you on the ship," she stuttered. Where're all these feelings coming from? she wondered.

"I just got on. I've been in St. Martin . . . just relaxing. It's beautiful here. I thought it would be nice to cruise back to Florida instead of flying."

"It is a nice way to travel, isn't it?" Lauren asked, thinking about her lazy days. "I love it."

"It is nice," he agreed. "I'm Darryl," he said as he held his hand out and Lauren introduced herself.

"You here by yourself?" she asked, then sucked in a stream of air, stunned by her boldness. Yet it didn't stop her from glancing at his ring finger for the tell-tale band; his finger was bare and a bolt of relief shot through her.

Darryl's eyes swept over her, starting at her eyes, lingering at her mouth, and dancing over her legs, then zooming back up to her breasts, where they lingered. "I'm by my-self," he answered quietly. "My wife and I divorced three years ago."

"Oh, I'm very sorry," Lauren said.

"It happens." Darryl gave a careless shrug. "We had different goals. Hers was seeing how much of my money she could spend at one time and mine was trying to make enough money to keep a roof over our heads. Oh well. Are you here with your husband?" Even before he sat down he noticed her three-carat engagement ring and wedding band.

Lauren hesitated, then, "I'm a runaway wife," she replied airily. "He's home with the kids and I'm here with my girl-friends, basking in the sun and acting like a teenager."

"If you were my wife I wouldn't let you go on vacation by yourself," Darryl said, then winked. "I'd keep you all to my-self," he drawled, causing Lauren to blush. Just then Madison sloshed up.

"Hey, Lor! Snorkeling is da bomb! The water is so warm. I hand-fed some of the prettiest fish. And the reefs—" Her words stumbled to a stop when she noticed Darryl.

"This is Darryl," Lauren stammered. "He's been keeping me company while you guys were in the water."

Madison gave Darryl a polite smile before excusing her-self, then grabbing Lauren's hand and pulling her to the side. "Whassup, girl? That man's looking at you like you're a juicy strawberry that he wants to eat."

Lauren glanced over Madison's shoulder; Darryl was sit-ting on the ground with his back against the tree, watching them. He jutted his chin when he noticed Lauren's gaze. "Nu-uh. He's just being flirtatious," she said, blushing.

"Yeah right, that's why you're acting like your ten-year-old daughter," Madison scoffed. "I think ole boy got something else on his mind. Just be careful. Besides, there's only three of us in the contest and we aren't taking any new players," Madison joked.

"So were there any octopuses down there?"

"I don't know. Why?"

"Because if there were, they should've eaten your smart ass!" Lauren teased, then jogged away from her. Madison picked up a flipper and playfully tossed it at her. Lauren turned on her heel and chased after her friend.

"Hey, hold up!" Lauren called breathlessly to Madison. "I think I have a problem," she squeaked as soon as she caught up with her friend. "And I need your advice."

Chapter 42

"This is incredible," LaShawn breathed; Terrance had surprised her. Instead of sitting in the main dining room, he had set up a table for them on deck. Snuggled in a dark corner, away from traffic, they sat under a blanket of stars. The small, round table was beautifully set for two. Calvin would never have done anything like this, she thought as she slid into the chair Terrance held out for her.

LaShawn was glad that she had borrowed Madison's dress. The black Tracy Reese halter-top dress was a little too tight for her taste, but Terrance couldn't take his eyes off her.

From the shadows, four of his fraternity brothers emerged and quietly placed silver-dome-covered platters of food on the table. One by one the tops were removed to reveal crab bisque, lobster, steak, rice pilaf, a vegetable mix, and two fluffy, white slices of three-layer coconut cake. They left just as silently as they arrived, leaving LaShawn and Terrance alone.

LaShawn nervously picked at her steak, occasionally peeking at Terrance. After being on the cruise for only three days, he had tanned. His skin had darkened to a spicy cayenne color.

"What's the craziest thing you've ever done?" Terrance asked.

LaShawn shook her head. "Nothing," she said, then her eyes widened and she chuckled.

"What? What did you do?" Terrance asked, curious to know the reason behind her naughty chuckle.

"Well it happened when I was sixteen—"

"Mmm, sweet sixteen," Terrance joked.

"You can't tell anybody that I told you this," LaShawn insisted. "Promise!"

"I promise, Miz Greene."

LaShawn settled back into her seat before clearing her throat. "My hometown had a huge water fountain right in the middle of downtown. It wasn't very deep, more of a wishing pond. But every weekend I'd always hear stories about people who went skinny-dipping."

"No! Not LaShawn," Terrance teased, in mock shock.

LaShawn grinned. "I wasn't actually butt naked, I kept my bra and panties on," she admitted. "But just my luck, the sheriff came. I was positive that we all were gonna be shipped off to jail. Luckily, all he did was give us a warning."

"That is crazy. LaShawn taking a walk on the *wild* side," Terrance teased and LaShawn flushed.

"What about you?"

"Who, *moi*? I would never do anything crazy. I'm a responsible adult," Terrance intoned.

"Just because you've got those incredibly sexy eyes that

can look downright innocent when you want doesn't mean that you're an angel," LaShawn flirted.

"You think my eyes are sexy?" Terrance drawled and LaShawn could only nod. Their gazes locked, then they slowly inched toward each other. Terrance tilted his head and suddenly a group of drunken passengers ambled by and jostled the table, nearly tipping over Terrance's wineglass. Their private hideaway had turned into a highway for the intoxicated. The spell was broken. "Shit!" Terrance muttered and LaShawn blinked her way out of a trance.

"We were talking about the craziest thing you've ever done," LaShawn said, composing herself.

"I can't think of anything."

"You started this, you'd better come up with something," she ordered.

"Aren't we a little feisty? Okay, something's coming to me, it's coming . . . I almost see it . . . it's here," he said, then shuddered as though every ounce of his energy was gone. "This was back in the day when Jheri curls ruled and LL Cool J had just learned that he had skills on a turntable."

"Tell! Tell!" LaShawn urged.

"I tried to fly," he sheepishly admitted.

LaShawn knew that he was too smart to ever think he was Superman and she told him so.

"I know that. But my boys and I made a glider, out of my momma's down comforter."

"Oh no!" LaShawn howled with laughter.

"Oh yeah! We thought since it was filled with feathers . . . well, you get the idea. Not only did I break both legs, but after they healed my momma whooped my butt so bad that I couldn't sit down for a week." He chuckled at the memory.

A couple hours later after they'd cleaned their plates, Terrance suggested that they take a walk. He rounded the table and pulled out her chair. LaShawn thought again, Calvin *definitely* wouldn't do this.

They leisurely strolled around the ship, passing several other couples and even more of his fraternity brothers. Terrance stopped at a small pool.

"That pool sure looks refreshing," Terrance said.

LaShawn nodded in agreement, then she looked up and their eyes caught. "No!" she squealed. "I'm not getting in the water, I'll ruin the dress," she protested as she glanced down at her gorgeous black outfit. Breaking off her wedding was one thing, but ruining Madison's dress was cause for war.

"Take it off," Terrance said, as causally as though he was suggesting she remove her sandals.

"Oh, and that's a double no," LaShawn huffed.

"Come on," Terrance coaxed. "There's no one around."

"Yeah, that's now. But what happens if someone comes by?"

"I'll shield you," Terrance promised.

"How? You have one of your magical capes underneath your clothes?" she asked, laughing.

"Oh, so you got jokes now?" Terrance asked, chuckling. "This is what I'll do," he said, then he hopped in front of her and spread his arms out wide, shielding LaShawn from an invisible passerby.

Then he did something that made LaShawn's breath catch in her throat. Locking his gaze on hers, he cupped her face in his hands and brought his mouth to hers. LaShawn sighed, then backed away, dazed. This wasn't anything like Calvin's hard and rushed kisses.

"I'll do it," she said. Well, you said you wanted to let loose, and you can't get much looser than this, she thought. It took her less than a minute to toe off her shoes and drop her purse. Her shoulders lifted slightly as she looked helplessly at Terrance.

"Let me," Terrance offered. He unzipped the dress and LaShawn nervously watched it slide off and puddle at her bare feet. She stood in front of him in nothing but her thong; her hands automatically popped up to cover her breasts.

Terrance drew in a shaky breath; she was even more beautiful than he had imagined. Before she could blink, he stripped down to his boxer briefs. Blood rushed to LaShawn's face so fast that it almost made her light-headed. She thought she had gotten a good look at his body at the gym, but that didn't compare to this.

"Ready?" Terrance asked, reaching for her hand and pulling her out of her daze. LaShawn nodded as she slowly lowered her arms and her breasts sprung free.

"Oh my!" LaShawn protested and was about to shield herself when Terrance grabbed her hand.

"They're beautiful . . . you're beautiful. Come on," he urged as he walked to the pool.

"Oooh, this is so cold." LaShawn gasped as she lowered herself in, the cool water encasing her like a chilly lover.

"I can warm you up," Terrance teased.

"Oh yeah? How?"

"Like this," he said, holding out his arms. "Lean back." LaShawn opened her mouth to protest, but Terrance pressed his lips against hers, silencing her. "Do it," he demanded when it looked like LaShawn was going to veto his suggestion. LaShawn silently scrutinized him and liked what she saw; his eyes shone with kindness and trust. She fell back into his arms.

Moments later she was floating on her back with Terrance's arms securely wrapped around her waist. She leisurely floated as she and Terrance navigated the small pool. LaShawn alternately looked at Terrance, then the star-filled night, and a sigh of happiness broke through her lips.

Terrance grinned at her, then his eyes inched down to her breasts. Terrance bent down and tenderly kissed the exposed skin, turning LaShawn's nipples into diamonds. This time the blood rushed to LaShawn's clit and she closed her eyes, her body tingling with desire. Her eyes snapped open when she felt Terrance's fingers easing into her panties. She stood up and waded away from him.

"Behave yourself," she scolded.

Terrance eased over to the edge and sat down on the top step. "Come here," he called to her.

"What?" LaShawn asked shyly.

"I wanna talk to you."

"I can hear you from here."

"I need to tell you a secret."

"Go ahead. As you can see there's nobody here," she said as she pointed to the empty deck.

"But the sea monster could be lurking and listening. And I don't want anybody to hear what I have to say," he said with such a serious face that LaShawn burst out laughing.

"Okay, but don't try anything," she demanded half-teasingly, the kiss still fresh on her mind and her breasts. She waded across the pool until she stood in front of Terrance. "Tell me."

"What? And risk the sea monster hearing me? Come

closer, then I'll tell you." LaShawn took two steps. "Closer."
She took two more. "Closer." Before she could protest, Terrance grabbed her wrist and pulled her between his legs.

"What did you have to tell me?" LaShawn asked breathlessly.

"This." He leaned down so that his mouth touched her
ear. "Are you listening?" he whispered and LaShawn trembled, then gave a shaky nod. "You're the most beautiful,
sexiest, smartest lady that I've met in a long time."

"Thank you," LaShawn whispered.

"It's true," Terrance said as he gently suckled her earlobe.

"Whoa! We need to stop," LaShawn said, pushing away
from Terrance. She floated out to the middle of the pool to
cool off. "That was getting heated," she called to him. "Let's
sit down," she said, pointing to a row of chaise lounges.

Terrance pulled her out of the pool and they padded
over to the chairs. He settled into one and she happily slid
between his legs and rested her head on his chest. Her lips
curved up into a smile; she loved the feel of his skin against
hers.

"I'm sorry," she repeated. "I'm not ready for all this."

"I'm not pressing you for anything. You should know
that."

"I know. It's just . . ." She took a deep breath. She had
only known him for a little while, but it felt like a lifetime. "I
haven't been with anyone in a while," she said.

"Me, either," Terrance admitted. "But I hear it's just like
riding a bicycle."

"Well, this bicycle has rusted and the chain has fallen
off."

"It's not that bad," Terrance soothed her.

"Try three years."

"Wow!" Terrance whistled.

"Yep, wow!"

"It's not a problem with me," Terrance was quick to reassure her.

"Thank you." They were silent as they enjoyed each other's presence. "Check out the sunrise," LaShawn suddenly said. The sky looked as though a child had stuck her fingers in pink paint and smeared it across the sky.

"We'd better get going." Terrance sighed; out of the corner of his eyes he had seen a crewmember stealthily walking across the deck. LaShawn agreed and they both shook the kinks out of their bodies before throwing on their clothes. He walked her back to her room and kissed her on the forehead before making sure she got in and locked the door behind her.

LaShawn stripped off the dress, which was wrinkled and had a tiny water spot on the front. I'll have our steward take it to have it dry-cleaned, she silently decided. And Madison will never know. LaShawn peeked at Lauren. She was snoring softly.

LaShawn reached into her suitcase for her lubricating gel, then eased into the microscopic bathroom. Easing the toilet seat down, she perched on top, then reclined and spread her legs.

"This is what I'm talking about." She moaned as her fingers danced across her clit, stroking it until she couldn't tell the difference between the gel and her own juices. Her body trembled slightly as her finger began making small number-eight movements across her button. Closing her eyes she pretended that it was Terrance's hand caressing her. Her body jerked and wave after wave of pleasure radiated from her mound.

"LaShawn, are you okay? I heard noises . . . LaShawn, open up!"

LaShawn jumped up at the sound of Lauren's voice on the other side of the door.

"Oh crap!"

Chapter 43

"Aren't you going to snorkel?" Trey asked Madison. They had taken a catamaran along the coastline of Antigua and it had stopped so that the passengers could snorkel in the clear Caribbean water or sunbathe on the sandy white beaches.

Trey and Madison had just finished the stingray excursion. They were resting on the beach watching another group of people swim with the slippery, stealthy animals.

"Nah, not today. I went with Shawn and Blair in Saint Martin, it was fun!" She smiled, then said sadly, "Only seven more days left on the cruise." Then she brightened: "Seven more days for us to hang out together." Madison whispered to Trey as she subtly pressed her behind against his groin and carefully shifted. Not less than ten feet away were a group of children building sand castles; the last thing she needed to do was give them a show.

Trey leaned down and brushed his lips against her ear, then responded in a voice just as low as hers. "And do what?" he teased.

Madison grew hot and she knew that it wasn't from the Caribbean sun. Images of her and Trey making love filtered in her head. "Umm, I can think of a hundred things that I want to do *to* you, but I bet half of them are illegal in Georgia."

Trey suddenly felt himself get as hard as a slab of marble. "So you're saying that we'd better do everything while we're on vacation?"

"Something like that," Madison drawled.

Trey angled his head so that his dreadlocks hid his mouth to any passersby. He gently probed Madison's ear with his tongue and she let out a low moan.

"Maybe we should take a walk," Madison said breathlessly.

"Give me a minute . . . or twenty," Trey answered. "If I get up now, I might end up poking somebody in the eye."

Madison giggled and rested against his chest. Ten minutes later Trey stood and pulled Madison up. "Come on. Let's go somewhere private. Thank God for these baggy trunks," Trey said. His excitement had diminished a little, but he still felt like he could put a dent into anything that stepped into his path.

"Oh, where's everybody going?" Madison asked. Suddenly as if on cue everybody was picking up their beach blankets and heading toward the catamaran.

"I guess it's time to go back to the ship," Trey said, disappointed. He would've enjoyed making love to Madison on the Caribbean beach.

"So what's your type?" Madison asked softly, surprising herself with the question. In the past she couldn't have cared less about what made a man get hard, but she wanted to know everything about Trey.

They each had gone to their rooms to shower, then met up later to eat after their return from Antigua, but they couldn't seem to stay out of the water.

She was sitting on the edge of the pool with Trey standing between her legs, gazing at her; at least she thought he was looking at her. His gray eyes were hidden behind mirrored aviator shades. "Hey, take these off," she demanded and before he could do it, she reached up and snatched them off his face. "Now I can see you. I felt like I was talking to a robot," she said tartly, then stuck the arm of his glasses in the top of her bikini so that they rested between her breasts.

Trey chuckled. Madison *always* had to have everything *her* way. "Type?" he asked, raising an eyebrow at her.

"Yeah, *type*. Everybody has a type." Madison slowly pedaled her feet, splattering dots of water over Trey, who didn't seem to mind; instead he ran his hand up and down her leg.

He stopped his hand movements. "That's easy, I don't have one."

"Yeah, you do. *Everybody* has a type."

"Not me." He shrugged.

"Yeah, you do," Madison insisted.

Trey sighed. "What do you mean when you say 'type'? Are you talking physical, spiritual, mental, sexual?"

"Yes, yes, yes, and yes!" Madison squealed like a five-year-old. "All of the above."

Trey looked up at Madison and studied her. By her furrowed brow and the intense look in her eyes, something told him that she wasn't going to let it go. "Do you really want to hear this?" he asked. Madison's mouth went dry as she somberly nodded her head. "Are you sure?" Trey insisted.

Madison stubbornly crossed her hands under her breasts, then said, "I'm sure. Tell me, you won't hurt my feelings or anything," she said, sounding braver than she felt.

"That's right, because you're big bad strong Madison," Trey taunted.

"Stop with the teasing. I'm not going to be sucked into your games. Just answer the question," Madison demanded, her heart pounding against her chest.

"Well, if you really want to know . . ."

"Trey!" Madison yelled, then began beating the water with her feet so hard that Trey was immediately drenched.

"Okay! Okay!" he sputtered before giving his dreads a couple good shakes. "You asked for it." He shot her a warning look before he continued. "I like a woman who is as clean as a fresh brook, one who is as tranquil as a clear blue sky, one who is as ferocious as a tiger, and as deep as that ocean," he finished, nodding at the water.

Madison was left speechless. His poetic response was totally different from what she had gotten from other guys in the past. Nowhere did he mention the size of a woman's breasts nor the color of her skin nor the length of her hair. "So am I all those?" she asked in a voice brimming with bravado but laced with shyness and uncertainty.

Instead of answering right away, Trey reached over and, before Madison realized what he was doing, his hand zipped out and grabbed her foot and began tickling it. He had found out that she was extremely ticklish.

"Stop!" she squealed and twisted her foot away from Trey, who held firm.

Trey pulled her into the water and into his arms. "I think you're all that and then some," he breathed against her lips.

"Better than a pimped-out Jetta?" Madison joked.

"Way better," Trey assured her. He leaned in and gently ran his lips over Madison's; she shivered. It wasn't like any kiss she had received in her life. Madison leaned in even closer and flattened her lips against his, and his teeth pressed against her lips, but she didn't care. He pulled his mouth away from Madison's.

"Please, kiss me again!" she whimpered, but suddenly there was a commotion. Trey broke away from Madison just in time to see a female passenger douse her boyfriend with her strawberry daiquiri. She stormed off but not before slapping him hard across his cheek. The man snatched up a napkin and angrily swiped off the gooey drink, then slunk away.

"Woo-hoo! He's wetter than a lady at a Chippendales show. There goes their vacation," Madison announced gleefully.

"Not necessarily," Trey said.

"It would be the end of mine. Obviously, he said or did something that pissed her off so much that she had to show her ass in front of everybody."

"Jesus said that any sin of man can be forgiven, even 'blasphemy against me.' So why can't either of them forgive each other and move on?" Trey asked, leaving Madison speechless.

Trey cradled Madison's face in his hands. He tenderly brushed her cheeks with the soft pads of his thumbs.

"That's something I want you to think about," he said before angling over and planting whispery soft kisses on her lips, crisscrossing repeatedly over them as though they were a delicacy.

Trey pressed his tongue against Madison's lips and she gladly granted him access. Her knees nearly buckled when Trey's tongue met hers, and he immediately steadied her with a vise-like grip around her waist.

Madison whimpered as her tongue delved deeper into Trey's mouth. Their tongues caressed each other and moved in a synchronized dance as though they had kissed each other a thousand times before.

"So," Madison said, panting as she pulled away from him, "you think I'm ferocious?" She peeked shyly up at him.

"What do you think?" Trey responded, then touched his lips to hers.

I want you to be my man, my soul mate, and my protector, floated through Madison's head, immediately shocking her into silence.

Trey gazed at her, waiting for a response.

Chapter 44

LaShawn stood at the door of the nightclub and peered inside. Bodies writhed to LL Cool J under a psychedelic disco ball. Those who weren't dancing were guzzling drinks. A cloud of cigarette smoke wafted in her direction and she promptly waved it away.

"Ready to dance?" Terrance asked.

LaShawn jerked; she was staring so intently around the club that she had forgotten he was standing next to her. "Umm, yeah," she nervously agreed while studying the crowd. It sounded like fun when Terrance had asked her out to the club. She had even dressed for it. She stole a peek down at her outfit; it was another one of Madison's. Jeans hung low on her hips, and a gold-sequined tube top clung to her breasts. I guess clothes don't turn you into a dancer, she silently mused.

"Come on . . . it'll be fun," Terrance urged as he dragged LaShawn into the club and onto the dance floor.

"I don't know how to dance," LaShawn protested and

stood as still as a statue while Terrance swayed easily to the music. "I don't have any rhythm," she replied enviously as he did a dance move that would even make Usher jealous.

Suddenly R. Kelly's voice filled the air, slowing down the pace, and several couples shimmied to the dance floor. "I know you can move to this," Terrance said confidently before pulling LaShawn into his arms. She stood stiffly against him. "Relax, and enjoy the music," he whispered in her ear. He grinned when her body loosened up and her movements became less robotic. "There you go. Let your body feel it," he soothed.

Sitting at a table on the fringe of the dance floor Madison and Lauren watched their friends. "Look at Blair!" Madison laughed. Blair was on the dance floor with an Antonio look-alike. "Who said white women can't dance?" Blair was standing in front of the man grinding her behind into his pelvis. Her face was shiny with perspiration and her hair swung wildly around her face. I need to get a picture of this, Madison thought. She snatched her camera off the table and was about to take the picture when Lauren swatted her hand.

"What the hell?!" Madison asked.

"Why would you want to take a picture of her?"

"I thought she'd like a memento," Madison said, grinning.

"Like hell!" Lauren admonished; knowing Madison, she would use it to torture Blair.

"Oh! Look at Shawn," Madison exclaimed. Walking across the dance floor in their direction was LaShawn and Terrance.

"That's Terrance," Lauren offered.

"You've met him already?" Madison asked.

Lauren nodded. "You must've been with Trey when LaShawn brought him around," she said, keeping her eye on the couple as they started slow dancing. "I think he's adorable, so much better for her than Calvin was."

"A cardboard man would've been better than Calvin," Madison retorted, then smiled as she watched the couple. "So you think she gave him any yet?"

"Madison!" Lauren said. "I'm beginning to agree with Shawn. I do think you have a one-track mind."

"Do not," Madison quipped, then sipped her drink. "I wanted to see where I was in the contest. It looks like Blair might have another contestant." Blair and her dance partner were dancing so close that they looked like Siamese twins.

Lauren whispered, "I know. Something might go down tonight. Our girl already had three margaritas, and you know how she gets when she drinks."

"You think she's gonna tell Rich?" Madison whispered back.

"I hope not—not that I'm condoning cheating," Lauren hastily explained. "But what good would it do? Rich would be totally pissed and it'll just hammer another nail in the coffin of their almost-dead marriage. I wouldn't tell if I were her," Lauren said with a firm shake of her head.

Madison agreed, then for the twentieth time that evening scanned the crowd for Trey. He was supposed to meet her in the club an hour ago.

"He's coming," Lauren assured Madison after seeing her look of distress.

"So what's going on with you and Boris?" Madison asked.

They hadn't talked about him since St. Martin, when Lauren confessed her attraction to Darryl.

"There's nothing going on with us. I haven't seen him since St. Martin," Lauren answered.

"What are you going to do?"

"I'm going to take your advice and enjoy my fantasies and not act on them."

"I didn't say that!" Madison laughingly protested. "I said to pretend that fine man is a surfboard and to ride his ass all the way to Hawaii."

"I know what you said, but I'm sure you meant for me to keep my legs closed. That's what a good friend would say."

"You're right. Everybody isn't meant to be a citizen of Slutville." She laughed.

"Yeah, besides, I heard there's a problem with overcrowding," she joked. But it sure would be nice to drive through, Lauren thought as she pictured Darryl's muscular chest and full lips.

Her musings were interrupted by Blair, who bounced over to the table. Her face was flushed and her curls bounced on her shoulders like streams of crimson.

"Damn, girl, you're good! You should be on *Soul Train*," Madison teased. "You're already dressed like you're there." Madison eyed Blair's ensemble, which only she could pull off. Her outfit of a pink satin halter top, black boot-cut jeans, and black pointy-toed shoes looked like a seventies flashback but on Blair it was trendy.

"I know," Blair squealed and pirouetted. "I *was* good," she boasted.

*   *   *

LaShawn peeked up at Terrance. "Thank you so much for the other night," she said and inhaled his cologne; he smelled luscious, unlike Calvin, who had always smelled as though he had bathed in a keg of beer.

"I enjoyed it," Terrance breathed into her ear, and her body shook with excitement. "You're such a wonderful lady, you make it easy for me to do stuff for you."

"Thanks," LaShawn said, then, "Remember what we talked about last night?"

"Yeah, when you showed your hometown goodies," Terrance joked and LaShawn pinched him gently in the ribs.

"Not that, silly, about—you know—my c-e-l-i-b-a-c-y," she whispered.

"Oh, your c-e-l-i-b-a-c-y," he said in mock seriousness. This time LaShawn punched him in the ribs. "Ouch! Keep that up and I'm going to have the captain arrest you for harassment."

LaShawn laughed, then blurted out, "I'm ready."

Terrance stopped dancing, forcing LaShawn to stop, as well. He looked down at her. "You sure?" LaShawn nodded. "You're positive?"

"Yeah!"

"I meant what I said last night, I can wait. That won't be a problem."

"I don't want to wait."

"So when?" Terrance asked and held his breath.

"Tomorrow night."

"Where?"

"Your cabin. Is that okay?" she asked shyly.

"Sure. I can get rid of my roomie."

LaShawn stepped into Terrance so that their bodies molded together. He wrapped his arms tightly around her.

Madison and Lauren watched the body-hugging couple sway together on the dance floor.

"What's that all about?" Madison asked. It looked like LaShawn and Terrance were ready to jump in bed.

"I think you're going to have some competition," Lauren said, a smirk forming on her face.

Chapter 45

Lauren had her head cocked to the side and was sucking on her bottom lip. Her pencil flew over her sketchpad as if it had a life of its own while she immortalized a senior citizen couple. Occasionally she broke into a victorious smile whenever she completed a difficult stroke.

Determination etched the man's face into a mask of confidence as he stuck his cane out, maneuvering his wife gently down the deck. It looked like his strength was coming from his knobby, wobbly knees.

Lauren was drawing squiggly lines for his hair when he gestured toward the nearest chaise. Before his legs could disobey, he slid down into it and his wife quickly threw a towel over his lower limbs, but Lauren could see them twitching mindlessly, as if they were still trying to walk. She wanted to give him a standing ovation, for his strength and courage, as she knew that it wasn't easy to struggle for something that might seem a little bit out of your grasp. She quietly finished her sketch while occasionally sneaking peeks at him out of the corner of her eye.

She made the last stroke, and her gaze went back and forth between her sketchpad and the man, who by now had fallen asleep, his soft snores blowing out to sea. "I can't wait to paint this, this is phenomenal," she muttered to herself, half awed and humbled by her talent. A gut feeling told her that it was going to look even better as a watercolor, maybe something good enough to exhibit or sell.

She was startled by the idea; something that she hadn't thought about since college, before Cleve, before the children. But she liked it, it felt good, it felt right, like long-lost friends coming to visit.

I can sell my paintings, she thought, then testing the words on her lips and they sounded even better out loud than just images in her head: "People will come from all over to see paintings done by Lauren!"

She settled back into the chaise and began outlining a marketing plan for her budding idea. In less than twenty minutes she had listed five galleries in the Atlanta area that might show her work, ten different specialty boutiques that could possibly showcase her work on a consignment basis, and a rough draft of a Web page.

Before now she had forgotten who she was. She knew that she was Lauren Hopson, married to Cleve and mother to C.J. and Debbie, but it'd been so long since she'd had time to herself that she had forgotten how to be Lauren, how to be the Lauren that could kick anybody's ass at the drop of a hat, how to be the Lauren that stayed up all night because she wanted to, not because it was dictated by circumstances.

I want Lauren back! I'm going to stop being everybody's personal assistant, on-call babysitter, and fucking caterer! And I know just how to do it! She began singing the theme song to *The Mary Tyler Moore Show*—"I'm gonna make it after all . . ."—as she gathered her things and nodded at the old man's wife before going to the dining room to join LaShawn, Madison, and Blair for breakfast.

Just as she was about to leave she heard her name, and she shivered slightly at the sound of the voice. Pictures of his face and body had been looping through her mind like a triple-X-rated DVD. "You're leaving?" Turning around she came face-to-face with Darryl.

"Hi there," Lauren said cheerfully. "I was on my way to meet my girlfriends for breakfast." Lauren watched Darryl as he sauntered over to a pile of folded towels. Her breath quickened at the way his muscular legs looked in his shorts. Darryl grabbed a towel, strolled back, and proceeded to wipe down the chaise. "You're like the invisible man, you're here one minute, gone the next," Lauren joked. "Where have you been?"

"I've been on the ship. Obviously not in the right places," he answered, his voice lowering to a sexy rumble; Lauren blushed. "But your friends are the talk of the ship."

"Oh Lord!" Lauren groaned. "If you're talking about Madison's top falling off in the whirlpool, it was an accident. She didn't intentionally do it. Or Blair tonguing down the bartender in front of a group of children; he kissed her first," Lauren heatedly defended her friends. "Or when LaShawn—"

Darryl chuckled. "It sounds like you ladies are enjoying your cruise. People are talking about how beautiful you all are. And I agree," he said and gave her a pointed gaze.

She was the first to look away, then silently cursed herself for her weakness. For a lady who was used to having everything from TV cameras to microphones crammed in her face, it was unnerving how just a glance from Darryl made her hot.

She began fiddling with her sketchbook. "What's this?" Darryl asked as he reached for her pad. "Do you mind?" Lauren shook her head and he eased the pad away from her and flipped through the pages. "Wow! These are fantastic!" he exclaimed.

"Thanks," Lauren replied modestly, but inside she glowed with pride.

"Is this your full-time gig?"

"I wish. I'm in public relations—well, kinda—I used to be," she stammered. "I've decided to go part-time and devote more time to my family and just now . . . painting."

"Not only beautiful but talented," Darryl drawled. "God truly loves you, because you've been doubly blessed."

Lauren automatically thanked him, not knowing what else to say.

"Would you like to have breakfast with me?"

Lauren hesitated, but then remembered her plans. She shook her head. "I'm meeting my friends, remember?"

Grinning, Darryl slapped his forehead. "See what you do to a brother. Got me forgetting things. What about lunch?"

Lauren shook her head. "I can't, my girlfriends want to hang out."

"Dinner?" Lauren shook her head. "Girlfriends, I know," Darryl said for her. "Listen, all I want to do is enjoy some time with you. You're intelligent and a wonderful conversationalist, and I haven't had anyone to mentally duel with in a long time."

"I'd love to," Lauren answered, then offered softly, "I'm sure there are a number of single women who would love to have you spend some time with them." As soon as it was out of her mouth, she immediately regretted it. She sounded like a jealous girlfriend.

"I'm sure there are. But you're the one I'm asking out."

"Okay, lunch," she agreed. Oh my God! I just made a lunch date, she thought as she gathered up her items again and hurried off to breakfast with her friends.

"I'm a big spender," Darryl joked before handing Lauren a plastic plate with two slices of pizza. They were visiting the twenty-four-hour pizza and ice-cream bar.

Darryl grabbed four slices for himself and led her over to a table hugging the railing. Lauren watched in amazement as Darryl cut the tip off a slice of his pizza, then speared it with his fork and placed it in his mouth. Lauren felt down-right ghetto as she held a slice of pizza in one hand and clutched a cup of cola with the other. "So are you happily married?" he inquired.

She stopped chewing, tilted her head, and studied Darryl. "I guess— I thought— Very!" she decided after stammering like a teenager.

"Are you sure?" Darryl teased. "He's a lucky man," he said and Lauren blushed; she could get used to his constant praising. "So what's your secret?" he asked.

"Time apart," Lauren answered without any hesitation.

"That's interesting. I thought married couples are supposed to be joined at the pelvis . . . that's how my wife and I were," he muttered.

Lauren shook her head and averted her eyes. "It gives

you time to rejuvenate yourself. I feel like a new person," she added.

"Really?"

"Yep, really," Lauren grinned. "Don't sound so surprised. A couple weeks ago I was a mess . . . a huge mess. I was a Superwoman on steroids. I was out of control," she admitted.

Darryl shrugged. "But what's that got to do with your marriage?"

"A lot," Lauren said softly. "This vacation made me realize that it's okay to say no . . . to let things go. I'm happier now and more rested. It's a process," she admitted. And to be open to new opportunities, she thought as she studied Darryl over the rim of her glass of soda. They were silent as they finished their pizza then went back for some ice cream. "So what happened to your marriage?"

"Caught up. We got caught up in our image, our careers, and money. All evils of the new millennium," he said and snickered nastily.

"Ain't that the truth! It's so easy to get attached to stuff."

"I bet if you were my wife, you would've kept me real," Darryl said in a seductive voice.

"You'd lose that bet." Lauren laughed. "Cleve, my husband, always complains how materialistic I am. That's why I got a Lexus sitting in my driveway and I'm begging him to let me buy a Range Rover."

"I bet you'd look nice in it. With the sun glinting off your face, and the wind blowing through your hair," he drawled and Lauren looked at him openmouthed, wondering how it would be to kiss him.

"Do you think you'll ever remarry?" she asked, pulling herself out of her daydreams. He stared down at the table as though the question was too painful to answer. When he raised his head, he was wearing a little smirk.

"Never again," he answered. Then he announced, "Only to you, that is, if you want a broken-down man like me."

"You're silly. You're far away from being considered broken-down," she teased and giggled girlishly, gently brushing her hand over his arm. "When I first saw you, I—" She clamped her mouth shut and looked at him with wide eyes.

"You what?" Darryl asked, grinning.

"I can't tell you," she protested.

"Yeah, you can. Go ahead," he urged. "I'll even help you. 'When I first saw you . . .' " he prompted.

Lauren took a deep breath, then said, "When I first saw you I thought Boris Kodjoe had stepped out of the water. I guess I got too much sun," she said, laughing.

"You thought that I was the object of millions of black women's wet dreams?"

"Oh yeah," Blair drawled.

"Really?" Darryl asked, pleased. He took a spoonful of his ice cream and held it out to Lauren. "Wanna try?" Lauren opened her mouth and slowly eased toward the dessert, then just as quickly pulled herself back.

"I can't," she objected, feeling as though she was taking something more than ice cream.

"It's only ice cream. Here," he offered and before she could refuse, he had the spoon to her lips. Darryl felt himself go hard as her lips closed around the spoon.

"Thank you. It was good," Lauren awkwardly replied.

"All the good women are taken," he moaned playfully, causing Lauren to laugh. "You have the whitest teeth," Darryl observed.

"It runs in my family," Lauren said, then blushed. "I'm sorry, that was a stupid thing to say."

"Was not. Big feet run in my family, wanna see them?" he leered and suddenly Lauren felt as though she had been doused with a bucketful of ice water.

What the hell are you doing, Lauren? "I'm happily married," Lauren said primly, then glanced down at her watch; it was getting late.

"Oh, my bad," Darryl quickly apologized. The air between them had grown colder than the ice cream they had just devoured. "Your husband is one lucky guy."

"Thanks," Lauren said as she stood up and extended her hand to him. "Thank you so much for dinner and your company. You have a wonderful evening."

"Let me walk you back to your room," Darryl offered as he hurried to stand up, but Lauren waved him down. "Come on now. I was out of line. The last thing on my mind was to offend you. Let me make it up to you," he pleaded.

"What do you have in mind?" she asked, nervously licking her lips.

Chapter 46

Madison sneaked a peek at Trey and did the same thing she'd been doing for the past couple of days—she scrutinized him, hard. She studied him the same way a little boy would examine a newly captured ant, thoroughly, objectively, and with every intention of dissecting it when the time was ripe.

She loved everything about him, especially the way he walked, with his pelvis jutted forward and his shoulders pulled back, as if he was making love to the world. She sheepishly glanced away when he caught her looking at him. Trey noticed that she had been doing that all day, like he was a piece of clothing that she was inspecting for a flaw that would give her an excuse to throw it away.

Trey smiled. His last girlfriend was like that; she thought he was too good to be true. Over and over, she'd wonder out loud why a black man his age, sporting an MBA, articulate and fine, would be unmarried, with no children to boot. She'd swear that there had to be something wrong with him. She'd used to regard him the same way Madison did, looking for a tear in him that she could stick her finger in and pull and poke at until it gaped open. That relationship quickly ended.

He and Madison had stopped in a little cubbyhole, really an awkward spot on the ship, wasted space between a door and the stairs that gave creative couples some privacy. Trey sat with his back against the wall, and Madison sat between his legs with his chin resting on her head.

"What's on your mind?" Trey asked lazily.

Madison pulled her knees against her chest and watched the parade of sandaled feet. "I was just wondering if half these people would've gotten a pedicure before putting on their sandals if they knew that somebody would be on foot patrol, because they're tore up," she cracked.

Trey laughed along with her and tightened his grip around her waist. Her body rippled against his and his tank top was no barrier to her body heat.

"That's not what you're thinking about. Tell me the truth."

Madison nestled against him and smiled. "I was wishing that we could stay like this forever," she said wistfully.

"Yeah," Trey mused. "People can shoot food at us, then hose us down once a week. We'd be the freaks in the cubbyhole."

Madison playfully pinched his calf. "That's not what I'm talking about, silly. I'm talking about me and you staying on the ship forever . . ."

"That would be cool, wouldn't it? We wouldn't have to work and our meals would be taken care of. And we don't

have to worry about clothes, because the only things we'd need is bathing suits."

"And shorts," Madison added. "I've got to have my shorts."

"You'll get whatever you want," Trey whispered in her ear.

"I can have *whatever* I want?" she asked and she felt Trey nod. "Then I want you," she said softly, then held her breath.

"What do you want from me?"

"I want your body."

"You have it."

"Then I want to feel you inside me."

"Come on, let's go to your cabin," Trey said and Madison's eyebrows shot up. "I'm not hiding a stowaway, if that's what you're concerned about," he said, laughing. "My roommate caught some type of bug and he can't get out of bed," he quickly explained.

"Dang, that's not pretty. I hope he feels better," Madison said politely, as Trey tucked her hand in his and they strolled to her room. Blair was just closing the door when they walked up. She pulled Madison by the elbow out of Trey's hearing range.

"You're so lucky," Blair whispered in her ear.

Madison giggled and muttered, "I am, aren't I? And he's all mine."

Blair gave Madison the thumbs-up before she turned on her heel and sauntered down the corridor.

"Hmmm, " Trey said, watching Blair's rear end. "Where's she off to, switching like that? Looking like she's in heat," he said as he watched her behind beat the hell out of her purple sarong.

Madison giggled and pulled Trey into the room. "She's probably off to meet Antonio."

"The one she picked up on deck?"

Madison nodded, then she eased closer to Trey so that their mouths touched. "You have such sexy lips," she breathed between kisses. "Such soft, sensuous, *juicy* lips," she murmured as her mouth danced over his.

While her hand was inching up to cup the back of his head, Trey's was slipping inside her tank top to cradle one of her breasts. She moaned softly.

"I can't do this." She shuddered suddenly, then pulled out of his arms.

"What—? Why—?" Trey asked stupidly.

She quickly apologized. "I don't want to have sex with you. I thought I did, but I can't. I don't know you like I want to know you. I want a soul-touching experience," Madison explained. She bit back a smile. Is this what self-respect feels like? she wondered. She had moved to Blair's bed and sat perched on the corner.

"Ahhh," Trey drawled. "Miss DuPree has a deep side. I like it. We don't have to do anything," Trey assured her. "To be honest with you, I didn't want to do anything either," he said, dropping down onto her bed.

Madison's jaw dropped. "You didn't want to do anything?" she asked incredulously. "But you were all in it a minute ago."

Trey shrugged, and patted the space next to him. "Baby, come sit next to me. What do you expect?" he asked when Madison was on the bed. She had stretched out and rested her head in his lap. "You offered me pussy, and it's been a long time for me. It's like waving a donut in front of a fat person. He knows that he doesn't need it, but he can't refuse. You can't get mad at him for that, can you?"

"So my pussy is just a donut? Something to fulfill a craving?" she hissed and struggled to get up, but Trey kept a gentle hand on her head and coaxed her back to his lap. He waited until her body relaxed before continuing.

"Baby, listen, you said it, I didn't. That's how *you* treat your body. But that's all going to end, tonight," he said. "Now take off all your clothes!"

"What!" She shot up before Trey had a chance to stop her.

"I want to give you a full-body massage. It'll be one of the most sensuous experiences of your life," he promised and Madison looked in his eyes and knew that he was telling the truth. Without another word she undressed. Not that there was a lot to remove—a tank top, short shorts, but she left her thong on. She watched in amazement as he gathered his locks with one hand and slipped a rubber band on the bunch with the other. He reached into his pocket and pulled out a vial of oil.

"You carry around your own supply of massage oil?" she asked dryly.

"Always be prepared," he murmured. "Now get on your stomach and be quiet," he commanded. Madison did as he requested and butterflies tickled her stomach when she heard the unsnapping of his watchband and then the soft swoosh of clothing falling to the floor. Her breath caught in her throat when the bed creaked and he straddled her, placing his knees on either side of her, locking her in between his legs so that she couldn't move, even if she wanted to. Madison inhaled deeply and slowly exhaled before she dared a peek over her right shoulder. She knew then that if his chest was the last thing she looked at before going blind, she could honestly say that she'd seen the finest piece of art that God created.

"You comfortable?" he asked as he poured massage oil in the palms of his hands and rubbed them together to warm the oil.

"I'm very—" Madison jumped slightly when he touched her shoulders; she was expecting the touch but not one so gentle. He was handling her as if she was a piece of china. His hands floated over her back as if it was uncharted lands and he wanted to take his time and explore every nook and cranny, and the attention that he paid to the back of her neck was sinful. He scooted back so that his butt rested on her calves and he redistributed his weight so that everything was in his ten fingers; he pushed, kneaded, and stroked her flesh until she felt like she was floating.

"Can you massage my butt?" Madison asked and she heard Trey chuckle, a knowing chuckle like her request was expected.

"I'd be mad at myself if I didn't," he said and chuckled again before he cupped her butt, then gently smacked it as if he was testing it for firmness. He poured the massage oil directly on her skin, causing Madison to yelp with surprise and pull her pelvis into the mattress as if she was trying to get away from him.

"That's cold," she complained.

"I'll warm it up for you, baby," Trey promised and just as he said it, his hands roamed over her behind, kneading her.

"That feels good," Madison squeaked as Trey's hand eased open her thighs and began stroking the fleshy spot that always made her eyes roll back in her head.

"You feelin' that," Trey teased and all Madison could do was nod, as he bent over and kissed her spot. She groaned even louder.

"Trey, that wasn't in our agreement," she complained, but not very forcefully.

"So we have agreements now, whassup wit' that? I didn't know we were so formal," Trey teased, then kissed her spot again.

Madison wanted to turn over on her back and open her legs to him, and finally feel him inside her, but instead she said, "Just stick to my back."

"Are you sure?"

"Yes," she said, then repeated it with more conviction.

"Your wish is my command, baby," Trey said. "But may I ask you something?"

Madison raised up just enough so that she could look at him over her shoulder; she could tell by the tone of his voice that he was going to be mischievous. "What?"

"May I kiss the small of your back?"

"No!"

"May I kiss the insides of your thighs?"

"A definite no!"

"Then may I kiss the part of your leg where your thigh and butt meet?"

"No!"

"May I kiss your calves?"

"No!"

"May I kiss the bottom of your feet?"

"No!"

"Well, may I kiss your toes?"

Madison pretended to consider his question, then she said, "No!"

"Can I kiss your lips?"

"Yes." Then, "Hey, which lips!"

"Ah, you're smart. So this time, I'll say the lips on your beautiful face."

"Now you're talking. Bring your lips over to me."

Chapter 47

Blair loosely gripped Antonio's hand as she let him lead her deeper into the ship, into a world where wallpaper and plush carpeting became nonexistent. If she and Madison were staying in the heart of the ship, this had to be the big toe, she thought as she eyed the paper-thin carpeting and the spackle-dotted walls that looked like they had a bad case of acne. She suddenly thought about the stupidity of her actions, following a stranger into a remote part of the ship; this wasn't one of her smartest moments.

"Umm, Antonio, where are we going?" she asked nervously.

He pulled his hand out of hers long enough to point to the floor. "Way down," he uttered, then placed his hand on her bikini-clad bottom.

"I hope I don't get you into any trouble," she said coyly, then giggled when he gave her butt an appreciative pinch.

"Trouble?" he asked, as if he didn't understand the meaning of the word.

"You know, because we're together," she said, poking him in the chest then pointing to herself. "You understand?"

"Oh no, no." He laughed, dismissing her worries. "They don't mind, as long as we don't make any babies." His words jabbed her in the stomach and his blasé attitude knocked her off kilter. "Here we go," Antonio said, stopping in front of a metal door. He indicated for her to stay put as he rushed into the room to tidy up. Blair craned her neck to try to catch his movements, but all she saw was him snatching up items off the floor as if he was picking up garbage. She stood on the threshold, feeling like she was teetering on the edge of a cliff. One sudden push was all it would take to send her skidding backward to safety, or plunging headfirst into trouble.

Antonio looked over his shoulder and saw indecision dancing across Blair's face; he rushed over and pulled her into his room.

"You have a roommate?" Blair asked, seeing two bunks, one neatly made up and the other looking as if the occupant had a wrestling match with the sheets. The room was a quarter the size of hers and Madison's.

"Yes, Ngoli from Nigeria. He's out chasing women," Antonio answered.

When Antonio didn't offer her a seat, Blair sat down on the bed, her eyes widening in surprise as she shot up, almost banging her head against the upper bunk.

"I shouldn't be here," she muttered and looked at Antonio. "I have to leave, I really have to leave," she babbled and moved toward the door, which was only two steps away from the bed.

In one step Antonio was at her side and stilled her movements with a parade of kisses down her cheeks. "Pretty lady, come stay with me tonight. Would you do that for me, pretty lady?" he pleaded gently against her face as his eyelashes tickled her cheek.

"I don't know . . ." Blair hesitated, but she slipped back onto the bed only to discover that her swimsuit had mysteriously disappeared, and she looked confused as she glanced down at her naked body. Somewhere between moving into his arms and his kisses he had vacuumed her bikini off. Antonio slipped a hand into her luscious red hair and drew her up to him.

"You are so beautiful, pretty lady," he murmured against her lips. With his free hand he took off his shorts and underwear in one swift movement, and their bare legs pressed against each other. Blair couldn't help but peek at his body. It was hairless; he was as smooth as a Ken doll.

"You shave?" she couldn't help asking, nor could she resist caressing his smooth chest and back. His body was much different from Rich's.

"I do. You like?"

"I *love,*" Blair murmured.

"I want to taste all of you," he said, then gently probed her mouth with his tongue. "Then I want you to taste all of me."

"I-I-I—" Blair stuttered.

"Shush," he whispered. Blair could feel his excitement hot against her leg, burning an imprint into her skin. "Antonio will take care of you," he reassured her as he cupped her face in his hands and his mouth moved over her face, kissing her forehead, her eyelids, the tip of her nose, and her cheeks. Blair grabbed his head and glued her lips to his and he pulled away. He wagged his finger playfully at her. "That's a no-no. Lay back, pretty lady, and let Antonio take care of you. Promise me that, will you?" His eyes begged for an answer and she could barely squeak out a response before he slipped down and began nipping at the inside of her thighs.

Blair's hands stole into his hair and she wrapped her legs around him, pulling him closer up to her essence; his movements suggested that he was gently prying open an oyster shell and he couldn't wait to taste the priceless pearl inside. Blair bucked wildly when he captured his prize, and slowly caught her breath as every inch of her body was pampered and indulged until she felt like she could melt into a big puddle of happiness. Antonio pulled himself up from his position and pointed to the floor, then said, "My turn."

Her euphoria quickly lifted and was replaced with trepidation as Blair and Antonio switched places. Blair nipped at his toes and kissed his feet until he begged her to stop; she kissed him to the top of his head, while at the same time strategically avoiding his penis. "Pretty lady," he moaned, "wrap those lips around me." Blair scrunched up her face, inched down, then quickly backtracked. She peeked up and saw his expectant expression when her mouth lowered again, and he moved his hips up to meet her. As soon as her lips touched his tip, she backed away and buried her face in her hands.

"I can't do it," she moaned, then looked piteously at Antonio. "My husband would kill me if he ever found out I did that to another man!" she wailed.

"Pretty lady," Antonio murmured, before gathering Blair

up in his arms. "Don't worry, we have all night to do whatever you want to do. If you don't want to do this, don't worry. See, I can make myself happy," he said, grabbing his penis and stroking it up and down.

"Stop, I want to do it," she said stubbornly. The picture of Rich making love to another woman flashed before her eyes.

"You sure, pretty lady?" he asked as he looked at her through heavy-lidded eyes. Her tanned skin shimmered in the soft light, her lips were puffy from his kisses, and her breast tips were glowing. Blair shook her head and bent down. Her lips skirted over the tip of his penis, then she pulled away, but she held her head a little bit higher, a little prouder.

"I almost did it," she said, looking at him like a little girl waiting for a pat on her head from Daddy.

"Yes, you did," Antonio murmured as his hand replaced her lips, gently stroking himself. He wasn't sure how much longer he was going to last. "Why don't we try this," he said and went over to a minirefrigerator. He pulled out a bottle of strawberry syrup, and poured it over himself, then he put some on his fingers and fed it to Blair.

"See, it isn't that bad, is it? It tastes good, doesn't it, pretty lady? Now you try it here," he said when she licked his fingers clean and he gently eased her head down. "You try it," he encouraged and brought his penis up to meet her mouth. Blair looked at the red gooey thing and nearly laughed, it looked like a double-size freezer pop and she licked it up.

"Oh, momma!" Antonio shouted, then grabbed Blair by the waist and pulled her up as easily as if he was picking up a ten-pound bag of fresh fruit, then plopped her down on him.

"So you want it this way?" she teased, a new courage taking over her. She had leaned back, thrust her breasts in the air, grabbed his ankles, and moved her hips against him, making a slow, exaggerated figure eight. Antonio's eyes widened at Blair's boldness, then he matched her movements, making his own figure eight with his hips.

"I want it any way you can give it," he panted. "Give it to me, pretty lady."

"Ooh, I like that. Antonio!" Blair moaned, and leaned forward and grasped his shoulders, then let nature take over. Her hands roamed over his muscled body.

"Aw, no-no-no," he gasped repeatedly, while Blair rode him until she couldn't go any further.

They lay spooned together on Antonio's bunk, with the sweat that they'd spent hours making drying in little waves across their bodies. After they'd made love for the fourth time, he pulled her into the bunk and laid his head on her chest and promptly fell asleep in her arms. But Blair was wide awake, and she was giving Antonio's sleeping body a thorough examination. She reached around and cupped his pecs, and then she grazed his nipples with her thumb, and giggled when he moaned in his sleep.

His stomach grumbled at her touch when she danced over it to get to her candy, which sprung to life under her touch. Wonderment softened her face when she stroked it and played with it like it was her favorite doll.

See, Rich, I'm an interesting person. She smirked, then a sudden chill went through her at the thought of her husband. She snatched her hands away from Antonio and clasped them to her chest as she warily rested her head against the wall. Is this what it feels like to cheat? she wondered guiltily.

She glanced at Antonio; he looked like a younger, more exotic version of her husband. Where Rich's hair was a dusty black, Antonio's black hair was glossy, as if someone had drizzled a capful of sunlight on it, making it glisten like a sunbeam. Muscles bulged from Antonio's lean body in places that Rich hadn't used in years, and the right muscle was working for Antonio, working very well indeed.

Blair slid off the bed, then slipped on her bikini and one of his T-shirts. She tiptoed toward the door.

"Where are you going?" Antonio called from the bed, his voice sleepy. "It's still early. Come on back to bed. I'm not finished with you yet."

Blair stood at the door, her face knotted with indecision.

Chapter 48

"So I get to hang out with a beautiful lady twice in one day, aren't I lucky?" Trey teased.

"You sure are," Madison said with a smile. "Did you have a good workout?" she asked Trey. They were back in Madison's cabin snuggling on her bed. Trey was sitting up with his back against the wall and Madison was sitting securely in between his legs. They fit together like a perfect puzzle.

"It was aw'ight. I would've had more fun if you were with me," Trey said as he nuzzled Madison's neck.

"That's sweet," she said, grateful that he was sitting behind her because she was cheesing like she had just won a lifetime supply of Pradas. "But you know the girls, they wanted to hang out together." She felt Trey nod in understanding. "And LaShawn and I are going to the spa in a couple of hours."

"This place is so freakin' huge," Trey observed. Her stateroom was bigger than most hotel rooms he had been in.

"I know. I really lucked out when I decided to bunk with

Blair. Usually I'm hanging with Lauren, but I figured that LaShawn needed her wisdom. So here I am."

"So Lauren didn't want to deal with you?" Trey joked.

"Ha-ha! Joke man." They were quiet for a couple of minutes, then Madison tugged herself out of Trey's arms.

"Where're you going?"

"To the bathroom . . . is that all right with you?" Madison asked saucily as she put her hands on her hips.

"You'd better take a little of that tartness out of your tone, lady."

"And if I don't?"

"I'm gonna spank you," Trey threatened.

"Promises, promises." Madison playfully stuck her tongue out at him, then sashayed off to the bathroom. As soon as she was done she slipped back into Trey's arms.

"You ready for that *spanking?*" Trey whispered, then turned Madison around so that she faced him.

"That depends," Madison drawled. "Are you gonna do it fast and hard or slow and steady?"

Trey's penis immediately swelled. "Which would you prefer?" he asked, chuckling softly. " 'Cause I can do it any way you want."

"Surprise me," Madison teased. "I can take it any way you give it."

"I can give it to you all night long," Trey boasted as he gently stroked her face. "What time is Blair supposed to be back?"

"Not any time soon. She's with Antonio and they usually spend hours together. Besides, the door is dead bolted. She can't get in unless we let her in."

"Oh yeah? So you're all mine?" Trey murmured. Madison nodded. That's all it took. Trey leaned forward and hungrily covered Madison's mouth with his. He ran his hand through her hair and was rewarded with a groan of desire from Madison as she pressed herself against him.

Trey pulled his hand from her hair and started easing her shorts off her hips. "Stop!" Madison demanded, squeezing her legs together.

Trey's hand froze. "What's wrong?"

"It's just that when I imagined us making love, there was always tons of candles around and KEM or Luther playing in the background."

Trey popped up off the bed. "I'll be right back."

"What? Where are you going?" Madison demanded.

"I'll be right back," Trey promised. "Give me ten minutes."

Madison gave him a curt nod, then he hurried out the door.

Seveal minutes later she heard a muffled knock on the door.

It took her only a second to hurry across the room and open the door to Trey. He strolled in carrying a couple of bags.

"You went shopping?" Madison asked incredulously.

"Kinda." Trey grinned. "I borrowed a couple things from my roommate. Ta da!" he announced as he pulled out three candles, a miniature CD player, and a box of condoms.

"Trey!" Madison squealed. "I can't believe you did this," she said, awed by his thoughtfulness.

"I remembered my roommate had all this." He grouped the candles on the mirrored dresser. Once they were lit it looked like they had half a dozen candles instead of three.

"Oh, it's beautiful," Madison gushed.

"Since it's not dark yet, why don't we do this?" Trey turned off the light and closed the heavy curtains over the plate glass window, leaving the room in a soft glow. "And I know this isn't KEM or Luther, but I think you might like this even more," he said, smiling smugly at her. Anita Baker's sultry voice filled the room.

"She's perfect . . . this is perfect," Madison said.

"I'm glad." Trey smiled as he sat down next to Madison.

"I'm sorry," Madison said.

"Why?"

"For making you do all this."

"You're a phenomenal lady. I'd give you the world if I could," Trey confessed, then brushed his lips against hers. He pulled away, then gently turned Madison on her stomach.

"You wanna do it that way the first time?"

Trey burst out laughing. "Hell no! I want to give you a massage."

"Oh!" Madison answered.

"You sound disappointed," Trey said as he worked Madison's top off, then her bra.

"I'm not," Madison said into the mattress, then turned her head so that he could hear her. "I'm not," she repeated. "It kinda caught me by surprise. I thought we were gonna do something. I mean, you've already given me a massage. And a very good one at that."

"Thanks," Trey said as he gently kneaded her neck and Madison groaned with pleasure.

"You really should take your clothes off, too," Madison suggested.

"You think?"

"I think."

Trey didn't need any more convincing; in the time it took for Madison to turn her head to watch the ministrip show, he had already taken off his T-shirt and shorts.

"Damn, you're fast. No underwear?" she observed. She could feel Trey's erection against her behind when he straddled her back.

"No need to, baby."

Madison grinned but said nothing as his strong hands moved over her shoulders, gently grabbing at her skin as though he was picking fruit.

"That feels luscious," Madison groaned.

"Anything for you, babe. Your skin is so soft." Her honey-dipped skin shimmered in the candlelight as though it had been dusted with fourteen-karat gold dust.

Trey's hands floated over her back, skipped over her butt, then kneaded her thighs and calves. "Saving the best for last," Trey said in answer to Madison's thoughts. He tenderly cupped her behind, then softly kneaded it until Madison whimpered softly. She parted her legs and lifted her behind off the mattress, giving him easy access to her mound. Trey chuckled and tenderly smacked her behind. "Aren't we in a hurry," he teased. "Turn over," he instructed. Madison did as told, and Trey straddled her again.

"Can we do it now?" Madison pleaded. Looking down at her, Trey nearly laughed out loud. She looked like an overgrown baby, her lips were in a pushed-out pout, and her eyes were squished shut.

"Chill! We have all day." Angling down, he rained kisses on her shoulder blades and her body shivered. "Hey, stop that," Trey scolded. Madison had reached out to stroke his penis. "This is all about you. Not me. I want you to enjoy!"

Trey shimmied down until he was level with her breasts, then he took a moment to admire their beauty. He gently swiped his tongue over her erect nipples, leaving a trail of heat. Madison arched her back, begging him to do more. He did; he took them in his mouth and enjoyed them as though they were ripe peaches.

"I want you in me now," Madison breathed.

"You sure? There's still a lot that I want to do to you."

Madison shook her head. "No, now!" she insisted. Trey passionately kissed her while he slipped on a condom, then he flattened himself against her and Madison opened her legs, urging him to enter.

Trey poised over her mound, then made a kissing sound, forcing Madison to open her eyes; her mouth opened with surprise when he plunged into her. She wrapped her legs around his waist, urging him to go deeper.

"Ah!" Trey moaned as he moved in and out of Madison's softness. "Tell me what you want me to do!" he demanded.

"Keep doing what you're doing," Madison panted and wrapped her legs tighter around his waist. "Just keep doing what you're doing," she repeated dreamily as Trey's pace increased.

He suddenly went rigid and his breath came out in little puffs. "I'm sorry," Trey sheepishly apologized. He hopped off the bed and skulked to the bathroom. After he cleaned himself off he returned to the bed.

"Don't worry about it, it was the first time," Madison consoled him, but silently prayed that she was right. Everybody has performance anxiety one time or another.

"I have a good explanation about what just happened," Trey said.

Madison's mouth went dry. "Do I want to hear it?" she squeaked.

Chapter 49

A feathery sigh of happiness escaped LaShawn's parted lips. "This is pure ecstasy. Just total heaven." She and Madison were in the ship's spa, lying side by side with seaweed-peppermint scrub smeared over their bodies. Etta James softly crooned them into deeper bliss. "Umm. I'm sooo glad you talked me into this," LaShawn said. She hadn't felt this relaxed in years. "And it's so nice that we have the room to ourselves."

"This is so delicious," Madison agreed. Every fiber of her body felt as though it had been kissed by gods; she was tingling as though she'd just had a twenty-four-hour sexing session.

"Madison?" LaShawn whispered.

"That be me," Madison joked in a sleepy voice.

"May I ask you something?"

"Sure."

"You won't laugh, will you?"

"If it's funny, I will," Madison replied.

"Please don't," LaShawn pleaded. Something in LaShawn's

voice made Madison peel the cucumber slices off her eyes and turn toward her friend.

"Whassup?" she asked. LaShawn whispered something that Madison didn't hear. "What?" she asked, craning her neck closer.

"Terrance and I are going to do it tonight," LaShawn shyly confessed as the blood rushed to her face.

"What?" Madison squealed and sat up so fast that she almost slipped off the table. "Wow! You're giving Terrance some. And you never even let Calvin sneak a peek into the secret garden. That's hilarious."

"I know," LaShawn said, and sighed. If she didn't have the green gunk slathered over her body, she would've hugged herself. "If you would've told me two weeks ago that I would be on a cruise ship, in the middle of a sex game, and making love to a man I barely knew, I'd call you crazy!" LaShawn shrugged. "But Terrance is the one I've been waiting for. It just feels right, it feels natural . . ."

"Can't argue with that," Madison said, then settled back down on the table. "See, I didn't laugh. What was so funny about that?"

"That wasn't the funny part—this is. I don't know what to do," LaShawn bashfully admitted.

"What do you mean, you don't know what to do?" Madison asked.

"I don't know what to do . . . at all . . . things probably changed a whole lot since I last had sex." LaShawn groaned. "No matter where I look, people are talking about sex, everything from how to make it sweet and steamy to how to have an off-the-scale orgasm. I'm not sure if I'm up to it," LaShawn wailed.

"I know!" Madison hooted. "It's been a gazillion years since you've had some. Your stuff is so dried up that Terrance is gonna have to presoak it before doing anything." Madison laughed so hard at her own joke that she teared up.

"See, that's why I didn't want to tell you," LaShawn huffed and turned on her side, showing Madison her back.

"Okay, I'll stop," Madison promised, but her laugh was reduced to bite-size chuckles.

"I guess that's the best I can expect from you," LaShawn acquiesced. "Tell me what to do!" she pleaded.

"It's easy. Trey admitted to me that he had been celibate for over a year, yet everything came back to him. It's not one of those use-it-or-lose-it skills. Basically, you do whatever you want," Madison answered.

"Huh?"

"It's not something that can be taught. All you got to do is relax and let the sensations take over. If you want to kiss him . . . kiss him, if you want to lick him . . . lick him. If you want to caress him—"

"Caress him," LaShawn finished. "Now I get it," she said, smiling.

"Remember, don't *think,* just do!"

"Don't think, just do," LaShawn whispered. It was her mantra for the day.

She repeated it to herself while she showered, hummed it to herself while dressing, and by the time she showed up at Terrance's cabin she was practically singing it.

"So what did you tell your roommate?" LaShawn asked, standing on the threshold of Terrance's door, peering in.

"That I had the most beautiful girl in the world coming

to visit me and I didn't want to see him until tomorrow morning."

LaShawn's brow crinkled. "Where's he gonna sleep?"

Terrance chuckled as he led her into the room. "I'm not that cruel. He can crash with a couple of our frat brothers. And there's a lot of ladies who'd be happy to help a brotha out. So don't worry . . . he's cool," he said as he sat on his bed, pulling LaShawn down next to him.

He turned toward her and took her face in his hands, gently cradling it. "We don't have to do this. I'll be just as happy if we go on deck and watch the stars."

"I want to do it," LaShawn gently insisted. To prove it, she pulled Terrance's mouth toward her until it was a mere tongue's length away. "I want to," she repeated, then she tenderly showered his lips with soft kisses.

"I'm glad you want to," Terrance said, then groaned against her lips. He pushed her gently on the bed then spread out on top of her. His tongue pressed its way past her lips and LaShawn gasped; he tasted so sweet. She froze, not sure what to do next. Sensing her hesitation, Terrance tenderly coaxed her tongue until it resumed its dance with his.

Terrance pulled his mouth off hers and dipped his head and before she knew what was happening his mouth was exploring her blouse, then her breast. It didn't take long for the white cotton to go transparent and her nipple peaked up as though it was saluting him. Terrance switched to the other, and soon she had two wet spots on the front of her blouse.

"You may take it off," LaShawn offered weakly. As soon as the words were uttered Terrance had both of their clothes off faster than a stripper on coke.

"You can still change your mind," Terrance offered as he nibbled at her lips.

"No way. Show me what you got," LaShawn moaned.

"Oh baby! I'm not from the show me state, but I'll be glad to give you what you want." Grinning, he reached down and cupped her breasts; her nipples reminded him of supersize Hershey's Kisses. Leaning down, he swiped his tongue across one and a shiver of desire ran through LaShawn.

"Your titties are so beautiful," Terrance whispered before he cupped one and brought it up to his mouth, gently rubbing the nipple across his lips.

He reached down between her legs and lightly inserted his finger. LaShawn took his hand. "Nu-uh, touch me like this," she said, showing him what she liked. She nearly fainted; it'd been too long since she felt anyone else's hand on her.

"I thought you said you haven't been intimate with anyone?" He peered down at her suspiciously.

"I haven't," LaShawn said as her hips shot up. "But I know what I like." She moaned as her legs spread wide and her hips danced with his hand. "Go faster!" she demanded. Terrance looked down at her as if she was the most beautiful woman in the world. Her body was arched like a bow, her head thrown back, her hair spread around her.

Oblivious to Terrance's eyes, LaShawn was in heaven. Her own fingers couldn't do what he was doing to her. Just do! She moved her hips higher. Just do! She grinded her pelvis into his hand. Just do! She felt the familiar flicker, and her lips curved up into a smile as the flicker turned into a flame and she burst into a three-alarm fire. "Oh my

God! Oh my God! Oh my God!" LaShawn babbled until the words rolled off her tongue and blended together into little whimpers.

When she stopped trembling, Terrance slowly stroked her body until it heated again. LaShawn watched through half-lidded eyes as he pulled back and slid on a condom. Their eyes met and LaShawn gave a small nod: Terrance winked in response.

He poised over her and slowly inched his way inside her. Every time LaShawn stiffened, he stopped until she relaxed a little; something was holding her back. He paused and glanced down at her, her eyes were closed. He ran his hand over her face, willing her eyes to open.

"Look at me," he softly commanded, and when she opened her eyes, Terrance saw fear. "It's okay, baby," he soothed. "It'll be okay. I won't do anything to hurt you. I promise I won't, just trust me," he begged. And with every word LaShawn's body relaxed a little bit more.

Terrance moved inside her, and LaShawn's eyes widened with wonderment and a thunderbolt shot through her. Don't think, don't think, don't think. She blindly reached out and her hands fell on his behind; she eagerly clutched it and urged him on.

Terrance followed her movements and he stiffened and she stiffened and they both came. Terrance stroked her face. "I didn't know, I didn't know," she repeated, tears pouring down her face. Terrance swiped his T-shirt off the floor and gently dabbed at her cheeks. When the river slowed to a stream he thumbed the last of the tears away.

"Thank you. Let me go clean up." Terrance hurried off to the bathroom. The condom wrapper was on the floor.

LaShawn hesitated for only a heartbeat before she snatched it up and stuffed it in her purse. When Terrance came out of the bathroom he found her sitting contently on the bed. "Are you ready for round two?"

LaShawn nodded her head. "Round two, three, *and* four," she said and gave him a big wink.

"Making up for lost time?"

LaShawn shook her head and crooked her finger, seductively motioning him toward the bed. Terrance grinned, then slipped in beside her. She reached out and grabbed both of his ears and tugged his face toward hers so that their lips were a breath apart. "Nope. Just making all the fantasies I had about you real." LaShawn watched as Terrance's eyes widened in shock, then pleasure.

"You fantasized about me?" he asked, incredulous that this beautiful but straitlaced lady had let a passionate thought enter her head.

LaShawn nodded. "I had a *lot* of fantasies about you," she boldly admitted.

Terrance was intrigued. "Like what?"

LaShawn looked demurely away. "I can't tell you," she said, pretending to be shy.

"Oh!" Terrance said disappointed.

"Maybe I can show you," LaShawn offered.

"Okay," Terrance said, then grew excited as LaShawn pulled him upright and moved him to the edge of the bed.

"Don't forget to wrap up," LaShawn reminded him, then tossed him a condom. As soon as he had it on, she was on him. With her arms wrapped around his neck and her legs encircling his waist, they looked like one.

LaShawn unlocked her arms from around his neck and

ran her hands through his hair, then gently massaged his scalp. Her hands continued to play in his hair as she leaned forward and took his left earlobe in her mouth. She alternated between sucking his earlobe and blowing in his ear.

"I think I like this fantasy," Terrance said, breathing against her neck. His hands reached down and cupped her rounded behind, softly kneading it.

"I love it." LaShawn groaned as she began moving her hips in little circles. He was buried deep inside her and she wanted every inch of him. She abruptly stopped her movements, then bore down and Terrance grunted as he dove into her velvety softness.

"Uh . . . Shawn," he stuttered. "Don't do that again."

"Why not?" she asked innocently, then did the movement on double time.

"This is why," Terrance said and, in one fluid movement, stood up, flipped her over on her back, then made love to her until both of them were soaking wet.

LaShawn gently scraped her fingernails over Terrance's chest, trying to wake him up. "Just like a man to go out like a light after sex," she murmured. Her fingernails dug deeper in his chest and he sleepily opened one eye and peered down at her. "Whassup, baby?"

Smiling, she propped up on one elbow and peered down at him. "I wanted to thank you."

"For what?" he asked.

"For making tonight so very special." She leaned down and pecked him on the lips. "You exceeded all my expectations."

"I did, did I?" he asked, fully awake.

"Yeah, you did. I was so scared . . . I was afraid I wouldn't know what to do," she admitted shyly.

"You did fine. *More* than fine." Terrance chuckled, then reached up, cupping the back of LaShawn's head and pulling her to him. Their lips met in a soul-tangling kiss.

"Are you okay?"

LaShawn nodded. "I'm fine . . . wonderful, really."

"You waited five years for this," Terrance said with a grin. "You gave me something tonight that your fiancé didn't get."

"Ex-fiancé," LaShawn corrected him. "This," she waved her hand back and forth between them, "feels right . . . it feels *so* right," she finished, kissing him to prove it.

Terrance carefully studied her face; the room was dim, but he could see the tranquil expression on her face. "You're fine now, but I don't want you waking up later and hating herself for what you did."

"Shhh," LaShawn whispered as she put a finger on Terrance's lips. "I'm truly blessed."

"Well, thank you."

LaShawn waited until he was asleep before she scooped up the empty condom wrappers and stuck them in her purse.

Chapter 50

Lauren pushed back her bed covers, swung her legs around, and gently placed them on the floor; with a peek over to LaShawn, she pushed herself up and tiptoed to the bathroom.

"Where you going?" LaShawn asked sleepily, and Lauren jumped as though someone was shooting at her feet.

"Damn!" she hissed. "Haven't you noticed we've docked?" Lauren said, avoiding LaShawn's question.

LaShawn kicked back her blankets, knelt on the bed, and peered out the porthole. "We sure did," she confirmed before plopping down and turning toward her friend. "So you're not going into St. Thomas with us?" LaShawn asked.

Lauren turned away and began pulling items from her evening bag and dropping them into an oversize straw purse. "No. I'm going with a friend."

"Darryl?" LaShawn asked excitedly and her sleepiness quickly dropped away. "So you're in the contest now?"

"No . . . I am not joining you all's nasty contest. I'm just visiting a beautiful city with a new friend."

"Wearing that? You've never worn anything like that for us, and we've known you for years," LaShawn said.

Lauren glanced down at her outfit. The shorts that showcased her long legs barely covered her butt, and the ends of her white cotton shirt were tied at the bottom, showing her midriff. She knew that she looked like a housewife gone bad, but the temperature was supposed to be in the high nineties, and that's just what she told LaShawn.

"Whatever. Just behave yourself. We aren't accepting any latecomers to the game," LaShawn teased.

Lauren inched over to the wall mirror and studied her reflection. "Do you really think Darryl might get the wrong idea about me?" she asked casually, already knowing how Darryl felt about her.

"I hope not. But you'd better not drop anything, because if you bend down you might be arrested for indecent exposure," LaShawn joked.

"Tee-hee, ha-ha," Lauren said in a flat voice as she pulled the door open. "I'll see you tonight." She closed the door on a giggling LaShawn.

Lauren and Darryl walked side by side down Main Street in Charlotte Amalie, St. Thomas. It was already two hours into their excursion and Lauren couldn't remember a single thing that they'd seen so far.

Lauren involuntarily shivered. Oh, there it goes again, she thought as her arm brushed against Darryl's. The feeling of his skin against hers almost made her clit explode. She glanced over at Darryl to see if he had the same reaction, but his face was turned away, his attention focused on the different shops.

"I've read that they have four hundred stores in this area," Darryl said, cutting into Lauren's thoughts.

"Yeah, and it feels like we've seen every one of them," Lauren joked.

"You tired?" Darryl asked.

"A little. Let's sit down," she said, nodding toward a bench.

Unbeknownst to Lauren he had a difficult time keeping his eyes off her. Occasionally he'd let her walk a little ways ahead of him so that he could watch the way her behind moved in her shorts. "You should've said something," he gently scolded her. "This sun is no joke. I don't want you getting a heat stroke," he said, then he thought how much he would love to be personally responsible for giving Lauren a heat stroke, knowing that they could easily start a fire under the sheets. "Better yet, we're close to the aquarium, do you think you can make it?"

"That sounds like fun!" Lauren said, suddenly reenergized. The thought of sitting on a bench next to Darryl, with the possibility of their bodies touching, was too much. An hour later she wished for the bench.

Coral World Ocean Park, the island's number-one tourist attraction, was jam-packed with tourists. So much so that Lauren found herself pressed against Darryl as though he was peanut butter and she was jelly, because they were definitely close enough to be a sandwich. Make that a Polish kielbasa sausage sandwich, Lauren mused. Her clit sizzled when she was repeatedly jostled against Darryl and his hardness pressed into her behind.

"Ready for the next exhibit?" Darryl breathed in her ear and she resisted the urge to lean into him. Instead she closed her eyes and took a steadying breath before nodding her agreement. "Lead the way."

Lauren turned and carved a tunnel through the crowd for her and Darryl. They were almost there when the lady walking in front of Lauren abruptly halted and Lauren smacked right into her. She stumbled, then flailed her hands, which made her look like a drunk pigeon, and tried to regain her balance.

Darryl wrapped his arms around her waist and pulled her against him and Lauren gasped. "It's okay, it's me, Darryl," he reassured her, mistaking her sharp inhale for fear.

Lauren remained silent. She couldn't tell him that her clit caught fire as soon as she was flush against him. Darryl's arms tightened around her waist, then pulled her closer against him, pressing his hard crotch into her butt. She swallowed a moan, then pressed her lips closed to make sure that it didn't escape. The lady resumed walking and Lauren pulled herself out of Darryl's arms.

"You okay?"

"It's a little tight in here, I'm beginning to feel claustrophobic. Let's go."

This time Darryl led the way through the crowd and back into the sunlight. Lauren blinked rapidly and sucked in the sweet air. "This feels good, there were too many people in there."

"Some might say too many people. I call it cozy," Darryl said with a knowing glint in his eye. Blood rushed to Lauren's head, her knees went weak, and she began to gently sway. "Lauren?" Darryl said before rushing to her side to steady her.

"You just seem to keep coming to my rescue," Lauren said in a shaky voice as she leaned against Darryl. "Let's sit down. I think you were right earlier, the sun is too much for me. Let's sit in the shade."

"Would you like me to carry you?" Darryl asked and an image of Darryl carrying her to her bed effortlessly popped into her head.

"I can make it," she reassured him. Once they were settled on a shaded bench, Darryl offered to get her something cool to drink. "That'll be perfect." She watched Darryl stroll away. What's wrong with you? You're a married woman, you have a husband at home who loves you with all his heart, and you love him just as much, she scolded herself. "But there's something about him," she whispered to herself. "He brings out a side to me that I never knew existed."

Lauren leaned back on the bench and pulled out her camera. By the time Darryl came back, she was feeling like her old self and she had gotten some awesome pictures of the buildings and locals.

"Here you go," he said, passing her a drink.

Lauren thirstily gulped it, and by the time she set the cup down, half the drink was gone.

"You were a little thirsty, I see," Darryl teased.

"I was. I didn't realize how much. Thanks," she said, smiling at him, and Darryl could feel himself getting hard.

Lauren shook her head. "I'm beginning to feel better already. Are you ready to walk some more?"

"Sure." He stood up and reached out for Lauren to take his hand; she hesitated before slipping her hand into his. He pulled her up, and as soon as she was standing, she discreetly pulled her hand out of his.

"Let's go."

Four hours later Lauren and Darryl were at her cabin door. Each had an armful of gifts and mementoes from St. Thomas. "Thank you so much for today. I really enjoyed it. You were an excellent tour guide."

"Any time," Darryl drawled. "See you around."

"Give me a second while I stick this stuff in the room." After much maneuvering and juggling, Lauren opened her door and dropped the items on her bed. Seconds later she was back in the hall standing in front of Darryl. "Let me thank you properly. Thank you," she said and opened her arms wide, inviting Darryl to step in.

"You're very welcome," Darryl said, hugging her hard. Then he bent down and swiped his mouth across hers. When she didn't protest, he gently applied pressure and slid his tongue past her parted lips. Lauren hesitatingly met his tongue and groaned when they touched.

When Darryl felt Lauren go limp in his arms, he guided her until her back was against her cabin door. Lauren's hands roamed over Darryl's shoulders, then down to his behind. She grabbed it and pulled his crotch closer to her; she wanted to feel every inch of him.

The sounds of her neighbors getting ready to exit their cabin broke through her haze of desire.

"What are you doing?" Lauren sputtered. She jumped out of Darryl's arms and angrily wiped her hand across her mouth. "What the fuck was that all about?"

"You wanted a kiss. So I kissed you."

"No I didn't," Lauren snapped. "I wanted to give you a thank-you hug. But it got turned into a tongue-ramming session."

"Tongue ramming? It was what you wanted."

"I did not. I think it's time for you to leave," Lauren retorted, but her legs were shaking so hard she was afraid she'd fall down again. Before Darryl could say anything she scooted into her cabin and slammed the door shut. She slid down onto her bed. While lying down she realized two things: That her head was pounding worse than the waves against the boat, and that her lips had touched a man's other than Cleve's, and not only had she liked it, but she'd encouraged it. "Oh shit!"

Chapter 51

Blair placed her hands on her hips and did one final knee bend, bending so far down that her butt nearly kissed the floor. Bouncing up, she stuck one foot in front of the other, repeating the motions until she fell into an easy rhythm. Blood roared softly in her ears every time her sneakered feet hit the deck. She grinned to herself; she hadn't run like this since college.

After one full lap around the boat, her hair was plastered to her head, her T-shirt clung to her body, glued by a strip of sweat, and a ribbon of perspiration made its way from her behind to her crotch, where it formed a dark spot in front. She looked like a drowned rat, but a triumphant one. Exhausted, she plopped down onto a bar stool and dropped her head in her hands. The glittering lights from the bar framed her.

Suddenly her time with Antonio popped into her head. *How could I have done something like that? Why am I jeopardizing my marriage? How could I have sucked that man's—*

"Is that my pretty lady?" she heard and Blair shot up as though she had been jolted with an electric current.

"Antonio?" she squeaked. She hadn't seen him in a couple of days. Something told her that he was either hiding out or maybe found somebody else to spend his time with. Surprisingly, neither possibility upset her.

"It's Antonio!" he grinned, then took in her appearance. She looked like a wrung-out washcloth. "Would you like something to drink?"

Blair nodded her head. "Just a ginger ale. I always seem to get into trouble if I drink something stronger," she said, laughing softly.

"Come on," Antonio chided. "A pretty lady like you has gotta have something—"

"—with an umbrella in it!" Blair finished for him. "Something small then," she decided. She nearly fell off her chair when Antonio slapped down in front of her a quart-size margarita with a purple umbrella swimming in the middle of it.

"Antonio, I told you something small," she protested while warily eyeing the drink.

He winked slyly at her. "I'll help you drink it."

"You can't. You're working and somebody might see us."

Antonio put a finger to his lips. Then he reached out and flicked a switch; suddenly all the twinkling lights went out, leaving them covered in darkness. "I'm off duty." He smirked, then motioned to her before disappearing behind the counter.

Blair suspiciously eyed the spot where he was standing.

"Come on down to my home away from home," Antonio called softly. "It'll be fun," he promised.

"I don't know," Blair whispered back, feeling silly, as though she was having a conversation with the Invisible Man. "What are we going to do down there?"

"What do you think?" came Antonio's teasing reply.

Blair leaned over the counter, conscious of the fact that any passerby would be getting an eyeful of her sweat-stained behind. "Antonio!" she hissed. "I can't do this anymore."

"What, have a drink with a friend? What's wrong with that?"

"That's not what I'm talking about and you know it," Blair said between clenched teeth. "If I—I mean, if we—" She stopped, looked over both shoulders to make sure no one was coming, then breathed out, "I can't come down there because if I do we're gonna do what we did a couple of nights ago and I don't want that to happen because I'm a married woman—a *very* married woman—and what we did was wrong and I don't want it to happen again, okay?"

There was a long pause, then, "I see," Antonio answered. "Well, come and finish your drink. You can leave after you're done."

Blair thought it over. "Okay . . . I'll come down, but I'm leaving as soon as I finish my drink." She grabbed her drink, took a few tentative steps around the counter, then bent down and peered behind the bar. "What the hell? Where are you?" she asked, her brow puckered in confusion.

"Have a seat," she heard and jumped so high that she almost spilled her drink. "Look down!" Antonio instructed and that's when Blair noticed an alcove behind the bar; it was large enough to seat four people.

"Oh, cozy," Blair whispered. The space was dark and just tall enough for them to comfortably sit upright and long enough to allow them to stretch out if they wanted. Just as she settled beside Antonio, a group of rowdy passengers trooped by. Blair went mannequin still.

"No one can see us," he assured her, then, "I missed you," he said, grabbing one of her breasts.

"Stop!" she ordered, while slapping his hand away. "You promised that you weren't going to do anything."

"No, I didn't. I told you to come and finish your drink," he answered in a contrite tone.

"But you *implied* that nothing was going to happen."

"But I missed you," Antonio drawled as he nuzzled her neck and made his way down to her chest.

"Antonio! I smell like a skunk," Blair protested, shrinking away from him.

"In my country, you have what we call a natural perfume," Antonio teased.

"Yeah, Eau de Piglet," Blair joked and suddenly turned serious. "I honestly don't want to do anything."

"I think you do," Antonio said. "And I love the way you smell," he whispered, as he plucked the margarita glass from her hand and placed it on the shelving behind them.

"Antonio," Blair protested as he pressed his lips to hers. "Antonio," she weakly objected as he peeled off her sweaty T-shirt. "Oh! Antonio . . ." She groaned as he fastened his lips to one of her nipples, then moved to the other one. "It'll be easier if you take these off," Blair said, as she helped Antonio peel off her musky sweatpants and panties. Her sneakers quickly followed.

By the time she looked up Antonio was stripped down to his underwear. "How do you do it?" she mouthed in amazement. The man was faster than the Road Runner. He simply grinned and nudged her shoulder, forcing her onto her back.

Leaning over her, Antonio's lips made a trail down the side of her face to her stomach. *"Bella,* you taste delicious," he declared, then tongued the inside of her thighs.

"How do you know? You've haven't eaten me yet," Blair murmured.

"Oh, I will," Antonio promised. "I—"
Suddenly there was a pounding on the bar, then Blair heard a male's voice. "Are you open? I thought I heard somebody," he muttered.

"You're hearing things again, Bob," a female replied in a dry tone.

"Is there anybody back there?" he bellowed.

"I think it's closed."

"I know I heard something," Bob insisted. "I'm half-drunk . . . not deaf. I'm gonna check it out."

"Don't move!" Antonio hissed unnecessarily in her ear. Blair was as motionless as a rock beneath him.

They both held their breath when they heard the flapping sound of Bob's flip-flops as he rounded the bar. He was almost in front of them when the woman said, "Would you come on! I'm taking you back to the room."

"But I did hear something," Bob whined.

"Come on," the lady said firmly, then half pulled and dragged Bob away from the bar.

Neither Blair nor Antonio breathed until his protests faded away.

"That was close!" Blair let out an uneasy laugh; this was beginning to feel like a bad idea.

"It was. But we should not have stopped." Antonio

breathed against her ear. "I should've done you. Then Bob *would've* heard something."

"You would not have done anything," Blair teased as she ran a finger over his nipple. "You were scared just like me."

"Antonio was not scared."

"Were, too," Blair taunted as she reached down between his legs and wrapped her hand around his cock. "You were acting like a little bitch," she mocked.

"I'll show you your bitch!" Antonio reached over to his pants, fished out a condom, and slid it on. "So who's a bitch?" he asked as he straddled her.

"You are!"

"Well, here is your *bitch!*" He grunted, then plunged into her and Blair's hips jerked up off the floor, nearly pushing Antonio off.

"Antonio!" she shouted, not caring who heard as he moved in and out of her so fast that his hips were a blur and all she could do was hold on for the ride. Their orgasms came so hard and fast that they both were left gasping for breath.

"Antonio is no bitch." He grinned down at her before he placed a kiss on her forehead.

Chapter 52

"So who won the contest?" Blair asked and Lauren let out a loud groan. She thought they had forgotten all about the contest and she said so.

"That was the whole point of the trip," Blair said. Then, "Okay, everybody," as her gaze slid over Lauren. "All participants, please show your tokens now!"

It was late afternoon and they were sitting on the deck taking in the scenery as the ship sailed to its last destination.

"Here?" Lauren shouted, looking at the crowd of passengers who meandered past their table. It looked as though everybody wanted to squeeze in as much sun as possible before leaving the ship.

"Sure, why not?" Madison shrugged. "Nobody's paying us any attention."

Lauren threw up her hands and settled back into the chair. "Don't ask me to count," she huffed and hid behind her magazine.

"You're supposed to," Madison snapped. Lauren glared at her over the top of her magazine. "You did say that you'd be a judge."

"Well, I duly resign," Lauren answered curtly before returning to her reading material.

"Fine. We'll do it without you," Madison said, sticking her tongue out at Lauren. "Who's first? Can't rely on anybody," she mumbled.

Blair grinned, then reached into her purse and pulled out six wrappers. "You're next," she said to Madison.

Madison pulled out ten and the table erupted in laughter. Lauren, unable to squelch her curiosity, laid down her magazine. "I was expecting *a lot* more from you," she said, snickering. They were so consumed in their contest that neither of the ladies noticed the attention they were getting from the nearby passengers.

"Oh, shut up! I thought you weren't interested," Madison said and balled up an empty foil and tossed it at her.

"Ewww!" Lauren screamed, batting it away with her hand. "Keep those things away from me."

"It's not like we *used* the wrappers, silly. There aren't any germies on them." Then, "You're next, girl," Madison said, nodding to LaShawn.

They suddenly got quiet as all eyes turned on LaShawn. Her lips were turned up into a mysterious smile as she reached into her purse, rummaged around for a couple of seconds, and pulled out a handful of wrappers. She unceremoniously dumped them on the table and confidently settled back in her chair.

All it took was a glance to see that she had more than Blair and Madison combined. Madison did the official count, but stopped after twelve. LaShawn was immediately crowned the Slut of the Caribbean.

"When you let loose, you really let loose," Lauren said. Looking at all the empty wrappers made her miss Cleve, but it also made her hot for Darryl.

"I had to make up for lost time," she said, laughing.

"Dang girl, you sure did. When did you find the time to do all that?" Madison asked, pointing to LaShawn's pile. She was a little jealous.

"Where there's two horny people, there's a way." LaShawn laughed again.

"I guess so! How many times a day were you and Terrance hitting it?" Madison asked.

"Obviously more than you and Trey," LaShawn quipped and Madison pulled off one of her sandals and tossed it in her direction.

"Let's get this cleaned up," Blair said. Just as she was about to swipe hers into the garbage, Terrance and Trey sauntered up. The incriminating piles of condom wrappers were still in front of Madison and LaShawn.

"Oh shit!" Lauren muttered under her breath, clamping her hand over her mouth to hide her grin. LaShawn and Madison were paralyzed. They couldn't have moved even if they were ordered to evacuate the ship.

"What's this?" Terrance asked.

LaShawn averted her eyes and muttered, "Nothing." She slouched down in her seat and began wishing with all her might that she was in the middle of a bad nightmare.

Terrance leaned down and hissed in LaShawn's ear, "Are these wrappers from all the condoms we used?" Too embarrassed to say anything, LaShawn could only nod. "Why,

Shawn? Why would you do something like this?" he whispered. LaShawn met his eyes and was struck by the anger that was there. Ashamed, she dropped her head.

"Why are those wrappers here?" Trey demanded. "Madison?" He turned to her and rested his hands on her shoulders, forcing her to look at him.

"We were just having fun," she offered lamely, then defiantly crossed her arms over her chest.

"Just having fun," Trey said to himself. "Oh, I see. I was just a toy to you."

"No, you weren't a toy," Madison said. "But you sure were fun," she joked. But when Trey didn't laugh, she muttered, "Guys do it all the time, I don't know why when women do it they get into trouble."

"I don't see a bunch of 'women' sitting at tables with a pile of condom wrappers in front of them, counting them as though they were prized dicks. I see only three confused children masquerading as women. I'll talk to you later," Trey snapped, then stalked off.

"I'll see you around," Terrance said to LaShawn before he turned around and followed Trey.

"We didn't do anything!" LaShawn yelled to his back. When he didn't turn around, she fell back in her seat.

"Oh shit! We have an audience," Madison announced, suddenly realizing that everybody within hearing distance had their eyes locked on them.

"I told y'all to take it to the cabin. But y'all wouldn't listen to me. Now, where did that get you?" Lauren gloated before snapping open her magazine.

Chapter 53

Rose slid into her seat at the dining room table. "So you finally got tired of playing with the beach toys," she joked to Madison and LaShawn. This was the first time they'd seen her on the ship in more than a week.

"Whatever," Madison grumbled and turned her head to gaze out of the plate glass window to watch the water. She was oblivious to the water's calming effects.

LaShawn gave Rose a slippery smile, then bowed her head and focused on her food. Occasionally her gaze would slip down to her lap . . . to her Bible.

"What's wrong with our little princesses?" Rose asked Blair and Lauren. "They don't seem quite as perky as they were, say, earlier today," she snickered and Madison's and LaShawn's eyes grew as big as their dinner plates.

"What are you talking about?" Madison squeaked.

"Oh, a little contest that has the ship buzzing." She glanced over at LaShawn. "Congratulations!" she sang.

LaShawn's fork clanked to her plate and her face turned

ashen. "Who told you?" she sputtered, embarrassed. This was a hundred times worse than the time she got caught swimming in her underwear. At least then she could blame her behavior on her age. She didn't have an excuse this time.

"You'd be surprised at what I know," she said in a sneaky voice. "First of all, y'all should've done it behind closed doors—"

"I told them to," Lauren added and Madison rolled her eyes. "Well, I did."

"A playette never puts her business out there like that."

"I'm not a 'playette,' " LaShawn protested. "We were only having fun."

"What would you have done, if, heaven forbid," Rose touched her hand to her chest and faked a swoon, "Terrance snatched your underwear and you saw him and his boys counting their stash. How would that have made you feel?"

"We didn't take their underwear," Madison snapped.

"It's the same thing," Rose insisted. "Condom wrappers and underwear, they're all prizes of the booty."

"Nu-uh," Madison said. "It's not the same."

"Well, it kinda is," Blair replied, then sat back in her chair when Madison glowered at her.

"That's bull!" Madison retorted.

"Hush!" Rose said to Madison. "Let's hear Miz Blair's reasoning. Do tell, we're all ears."

Blair flushed brightly at being the center of attention, but she forged on. "Y'all making us sound like the kind of boys my momma warned me about." LaShawn gave her a questioning look and Blair hurried to explain. "The ones who took girls' cherries as though they were at a twenty-four-hour Dairy Queen. See, they did it for the sport of it. They could care less about the girls' feelings."

"That's not me," LaShawn protested. "I care for Terrance. I might even love him," she admitted softly.

"Bravo!" Rose clapped. "What about Miz Thang?" she asked, locking her gaze on Madison.

"I don't know why everybody is picking on me and LaShawn. Blair did it, too," she huffed.

Blair shrugged nonchalantly. "I'll admit it. It was all about the dick with me."

"Oh, no she didn't!" Rose squealed. Lauren, Madison, and LaShawn cracked up.

"It was. I'm not going to lie to y'all. I needed someone to make me feel like a desirable woman again . . . and he did one hell of a job making sure that I felt that way. Madison?"

"It was never about the contest with Trey. Well, at first it was," she admitted. "I was stupid to collect those wrappers. It seemed fun at the time," she admitted. "Okay." She held her arms up as though she was being arrested. "Now the whole thing just seems stupid."

Rose shook her head. "Naw, it wasn't stupid, you ladies came on board with a mission in mind . . . to get dicks. And you got them. So no one can ever say you ladies aren't goal-oriented," she teased. "But realize that all actions have consequences. Sometimes they're good and sometimes they're bad. Either way y'all better be ready to face the repercussions."

"Well said," Lauren chimed in.

"How am I gonna get Terrance back?" LaShawn whined.

"By dropping the games and being honest."

"We *were* honest," Madison said.

"Yeah, but your actions say otherwise. Those men are feeling like they were played like a raggedy deck of cards. Just tell them the truth and pray that they'll believe you," Rose offered.

Chapter 54

"So how long you think they're gonna punish us?" LaShawn asked Madison as she watched the ship's cheesy version of the newlywed game unfold on stage.

LaShawn shifted to a more comfortable position, her legs aching as though she'd done laps around the ocean. Since the incident with Terrance she had been acting worse than an Usher groupie staking out the gym for hours at a time, hoping that Terrance would show up.

"Damned if I know. It can't be long—we only have a couple more days left on the cruise."

"That doesn't mean anything. You know how men are, they can carry a grudge for years."

"I know. Did you see how they totally ignored us in the café? You waved at them like you were flagging down a plane and they ran to the other side of the restaurant. I can't believe they're frat brothers, never mind such close friends," Madison said.

"I still can't believe they ignored us like that," LaShawn said.

Madison rolled her eyes. "They both can jump in the ocean for all I care."

LaShawn turned to her friend. "You care. You love you some Trey," she teased.

"Do not!"

"Yeah, you do!"

"Men are like milk to you, after a couple dates they go sour. Then they're history. So Trey must be doing something right for you to keep him around."

"It must be the salt water," Madison joked.

"Yeah, that and the fact that neither one of you can run anywhere. Your butt is forced to work things out."

"Whatever," Madison said, then focused her attention on the activities on stage.

They watched the show a couple of minutes, chuckling at all the right spots. Then LaShawn said, "You didn't answer my question. How long do you think they're gonna make us sweat?"

Madison lifted her shoulders and let them casually drop. "Maybe they're not coming back."

"The hell they're not. I'll go Jennifer Holiday on his butt. I'll tell him I'm not going nowhere."

"Look at you . . . Miss Feisty," Madison said with admiration. The LaShawn she knew a month ago wouldn't be talking like this.

A distraction a couple rows ahead caught LaShawn's eyes. A wave of grumbles reached her as people unstuck themselves from their seat to let a group of four in, two men and two women. Something about the way the men walked made her heart skip a beat. Leaning forward she squinted, then nudged Madison in the ribs. "Isn't that Terrance and Trey?" she asked, stunned. She wanted to cry. "They're seeing other people already?"

Madison leaned forward in her seat. "Yep, that's them," she confirmed calmly. But if LaShawn had looked down, she would've seen Madison wringing her hands like a white-collar embezzler with the auditors hot on his tail.

"Let's go talk to them." LaShawn shot up in her seat and was turning to leave when Madison pulled her by the arm.

"I don't want no shit," she hissed in her ear. But her eyes lied; they were sparkling with excitement.

"Oh, there will be shit," LaShawn promised. Her eyes narrowed dangerously.

A smile crept across Madison's face. "I'm loving the new LaShawn. This is your show . . . you're the star and I'm just a peon. Let's go get 'em."

LaShawn and Madison converged on the group. Terrance feigned a yawn, then wrapped his arm around his date's shoulders. Trey shot Madison a defiant look before mirroring Terrance's movement. But their dates exchanged nervous glances.

LaShawn gritted her teeth, then bent down in front of Terrance. "So did you enjoy last night?" she asked in a sultry voice. Terrance's eyes widened with confusion and Madison saw Trey's lip twitch with amusement.

Just then Terrance's date jumped out of her seat, her whole body trembling. "Who the hell are you?" she yelled.

LaShawn's eyes slowly roved over the lady, taking in her clownish makeup and her three-month-old weave, noting that she looked like a watered-down version of Beyoncé. "I'm his girlfriend. Do you have a problem with that?" she asked casually.

"Damn! Shawn is going Jerry Springer on the chick," Madison said and chuckled.

"His girlfriend!" she shrieked.

"Yes, his girlfriend," LaShawn confirmed as she looked in Terrance's eyes, daring him to dispute it. He didn't. Nor did he budge when LaShawn grabbed his hand and gently kissed his palm. While looking in his eyes, she wet her finger and drew a heart in the middle of his hand. She closed it and placed it on Terrance's chest, then hopped up. She turned to Madison. "Do you have something to say to Trey? Otherwise we're gone."

"Um, er, I guess," Madison stuttered, her bravado gone. Trey watched her discomfort with amusement. Something told her that kissing his hand wouldn't work. She looked him squarely in the eyes and said, "Somebody once told me that any sin of man can be forgiven."

Madison's face fell as Trey shook his head and focused on the show.

LaShawn said, "We're out!" She sauntered out with Madison close on her heel, and the earth-shattering shouts of Terrance's friend ringing in her ears.

Chapter 55

Blair and Lauren casually strolled down the sidewalk, their hips synchronized in an unconscious dance that drew stares from men and women, broken only when one of them stopped to stroke or inspect whatever trinket caught their attention on the Nassau streets.

Right on Blair's and Lauren's heel were LaShawn and Madison, who were snapping back and forth at each other like two underfed piranhas. They were blaming each other for the breakup of their shipboard romances. Their behavior drew more than one sharp reprimand from Lauren before they all stopped in front of a booth selling sewn-together gauze masquerading as twenty-dollar T-shirts.

Neither of the women was aware of the set of eyes that followed their progress through the city. If they had, they would've made a beeline to the nearest police precinct.

Two women sat behind the T-shirt booth, one looked like Father Time's wife and the other looked like her twin. Their artificial smiles pushed their cheekbones high up on their faces, squeezing their eyes into little slits that made it hard for customers to tell whether they were looking at them. The overpriced T-shirts looked perfect to Blair, who hadn't gotten her kids any souvenirs yet. She picked up a bright red T-shirt and studied it.

"I miss my family," she said quietly as she held the T-shirt against her chest and ran her hand down the front, smoothing out the wrinkles. Then she held it out in front of her, twisting and turning it back and forth while she tried to imagine the blood red T-shirt schmoozing its way into Caitlyn's wardrobe. She picked through the piles for two more, then handed one of the ladies a hundred-dollar bill before she changed her mind.

"Girl, why don't you call your children? They'd be glad to hear from Mommy," Lauren assured her. "There's a Subway right over there. I bet they have a pay phone." Lauren pointed across the street to the famous sandwich chain.

"I can't," Blair groaned as she slid between two men and sidled up to Lauren. "Not right now. I feel so guilty. I think that if I hear Rich's voice I'll confess to everything and I don't—I *can't*," she corrected herself, "do that."

Lauren thought of her and Darryl's kiss and immediately pushed it out of her mind. Suddenly, her stomach grumbled and she stopped walking and jutted her chin toward a popular fast-food restaurant. "Come on, y'all, there's the golden arches." The crowd had thinned a little and Madison and LaShawn were back to squabbling like two five-year-olds. "I'm hungry, and if I don't eat I'm going to get real bitchy," she teased.

Madison saw their destination and immediately began whining. "I don't want to eat there. We can eat burgers and fries anytime, let's get some authentic Caribbean food."

"You know, Madison," Lauren began as she and the group made a U-turn to a restaurant that advertised genuine Caribbean food. "It's not very attractive the way you pout every time you want something. You're an adult, so you should act like one," she said softly, but in a serious enough tone to let Madison know that she had better heed her words.

LaShawn poked Madison in her side, and said, "Yeah, that's right, act like one." LaShawn giggled and stuck her tongue out.

Madison's eyes grew as round as beef patties, then they narrowed to snap pea size. "Lauren! Did you see that? LaShawn stuck her nasty tongue out at me! Who's the child now?" she whined.

Blair nudged her shoulder against Lauren's and whispered in her ear, "Don't you feel like we have the kids with us?" Lauren nodded in agreement.

"I like him," Madison said out of the blue. They had just finished their dinner and were on their way back to the ship. Nobody had to ask who she was talking about, they all knew. "I'm just so mad that he had to see the condom thing."

"Yeah, we shouldn't've done it," LaShawn agreed.

"Yeah, we should've," Madison argued. "And I'm kinda glad we did. I mean, everything didn't go the way we wanted, some shit went down that we weren't expecting, but I met an awesome guy, Blair got her world rocked, and Shawn finally got some."

"What happens if Terrance and I don't . . . you know . . ." LaShawn asked.

"Make love until you can't walk?" Madison offered.

"No," LaShawn answered, vigorously shaking her head, then, "Yeah, that too," she admitted. "But what I was gonna say was 'end up together.' He doesn't know how much I really like him."

"Well, you gotta tell him," Lauren chimed in. "It's not that hard, you can do it."

The night sky was so clear that it looked as if someone had taken a napkin and swiped away all the clouds and pollution, leaving behind a twinkling wonderland. By now storeowners had brought out boom boxes and reggae and hip-hop music spewed at them from every direction. Every few steps flyers advertising the local clubs were stuffed into their hands by industrious promoters. They wanted the pretty American ladies, who were sure to draw the men, to visit their clubs.

Lauren turned to Madison. "Trey seems nice," she said carefully, digging into her bag of words for something that wouldn't offend her friend. "How do you *really* feel about him?"

Madison flushed and she knew that the heat wasn't caused by the warm temperature. "He's one awesome, phenomenal brother!"

"Wow! This sounds promising."

Madison giggled, a sound that made them all stop dead in their tracks and stare at her.

"Are you okay?" LaShawn asked. "Maybe you drank too much at dinner." LaShawn studied her friend's eyes for signs of inebriation, but they were startlingly clear.

Lauren laughed at LaShawn's reaction. "Madison is fine, she didn't drink too much. Our baby is in love." Lauren smiled, happy that Madison wasn't sucked into the deep abyss of hate for black men that so many of her sisters had fallen into. "He'll get over the condom thingie," Lauren said confidently.

"How do you know?" Blair asked. "Did you develop some type of superpowers that you didn't tell us about?" she teased.

"I *am* Superwoman," Lauren joked. "But seriously, he likes her, a lot; I see the way he looks at her."

"You can always call him," Blair offered.

Madison snorted. "Madison DuPree *never* calls a man to apologize, they always call her." Just then Madison spied a small candy stand. "Hey, hold up, I want to get some fudge for my Aunt Pearl," she said.

"I'll walk with you," LaShawn offered, but Madison waved her off.

"Stay here. I'll be back in two minutes," she quickly reassured them before trotting off.

"Hurry up!" Lauren called to her. "We need to be on the ship soon. I promised Rose a game of bid whist."

Madison entered the tiny candy store and smiled at the man behind the counter. Taking in the lush smell of chocolate, she perused the dozen different types of flavored fudge.

"I think Aunt Pearl would love this," she said, as she exited the store. "If not she can always give it—" She bounced forward and stumbled. Madison glanced over her shoulder.

The man who bumped into her was a little over five eight, as thin as a palm tree, and the color of one. He eyed her dispassionately as one would a broken zipper, and the sounds of the Bahamas fell away. It was just her and the man, locked in time. Everything moved at the speed of molasses.

Madison watched helplessly as the man reached out and grabbed her purse; Madison clamped it to her chest. He grinned as though he welcomed the challenge. You're not getting my purse, Madison's eyes screamed. Everything was in it, her passport, her identification card to get on the ship, and most importantly her money, almost a thousand dollars.

Oh, yes I am, his eyes yelled in response. Bringing his arm up, he used his elbow as a weapon to jab her sharply in her ribs.

"Ow!" Madison wailed. Her purse and candy dropped from her hands as she bent over and clutched her side. She could only watch as he leaned down to scoop up both items.

The whole thing took less than a minute, but to Madison, it felt like ten times as long. He pushed through the crowd with her purse tucked in the crook of his elbow as though it was a football. "Catch him!" Madison frantically yelled. "He has my purse! Somebody, please catch him!"

Chapter 56

Lauren wrapped her arms around Madison's shoulders, which were shaking from shock. "It'll be okay," she gently soothed. Everyone was crowded in Blair's and Madison's stateroom. "They'll find your purse," she murmured, even though she didn't believe it.

"No they won't," Madison answered. As far as she was concerned, her purse was long gone. "I can't believe it happened right in front of everybody. Has the world gotten so bad that a man has to steal an innocent woman's purse? I'm so mad. I wanna kick that man's ass. How dare he take my purse! Then he had the audacity to take my fudge. Did y'all see him? He bent down and picked up *my* fudge."

"I wish I would've gone in with you," LaShawn said.

"I don't think that would've mattered. He would've done it anyway. Oh crap, now I have to order a new passport, get a new Georgia license, cancel credit cards—"

"Hush!" Lauren advised, "Don't think about it. I'll help you get the new documents as soon as we get home. Let's go up to the deck and relax," she said, standing up and lifting her arms for a full-body stretch.

"That sounds terrific," LaShawn concurred. "Let me just—"

There was a loud rapping at the door. "I'll get it," Lauren offered. She strolled over to the door and peeked through the peephole. On the threshold was a man in a freshly starched uniform, holding a rectangular object in his hand. "It's security," she announced. "And it looks like he might have Madison's purse."

"Oh God, I hope so!" Madison squealed.

Lauren pulled the door open and found that there wasn't much difference between the speck of a man she saw through the peephole and the one who stood in front of her. He barely came up to her chest. Lauren smothered a laugh, then moved aside, allowing him to enter the cabin. The chatter halted to a stop as soon as three other pairs of eyes fell on the half-pint security guard. He looked like a miniaturized Ricardo Montalban.

"Hi. I'm Javier, ship security," he announced in short clipped tones, oblivious to their looks of amusement. A little taller than Lauren's son C.J., he had to tilt his head back to look them each in their eyes. "I'm looking for Ms. Madison DuPree," he said.

"That's me!" Madison announced, eyeing her purse in his hands. It looked a little dusty, but otherwise it was fine. So intent on her newly found purse, Madison didn't notice the way Javier's gaze slithered over her body.

"I have your purse," he stated flatly.

"I know! I never thought that I'd see it again." Madison stuck her hand out for her purse, but Javier tucked it under his arm, out of her reach. Madison's brow furrowed with confusion.

"So how did you end up with it?" LaShawn asked Javier.

"One of the passengers found it on the ground. He recognized the ship's access card and he turned the purse in as soon as he returned to the ship."

"May I have my purse?"

Javier shook his head. "Not just yet. I need to do a positive identification."

"What!" Madison nearly shouted. Her eyes closed to paper-thin slits, then she put her hands on her hips. "It's me. I'm the one who reported the missing purse to security. I'm the one who gave you the description of the purse. I'm the one—"

"Okay, calm down. We can get this worked out," Lauren said before turning to Javier. "Open up the purse. Hopefully her license is still there."

Javier backed toward the door. "Follow me," he said to Madison.

"I'm not going anywhere with you until you give me my fucking purse!"

"We're only going outside into the corridor."

"What the . . . ?" Madison mumbled.

"Just go," Blair said. "We're right here, baby."

Madison angrily shook her head and followed Javier out into the hall, where he handed her her purse.

"Look through it to make sure everything's there."

Madison glared at him. "Why couldn't you just . . . ? Oh, forget it." She opened her purse and the first thing she saw was her license. "Thank goodness," she exclaimed. But her relief was short-lived. "All my money, credit, and debit cards are gone," she wailed as she slid down the wall and onto the carpeted floor.

Javier glanced down at her and said, "I heard about the contest. What do you say, could I become a contestant?"

Chapter 57

Whop! Whop! Whop! LaShawn took a deep breath, then drew her arm back and walloped the punching bag so hard that her teeth shook. She stopped every so often to swipe at the rivulets of sweat running down her face, then began bouncing around the leather dummy as though it was her dance partner. Every time the image of Terrance's face popped up, she jabbed the bag with a left-right combo that left her shoulders tingling.

"I'm so stupid! Stupid! Stupid!" she chanted under her breath as she pounded the punching bag. "This is all Madison's fault. I should not have let her talk me into playing her stupid game."

Two guys were strolling by, then slowed to a crawl when they passed her. "I can give you a better way to work out your frustrations," one quipped as his friend stood on the side laughing.

"Screw you!" LaShawn quipped, then smacked the punching bag.

"I'd rather *do* you," the man threw over his shoulder as he and his friend sauntered out of the gym.

"In your freaking dreams," she muttered, then gave the punching bag one last blow before staggering to a mat, flopping down, and dropping her head in her hands. She and Terrance hadn't seen each other since she'd called herself his girlfriend. The ship was a minicity on water, but it wasn't so big that their paths wouldn't cross. Something told her that he was purposely ignoring her. She moaned and rubbed her temples; her head was killing her and her arms and hands were beginning to feel like they'd gone through the wringer.

"Come on now, it can't be that bad."

LaShawn whipped her head up so fast that it made her dizzy and a brown ball spun before her eyes. Groaning, she clamped her eyes shut until the world stopped spinning, then she cautiously opened one eye, then the other. Staring at her with the kindest eyes she'd ever seen was a man who was giving her an equally kind smile.

"It's not life threatening, if that's what you mean," LaShawn snapped and he stepped back as though she had slapped him. She immediately regretted her behavior. "I'm sorry. I didn't mean to be rude," she apologized. What's wrong with me? When he didn't say anything she rolled her eyes, then dropped her head, signaling him to leave. But when she opened her eyes she saw the tops of his sneakers. Lifting her head, she glared at him.

"We can talk about it if you want," he offered.

"How come you're not at the club?" she grumbled.

"Why aren't you?" he tossed back and LaShawn shrugged. "You mind if I sit down?" LaShawn shook her head no and he plopped down next to her. He had to be close to seven feet tall, because even sitting down she had to look up to him.

"I'm Walter."

Her mind went into overdrive. Give him a fake name. "Madi—I mean, LaShawn," she said, smiling sheepishly. "Madi is my middle name."

"Okay, LaShawn Madi, what's up? Why is a pretty lady sitting in the middle of the gym in the middle of the night by herself?"

"Kicking ass!" she replied emotionlessly.

"Are you winning?" Walter joked. "It has to be a man," he concluded.

LaShawn's lips twitched with amusement. "Why would you say that?" she asked, neither confirming nor denying his assessment.

"Why else would a beautiful lady be beating on a helpless piece of leather at one in the morning?"

The twitch blossomed into a full-fledged smile. "It's not helpless. That's the price it pays for wanting to see the world," she joked about the punching bag. "He has the best seat on the ship." LaShawn motioned toward the huge window. They laughed until Walter pulled her back to his question.

"What's his name?"

"Why do you care?" LaShawn asked, dodging the question faster than a weave-wearing woman dodges raindrops.

"I hate to see a pretty lady sad."

This was the third time he'd complimented her looks. She didn't comment; instead she simply said, "Terrance."

"So what did he do?"

"What makes you think it was him?"

"It wasn't?" he asked, perplexed.

LaShawn shook her head, then decided to fill him in on all the gory details, hoping to get a male's perspective.

"So he caught you with the booty? No pun intended." Walter chuckled and LaShawn echoed him.

"I was seriously busted. I waited five years," LaShawn offered, as an afterthought.

"For what? . . . oh!" Walter said, understanding.

"He thinks I'm playing games."

"Are you?" he asked, the question so simple that it was difficult.

"On one level—"

"Were you playing a game?"

"It didn't—"

"Yes or no," Walter asked firmly.

LaShawn glared at him before answering. "Yes! But it didn't start off like that," she insisted.

"He doesn't know that. All the brother knows is that you were collecting little souvenirs from your time together. And all he was doing was catching feelings for you."

"You think he likes me?" LaShawn asked and allowed herself a giggle.

"I think he's into you. He wouldn't be acting like this if he wasn't. So what's the next step for you two?"

LaShawn shrugged and looked outside. It was too dark to see the water and the ship was too far away to see any lights from the islands; it looked like she was looking into a big pit, which matched her mood. "He doesn't want to talk to me."

"Make him. Here's what you should do." Walter winked,

then began speaking in a low voice. "Lasso that man. The next time you see him, wrap a piece of rope around him and pull him in."

"Just rope him in. Call me cowgirl LaShawn." She laughed, then began twirling an imaginary rope.

"I was speaking figuratively." Walter laughed. "But I know a lot of men who wouldn't have a problem with getting tied up," Walter roared and had LaShawn laughing so hard that she began crying. "But that's another tip."

"Is he another contestant?" A familiar voice asked snidely. LaShawn jumped; she hadn't seen Terrance come in. Walter gave her a look that asked, is that him? LaShawn nodded miserably. Terrance sneered down at her before he turned on his heel and stalked over to the weight equipment.

"He got it bad!" Walter remarked. They were both watching Terrance as he loaded the weight bench, settled himself down, and lifted the barbells over his head. LaShawn was no expert, but she knew enough about weights to guess that he had to have been pumping over two hundred pounds.

"Why do you say that?" LaShawn asked, keeping her eyes on Terrance. Every time he lifted the weights, the muscles in his arm rippled with the effort.

"What else would run a brother to the gym? He's working off some frustration. Just like you were," Walter said. "Go get your man."

"I can't," LaShawn said, shaking her head. "I tried talking to him before and he wasn't hearing it," she said. LaShawn looked fearfully at Terrance. He had moved to the bar and was doing chin-ups and she could see every one of the muscles in his back. "What happens if he tells me to jump off the ship?"

"He won't," Walter assured her. "Just go." He stood up, then reached down for LaShawn's hand, tugging her up. "Go!" he insisted, then gently nudged her toward Terrance.

LaShawn turned around and looked at her new friend. "Thanks, Walter. I won't forget you." She took a step toward him and pulled him into a hug; neither one of them saw the glare that Terrance shot them.

"Go on!" Walter said and pushed LaShawn toward Terrance. LaShawn inched her way over to Terrance. She looked over to Walter for encouragement, but he was gone. LaShawn stood over Terrance as he lifted the heavy weights. Neither said anything, but she knew that Terrance was aware of her standing over him.

"Who was your friend?" Terrance grunted through his bicep curls. LaShawn had to suppress a smile; he *was* jealous.

"That's Walter. And he *wasn't* a contestant," she quickly reassured him. "I just met him tonight. He's really nice." She knew she was babbling, but she couldn't stop. All Terrance did was make a sound, then he strolled over to the mats and began stretching. LaShawn was close on his heels.

"I'm so sorry," LaShawn said for the millionth time. Terrance was silent as he touched his toes. "I care for you so much. It wasn't a game to me. I haven't been this crazy about anybody in a long time, not even Calvin," she admitted softly. "Call me someone who's sometimes easily swayed by her friends, but don't ever call me fake. Because I was one hundred percent real with you." Terrance stood up and did side stretches. LaShawn wanted to touch him; instead she balled her hands into fists and kept them closely at her sides. He finished his stretching and towel-dried himself before he finally looked at her.

"I'm past your little game," he started. "But what gets me, and you've already said it, is how easily swayed you are. You knew what you were doing was wrong, but you didn't stop."

"It was harmless fun," LaShawn said, defending herself. "We—I never expected you to see anything."

"I know, you thought you could get away with it. Besides, I need a lady . . . no, I *want* a lady who can think for herself. There's going to be times when we're having problems. I want you to come to me first, not your girls. I want us to work this out between us. The lady in my arms can't be easily sucked into other people's worlds. I need for her to stay in ours."

LaShawn's eyes welled up and turned glassy and Terrance wrapped his arms around her and led her back to the bench. He left her there while he went over and grabbed some industrial-strength paper towels.

"Does this mean you forgive me?" LaShawn asked as she dabbed at her face. Terrance nodded yes and her tears turned to tears of joy. "And does it mean I'm your lady?" she asked, giving him a soggy grin.

In response Terrance brushed his lips against her salt-tinged ones. "You're my lady," Terrance said. "What happened was like a flashback."

"Somebody did this to you before?" LaShawn asked bewildered.

"No. Not exactly," he answered, shaking his head. "It reminded me of my ex-wife, who was manipulative as hell. When I first met her, she was the sweetest person, or so I thought, but it was all an act. As soon as I said 'I do' she changed. She brought all her girlfriends into our marriage, every time we had a little disagreement—it was always, 'Kara says I should do this, Sheryl says I should do that.'" And if that wasn't bad enough, everything she did was calculated, even when she got pregnant with Terry."

"Oh no!" LaShawn gripped his hand.

"Yeah. As soon as her true self started showing I was ready to go, and she knew that I wanted out. So she did the only thing she knew that would make me stay. She got pregnant."

"Well, she didn't do it on her own," LaShawn admonished.

"She told me she was taking the pill," Terrance said between clenched teeth. "We stayed together for about two years after Terry was born, but finally I couldn't take it anymore, I had to go. So when I saw the condom wrappers, I saw another lady with a hidden agenda and someone who couldn't think for herself."

"I can see how you thought what you did," LaShawn offered. "But can't you see that it was all a game? I won't ever do anything to intentionally hurt you. It was just a silly game," she repeated and the tears started again.

"You leak more than a toddler's diaper," Terrance joked, but he believed her. "You ladies need to find something better to do."

"It's been an emotional day. Earlier today Maddy was mugged and now this."

Terrance's eyes widened with surprise. "Madison mugged? What happened?"

LaShawn filled him in on Madison's ordeal.

"I'm glad she was able to get her stuff back," Terrance murmured.

"She is, too," LaShawn answered, feeling better, so much so that she had to ask him something that had been bothering her. "What was up with that chick you were hanging out with?"

"Were you jealous?" Terrance chuckled.

"Yeah, I was," LaShawn admitted. "If I couldn't have you, I didn't want anybody else to. Besides, I missed you."

"You did?" Terrance asked as his hand snaked underneath her T-shirt and cupped one of her breasts. LaShawn leaned into his embrace.

"Let's go back to your room," LaShawn whispered. Terrance nodded, then pulled her up and they practically ran back to his cabin.

Chapter 58

Lauren's mouth was drawn tightly and her brow was furrowed as she slowly sketched a picture of the ocean. Thoughts were running through her mind at lightning speed and occasionally some would randomly pop out.

"Attraction is a very human emotion," she muttered as the pencil moved skillfully over the paper. "Just because I kissed him doesn't mean that I love Cleve any less. And just because I was attracted to him doesn't mean that I'm not attracted to Cleve. And just because I want to ride his body like a surfboard doesn't mean that I'm not attracted to Cleve," she decided. Lauren was still having her one-sided conversation when Darryl walked up.

He stood watching her, undecided whether to say anything to her. He hadn't seen her since the kiss. "So do all artistic people talk to themselves?"

Lauren stiffened at the sound of Darryl's voice. "Only the crazy ones," she said, then smiled warily at him. She motioned for him to sit down. "I'm sorry about everything," she said.

"You mean you weren't part of the contest?" he asked and Lauren opened her mouth to protest, but then she saw Darryl's lips twitching with amusement. He shrugged. "Things like this happen all the time on cruises. I believe they call them shipboard romances."

Lauren vigorously shook her head. "You don't understand. Things like this *never* happen to me. I never *let* them happen," she said forcibly.

"I hate to throw around clichés," Darryl started, "but don't be so hard on yourself. You're only human."

"Yeah, a human who nearly put her marriage in jeopardy," Lauren said glumly. She slumped back in her chaise and her eyes became glassy with unshed tears. "And the sad thing is that I can't even blame it on alcohol. I wasn't even drunk."

"Your marriage is intact," Darryl calmly reassured her. "And hopefully when you get back it'll be stronger than ever."

"You know what really scared me?" Lauren asked. She looked Darryl right in the eye. He shook his head no. "My attraction for you consumed me. All I could think of was making love; hell, not even making love, but screwing you until neither one of us could walk," Lauren admitted.

Darryl blinked his eyes in surprise and he got as hard as an iron pole. He didn't realize that Lauren's feelings for him went that deep. From the time he had seen her on the beach he knew that he wanted her in his bed with her ass up in the air. "But nothing happened," Darryl insisted. "A kiss isn't considered cheating."

"Oh, isn't it?" Lauren asked while arching an eyebrow. "Cheating is like lying, it's not measurable. They are both things that are either black or white. There are no shaded areas."

Darryl settled back in his chair and silently regarded her, then he said, "Well, given that reasoning, your kiss means that you've cheated. So why don't you go all the way? Come back to my cabin. Make love with me, Lauren."

Chapter 59

"Thanks for seeing me," Madison said stiffly. "I don't usually do this . . . call men to meet with me. Usually it's the other way around," Madison added arrogantly.

"Well, I just feel so special," Trey said sarcastically, then took a sip of his rum.

"Yeah, whatever. This is our last day on the ship and I didn't want to leave without telling you that I'm sorry."

Trey looked at her blankly before taking another sip of his drink. They were in the ship's library, neither one of them interested in the popular fiction that lined the shelves. But they needed a quiet spot to talk.

"Didn't you hear me?" Madison screeched. "I just apologized. Isn't that what you wanted?"

"I want a *sincere* apology, not something that sounds like you were apologizing for giving me the wrong color socks."

"That was sincere. Besides, what happened to 'any sin can be forgiven'?" Madison asked.

"Nothing. But Jesus didn't have his condom wrappers all out for everybody to see," Trey retorted.

"That's a messed-up comparison. People make mistakes. Why are you acting like this?" Madison demanded.

"Because *you're* acting like a child, so I'm going to treat you like one."

"It was a silly game. Why don't you believe me?"

"Oh, I believe you, that's the sad part. What I can't believe is how childish you are."

"Am not!" Madison pouted, then crossed her arms over her chest. Trey held back a smile.

"Look at you. I wish I had my camera, so we can freeze this moment in time. Highlight at eleven o'clock news: Thirty-year-old lady turns back the hands of time, turns three."

"I'm very, very sorry," Madison pushed out between her clenched teeth.

"Put more heart into it."

"Trey! I'm trying."

"No, you're not. Speak from your heart. I know you can do it," he said as he looked in her eyes.

Madison took a deep breath, then said, "I'm sorry that you felt like I played you like a Game Boy. I'm sorry that all my girls saw that I had *medium*-size condoms. I'm sorry that—"

"Madison!" Trey warned and she burst out laughing.

She walked around the table and settled down on his lap. She wrapped her arms around his neck, then brought her mouth to his ear. "And I'm very, very sorry if I did anything to offend you. That wasn't my intent."

"Hmmm, I'm loving the sound of this. What *was* your intent?" Trey moaned as Madison gently blew in his ear, then took his earlobe in her mouth.

She breathed into his ear and said, "To love every inch of your body."

"Show me your intentions, not tell me," Trey said, feeling himself harden.

"Okay." Madison slipped off his lap and reached for his hand, but was promptly pulled back. Her eyes widened with understanding. "Here?" she asked and Trey nodded. "Somebody might come in," she said nervously, but was excited at the same time.

"And?"

"They'll catch us."

"We'll just have to be fast about it."

"Nu-uh. I'm not doing anything," Madison protested as she tried to pull herself off Trey's lap.

"We'll do it fast," Trey promised, then grabbed her hand and placed it on his crotch. It was hard as steel. "See, feel me. I'm halfway done."

Madison grinned as she lightly stroked his bulge. "Yes, you are."

"So you know it's not going to take me that long. Now all you have to do is lift up that dress of yours and jump up on my lap."

"Just jump up on you, huh? I think I can do that," Madison smiled at the thought of what was waiting for her. She sashayed over to a corner and pulled off her panties and toed them against the wall. She strutted back to a waiting Trey. He grinned as he watched her progress across the room; she was better than a stripper. He never took his eyes off her as she inched up her dress and settled on his lap.

"Are you all wrapped up?" she asked, reaching behind her to check. She felt the latex. "Ready, set, go!" she joked.

Trey grabbed her by the waist and gently picked her up, holding her over his penis. "You ready?" he asked. As soon as Madison nodded he slowly lowered her down onto his hard rod. Trey clenched his lips as he slowly pushed his way into Madison. It took all his willpower not to plunge himself into her. Every couple of seconds Madison moaned softly. Once he was fully in, Madison leaned her back against his chest and wiggled her behind against his lap. "Keep doing that and I'm gonna be done faster than we both want."

"You wouldn't dare."

Madison let out a sigh as Trey lifted her braids and gently nibbled her neck and covered her shoulders with butterfly kisses. He grabbed her grapefruit-size breasts and softly caressed them before he thumbed her nipples. Madison sucked in a stream of air as she and Trey gently rocked together.

"I wish you'd turn around so that I can put one of these in my mouth," Trey said and Madison shuddered with desire at the thought of his luscious lips on her hard peaks.

"I can if you want me to," Madison panted. "I'll do whatever you want."

"Right now I just want you to keep doing what you're doing. But I'll remember you said that. It might come in handy." Trey chuckled.

"I know what I can do that you like a lot," Madison teased, then she reached down and cupped his sack, causing Trey to whimper. Madison rested the back of her head on his shoulder.

"Oh, you'd better stop, otherwise I'm going to blow you right into the ceiling." Trey moaned as his thrusts became faster and deeper.

Suddenly Madison stiffened. "I heard something," she hissed. "Stop!" she punched his thigh.

"I can't." Trey moaned. His hips had taken on a life of their own, they couldn't stay still.

"Please stop." Madison threw her head back and groaned. "They might throw us in the Atlantic Ocean."

Trey finally heard what Madison was hearing, the voices sounded like they were getting closer. "I hear them," Trey whispered. "I hear them."

Chapter 60

"You just don't want to deal with Rose," Madison taunted. "That's why you want to have dinner here."

"Stop trippin', it's not like that," LaShawn called over her shoulder. "I don't have anything against her, other than the fact that she talks too much. Besides, this was Blair's idea, and she's the one who wanted dinner in her stateroom," LaShawn said, smiling. She tipped the steward, then wheeled in the cart holding their dinners, drinks, and desserts.

Blair leaned against the cart and looked around her cabin at her friends, who were sprawled around the room, and sighed happily. She'd coordinated this, their last get-together before the ship docked tomorrow morning.

The last thirteen days had been the most introspective days of her life. She lifted the steel-dome tops and passed the food out. Since it was their last night everybody decided to splurge and tonight "diet" was a four-letter word.

She and Madison ordered filet mignon, Lauren got

shrimp scampi, and LaShawn had grilled salmon with asparagus. The desserts lay untouched, but not forgotten, on the cart.

Lauren studied the stateroom for the tenth time. "Hey, you guys have a freakin' palace here, whassup with that? Compared to you two, me and LaShawn are living in the projects."

"We got the hookup!" Blair responded, as she settled on the floor. Madison, Lauren, and LaShawn looked at one another and laughed.

"You've been around us *way* too long," Madison teased.

"I know, but God, I've had so much friggin' fun!" Blair enthused and threw her hands up in the air and everybody nodded their agreement.

Lauren spied a bottle of Cristal sitting on top of a fully stocked wet bar. "You guys got a bar. All Shawn and I got is an ice bucket and two bottles of Coke."

"I think it's time for a toast," Madison announced as she grabbed the champagne and four glasses. It took less than two minutes for her to have them filled and passed out. "To friendships, to sanity, to fine-ass men . . . and to my girls," she finished.

"To my girls" was echoed throughout the room as they clinked glasses. They were quiet as they enjoyed the champagne.

"Do any of y'all believe in soul mates?" Madison asked softly, breaking the silence.

"You mean someone who turns you into a puddle of nerves? Or someone who has such a connection to you that there are times when words aren't needed?" Lauren asked, and thought of Cleve. Even though he wasn't either of those things, he was, by default, her soul mate. Why else would she put up with him all these years?

"Yeah," LaShawn whispered, thinking of Terrance. Her soul laughed whenever they were together. "I do. Terrance is my reflection. When I look at him, I see me. He and Calvin are so different. I can't believe you guys were going to let me marry him."

"I was going to tell you, girl . . . but they told me not to," Madison admitted while jutting her chin toward Lauren and Blair. "They said that you'd end up hating me for telling you. But I say, 'Don't hate the messenger, hate the message.'"

Lauren shook her head and turned to LaShawn. "I wanted to tell you—I mean, we all wanted to tell you, but we all know that you're a smart lady and you were going to find out on your own . . . and you did. But if you didn't . . . we were gonna kidnap you on your wedding day and take you far, far away."

Blair turned to Madison. "What about you? Do you believe in soul mates?"

"Yep!" Madison answered, and a collective gasp went up.

"Oh my God! Madison has slowed down long enough to be caught. Wow!" Blair sounded amazed, but Lauren smiled secretly to herself; she knew the day would come for her friend. "So Trey's the one?"

"Yeah," Madison answered in a dreamy voice.

"Why Trey?" Blair asked.

"Because he's the only man brave enough to cover her mouth with duct tape as soon as she starts whining," LaShawn joked and everybody laughed.

Madison stuck her tongue out at her friend. "It feels

right. When I'm talking to him, it's like I'm talking to my other half. The best thing is that I can be vulnerable with him. I know that if I fall, he'll be there to pick me up."

"Look out, world, Maddy's in love," Blair declared.

"I'm *not* in love!" Madison protested. "Well, maybe a little . . . no, I mean kinda, sorta . . . hell, I got it bad!" she admitted, then sheepishly hung her head.

"There's nothing to be ashamed about," Lauren said as she slid down next to her friend and Madison rested her head on her shoulder. "So you're gonna give him a chance?" Madison nodded. "You're not going to push him away?" Madison shook her head.

"I'm ready for love," she answered softly. "And I think Trey is ready, too. I think that he'll stick around."

"I'm proud of you, girl," Lauren said, knowing the length and difficulty of Madison's journey to knowing herself.

"What are you gonna do about Rich?" Lauren asked Blair.

"Counseling. I want us to go to counseling," Blair answered firmly.

"So you're not going to leave the bastard?" Madison asked. If it was her, the man would be living in the nearest motel.

Blair shook her head. "I still love him, I don't know why, but I do, and I want to make this marriage work. Just because something's broken doesn't mean that it can't be fixed."

"Ain't that the truth! But you know, trusting him is going to be a bitch!" Lauren added. "And you guys have been together *forever*. I tell you what, though, I bet he's scared shitless, not knowing what you're going to do."

"I'd leave his ass," Madison huffed.

"Oh, hush!" Lauren admonished. "No, you wouldn't. This is coming from someone whose relationships never lasted longer than a box of chocolate-chip cookies at a Weight Watchers meeting. Come talk to me after you've cleaned up your man's vomit. Or after you've seen him cry like a baby. Or after you've seen him rock your sick child to sleep. Come talk to me then," she finished and shared a knowing glance with Blair. "Besides, what happened to the softer side of Madison?"

Lauren settled back on the bed. She felt wonderful. In the past week her hives had cleared up, she slept more soundly and deeply than she could ever remember, and her libido had kicked up three notches.

"She's here," Madison answered, still doubtful. "But he hurt her and I hate to see my girl hurting."

"Thanks, Maddy," Blair said.

"Anyway, Blair, you have those kids to think about. They'd be really messed up without their daddy. I don't know what my childhood would've been like if my daddy wasn't in it," Lauren mused.

"I know," Blair said.

Madison cleared her throat, then turned to Blair. "Hey, how was your good-bye to Antonio? Good-bye sex is the best, huh?"

"It was groovy," Blair said, and Madison resisted the urge to roll her eyes. "I mean, he was so cool about it. We went back to his cabin and had some really hot sex. Man, he really knows how to work his thing, he put it—"

"Hey! Slow it down, Blair," Lauren urged. "I really don't want to hear all the details. You two went back to his cabin, had sex, and said good-bye. That's all I need to know."

"My bad," Blair said, then poked her bottom lip out. "And I think I saw him this morning exchanging spit with one of the waitresses," she said quickly.

"Are you gonna tell Rich?" Madison asked.

Blair turned around so that she faced Madison and cocked her head to the side. *"Humph!* Do you see me waving a banner that says 'I'm stupid'? I wanna live. Being with Antonio proved two things, that I'm not a piece of cardboard in bed. And I'm one hundred percent woman. *All woman."* Her skin heated at saying that. "If I tell Rich what happened, I might as well just sign a divorce decree, because Mr. Ricci would not take too kindly to somebody other than himself banging his wife."

"Talking about exchanging spit . . ." Lauren's voice drifted off and she looked guiltily down at her plate.

"You!?" LaShawn squealed, shocked and a little intrigued by her friend's confession. "Who with?" she asked, then suddenly her mouth widened to a minitunnel and she vigorously shook her head. "Naw, girl, tell me it ain't so. You didn't play tongue tango with the Boris look-alike . . . did you?"

"Once, after we'd gone to St. Thomas," Lauren admitted. "Girls!" She shook her head. "I had an attraction to him that couldn't be explained. I didn't understand it. It's like I was a cat and he was catnip!"

"Dayum!" Madison laughed.

"I was so hot and horny for him. I couldn't get him out of my head. And then when the opportunity came up to kiss those luscious lips of his . . ." She gazed helplessly at her friends. "I couldn't resist."

"Well, was it good?" Madison asked. "Was he a better kisser than Cleve?"

"Madison!" LaShawn and Blair shouted.

"What? You know you were thinking it." They were silent for a second. "Well, was he?" Madison pressed.

Lauren thought for a minute, then said, "It was different, not better, just different. There was a spark there."

"A spark?" Blair asked and she worried her bottom lip. "This is one time when sparks aren't good."

"It was probably from being together all day," LaShawn decided.

"Yeah, maybe," Lauren answered. "But I feel like I cheated on Cleve," she said sadly.

Blair was the first to console her friend. "You didn't cheat," Blair reassured her. "Try seeing a woman riding your husband as though he was a horse. That's cheating. And sleeping with an Italian bartender, that's cheating."

"Yeah," LaShawn chimed in, thinking about Calvin.

"That wasn't cheating, that was revenge," Madison chimed in. "Don't misunderstand me." Madison was quick to put everything into perspective. "Lauren, what you did was wrong, and you know it was. So chalk it up to bad judgment and move on."

"I understand everything you guys are saying, but I want to know where this attraction came from, and will it happen again?" Lauren asked.

The ladies looked at one another at a loss for words.

"I wish I could tell you that it won't," Blair finally answered. "But I don't know."

Lauren nodded her head. "He wanted me to go back to his cabin and make love with him."

"No!" LaShawn said shocked.

"And I almost went. I contemplated it. I even went as far

as to tell myself that I deserve to let loose once in a while because I'm the one always in control. But then Cleve, C.J., and Debbie popped into my head. And there was no way on earth that I could be so selfish to do something like that to them."

"But they would've never known," Madison said.

"But *I* would've known," Lauren said quietly.

Chapter 61

As soon as the soft *ding* sounded, Lauren flicked off her seat belt and impatiently hopped from one foot to the other until the door was pulled open.

Her lips formed into a smile. Home. She strode into the airport where she hit a wall of people. Lauren humphed, then stood on tiptoe, looking around the gaggle of people for Cleve and the kids.

She was almost finished with her search when she saw Cleve, with the kids in tow, slicing through the people as easily as if they were the tropical green-blue water that she fell in love with on the cruise.

"You look beautiful, baby. Damn, you look good!" Cleve said as he reached for her and enveloped her in a hug that she was sure was going to crack her spine. He held her that way for a full two minutes, and she sighed softly when she felt his hardness pressing against her hips. "It's been a long time," he whispered against her hair, then moved his pelvis

against her in a subtle grind that was imperceptible to anyone walking by, but felt like fire to her.

"Hi," Lauren said, blushing. There was a radiance in her
that outshone the sun.

"I *really* missed you, baby," he whispered in his wife's ear
and in those five little words Lauren heard a million times
over what he was saying.

"I missed you, too," Lauren said, and then knelt down to
pull her children into her embrace. "I've missed you two so
much," she said, her voice thickening.

Just as Lauren stood up, Darryl was strolling past and all
of a sudden her legs felt like the pasta she'd stuffed herself
with for the last fourteen days. He faltered and without
warning Lauren found that she couldn't breathe. She
gasped, then expelled a burst of air when he quickly regained his composure. They locked gazes. It took him less
than ten seconds to watch Lauren with her family and for
him to see that's where she belonged. He gave her a small
smile before gliding by.

Lauren shot a guilty look at Cleve. He didn't notice anything. "Wait, I need to tell you something—"

"Can't it wait until we get home? I have a special treat
waiting for you."

Lauren stepped back a few feet, put her hands on her
hips, and dipped her head back to look Cleve in the face.
"Cleve, I really need to talk to you," she said, desperation
burning in her eyes.

"C.J., watch your sister," Cleve instructed before he
pulled Lauren a few feet away from the kids; it was just
enough space to give them privacy, and enough for them to
keep an eye on their kids. He cupped Lauren's face in his

hands and tilted it up to his. She thought that he was going to kiss her, and she was surprised when he spoke.

"What's wrong, baby? You come off the plane looking even more beautiful than the day I married you, then all of a sudden you're acting like the world is gonna end. Baby, tell me what's wrong," he pleaded.

I wanted to jump another man's bones and I almost inhaled his tongue was on the tip of her tongue, but no matter how she worked her mouth it wouldn't come out. Instead she said, "We should make plans to get away . . . just you and me. No kids."

"Is that all? You're upset over that? I would love to go on vacation with my baby. Then I'll get a chance to make love to you on the beach. I've always wanted to do that," Cleve admitted.

"Yummy, that sounds delicious. Whisper in my ear . . . and tell me what you're gonna do to me on the beach," Lauren flirted.

Cleve and Lauren linked hands and strolled through the airport, with C.J. and Debbie trailing behind them, while Cleve made his wife promises that made her body hot.

LaShawn grabbed Terrance's hand as they headed toward his car. "Man, I've just had the best two weeks of my life. I'm no longer celibate, I lived a little on the wild side, and I've got the finest man in Atlanta. Let's do something crazy," LaShawn gushed.

Terrance gave her a sidelong glance. "What do you have in mind?"

LaShawn shrugged. "I don't know . . . hot-air ballooning or white-water rafting."

"Lord, I've created a monster," Terrance joked as he groaned.

LaShawn spotted an advertisement for skydiving. "Ooh! That looks fun!" She excitedly pointed at the sign.

"Oh, hell naw!" Terrance exclaimed as he vehemently shook his head.

"Come on, it'll be fun, everybody's doing it."

"I know you think I'm an angel. But do you see any wings on me?"

"Please!" LaShawn begged.

"Nope."

"What do I have to do to make you change your mind?" LaShawn asked and looked seductively up at Terrance.

Terrance glanced down at LaShawn, a naughty smile warming his face. "A couple things come to mind."

After hugging LaShawn and Blair good-bye, Madison snaked her way through the crowd over to ground transportation, where she was supposed to meet Trey. His Air Tran flight had landed five minutes before hers. She was walking, trying to call Trey on her cellphone, while at the same time scanning the crowd for him.

"Where is he? I bet he's still at baggage claim. Dammit!" she growled when he didn't answer his phone and she impatiently clicked hers off. "I hate all these people. Everybody's walking around like animals in a zoo. And some of them act like it," Madison grumbled, then walked directly into a man's chest. "Excuse me!" she said curtly and quickly stepped aside. He immediately mirrored her steps. Irritated, she glanced up and was promptly stunned into silence. Then she squeaked out, "Daddy?"

"It's me," Lucius answered.

"What are you doing at the airport? How did you know I was here?" Madison stuttered.

"Pearl."

"Aunt Pearl?"

Lucius nodded. "She called me, telling me that I needed to talk to you."

"I'm fine," Madison said in a brisk tone. "You didn't have to make the trip out here. Everything is okay."

Someone jostled them, nearly knocking Madison over.

"Let's go sit down," Lucius suggested and they both dropped down on the nearest bench. But Madison perched on the edge, ready to flee. "I want to tell you that I'm sorry. I'm sorry for every birthday I missed, I'm sorry for thinking that you were Bank of America, I'm sorry for not ever being there for you. I'm really sorry."

For the first time Madison noticed that her father looked like someone's father. Gone was all the jewelry, the hip-hop clothes and shoes. In their place were soft wool pants and a striped button-down that was starched so heavily that it looked like it might break into pieces if you touched it. His feet were covered in soft leather loafers. Her eyes made their way back up to his face. His eyes were shiny.

"Any sin of man can be forgiven," Madison mumbled. "Oh . . . Daddy," Madison cried and wrapped her arms around him. All the years of his absence melted away. "And you're my real daddy . . . not that other man."

Trey sauntered through the airport wearing a satisfied

smile, after finally getting his luggage. He got to his and Madison's meeting spot, then froze in his steps. Ten steps away Madison was sitting on a bench with her head resting against a stranger's chest.

Trey jumped into motion, making it to the bench in three steps. "Whassup, Madison?" he asked in a controlled voice.

Madison opened up a tear-stained eye to find Trey looking down at her, his gray eyes dark with worry. "Hey, baby. This is my daddy," Madison said proudly. Madison lifted her head so that Lucius could stand up to shake Trey's hand. They quickly sized each other up, then gave each other a tentative nod.

Can't ask for more than that, Madison silently mused.

"Well, let's get going," Madison said as she headed toward the taxi stand, but Lucius grabbed her elbow and steered her toward the parking lot. Madison's brow shot up in bewilderment.

"I got a car," he admitted. "It's not much, but it's mine."

"Wow!" Madison said. "Come on, Trey, *my daddy* is gonna drive us home," she said, smiling as she walked to the parking lot, flanked by her two guys.

Blair inched her way toward baggage claim, where it seemed like the whole city was returning home. There were more people there than at a Wal-Mart after-Christmas sale. She was surprised when Rich had called her and told her that he was going to pick her up. She quickly scanned the crowd and it took her only a moment to find them. Rich and the children were standing by the luggage carousel with her bags piled neatly at their feet. Blair quickly scrutinized her husband. He looks like he lost weight, she noticed. Blair didn't miss the dark bags under his eyes. She almost felt sorry for him. "Well, he did this to himself," she muttered.

The children were the first to see her, and she was surprised when her normally undemonstrative children sprinted toward her and almost knocked her down.

"Mommy!" came out of three mouths as one endearment. "We missed you!"

"I missed you, too," Blair gushed, giving each one a kiss, and was doubly astonished when none of them scrunched their face in disgust or wiped her kiss off.

After a quick nod to Rich, he scooped up her bags and fell into place behind Blair and the kids, who were loudly filling her in on everything that she had missed in the last two weeks.

She didn't say anything to him on the ride home. He patiently listened while she regaled the children with stories of her trip and passed out the gifts she had gotten them. He was even closemouthed when he discovered that she didn't have anything for him.

She didn't say anything to him until she'd showered and slipped into bed. "You're not sleeping in here with me!" she announced when Rich came into the bedroom. On the cruise, she had decided that she wasn't going to be banished to the guest bedroom; she hadn't done anything wrong.

"That's fine," he conceded. He was glad that she was home and he'd do anything to keep her happy. Rich immediately did an about-face and walked toward the door. Blair called out to him.

"Why did you do it, Rich?" she quietly asked.

Rich ran a hand through his hair, then, "Because I could," he answered, his tone matter-of-fact.

The honesty and simplicity of his words momentarily stunned Blair into silence. "What!" Blair screamed, incredulous. "Fuck you!"

"No, listen," Rich said, softly trying to soothe her. He stepped toward her, but her narrowed eyes, clenched hands, and pursed lips made him quickly change his mind. He immediately retreated across the room. "I thought about it, and I realized that I had a sense of entitlement. I told myself that I worked hard all day to pay for this house and everything in it. I deserved to have a little fun once in a while."

"You were supposed to do all those things—with *me.* You vowed to do so when you married me," Blair said, tears suddenly streaming down her face. She angrily swiped them away. "You promised to love, honor, and cherish me—"

"I know," Rich said, interrupting her. "I realized that when you were gone. I had a lot of time to think. I fucked up, baby. I fucked up bad and I hurt you. I didn't mean to hurt you. You believe that, don't you?" Rich asked, and he suddenly started crying, thick heavy sobs that made his body tremble and shake. He slumped against the wall for support.

"But you did hurt me, Rich!" Blair hissed. "I was living like an ostrich with her head in the sand. I didn't see the affairs coming. They were right under my nose like a pile of shit and I couldn't smell them for the life of me. Your actions took something away from me, from us, that took over fifteen years to build."

"I'm sorry, I'm—"

"So," Blair said sharply, cutting through his pleadings. "You tell me that you didn't mean to hurt me. I don't believe that, Rich, I don't believe that for one minute. On some level you did. Somewhere inside you, you wanted to hurt me."

"I didn't!" Rich said, his normally handsome face tight with agony. "I love you too much. And I don't ever want you to leave me. I'll do anything to make this up to you."

"I think we should go to counseling," she announced. "My heart is telling me that you love me. I want us to understand why you did what you did. I think counseling will make us a better couple, a stronger couple."

"I think so, too," he said, so agreeably that a fresh batch of tears fell down Blair's face. Rich inched toward the bed and sat on the edge.

"And I want you home every night to have dinner with the kids and me. I want the lies to stop. I don't want to hear about you screwing anybody else, 'cause if I do people are gonna start calling you Richardine," she warned. "And I want the man I married back. I want *you* back."

"It's done," Rich answered contritely.

"And I want—I want—I want for us to be a family again. I love you so much," she cried, then shoved the blankets aside and crawled over to Rich, wrapping her arms around his neck. He tenderly kissed her tears away.

"I want that, too, honey," he murmured. "I really do. And we'll have it," he said firmly. "I love you with all my heart."

If you enjoyed *Cruising,*
pick up Desiree Day's debut novel

CRAZY LOVE

Desiree Day

Available from
Pocket Books

Here's an excerpt from
Crazy Love. . . .

1
What I Want in a Man

1. Must be nine inches or bigger
2. He must be six-foot-one-inch or taller
3. He must have light eyes, green or gray
4. Must have soft curly hair—none of that nappy shit
5. Gotta have Shemar Moore's cheekbones
6. Gotta be able to wear a mesh muscle shirt and look good in it
7. His ride gotta be phat
8. He must be making at least $80K (after taxes)
9. No kids—I don't need any baby momma drama
10. He'd better be a freak in bed

Stacie Long ran her index finger down the list and mentally placed a check mark after nine of the items. This was her list. The nonnegotiable items she wanted in a man. It had been revised, scrutinized, and analyzed more than Bill Clinton's love life. A frown marred her pretty face, so much so that the space between her eyebrows looked like a halved prune. She was draped across a velvet couch, reviewing her list as if it was the Holy Grail. So intent on her list, she missed the hateful glares that were shot at her from the women who wanted to sit and rest their feet.

"Nine out of ten . . . not bad. Not bad at all," she said, laughing softly. Her body tingled with excitement. If she hadn't been sitting in the ladies' lounge in the Marriott Marquis in downtown Atlanta on New Year's Eve, she'd be howling with joy. Right now all she dared was a smug laugh. It was too easy . . . way too fucking easy, she thought.

Men usually sniffed after her the same way a fat man sniffed after a Big Mac, with desire, longing, greed, and lust. At five-feet-nine and one hundred thirty-five pounds, she was all woman; the red sequined dress she had slithered into earlier that evening *loved* her because it hugged every inch of her body. The color of warmed honey, with high cheekbones and full lips, she had a butt that made many a man stop dead in his tracks. Depending on when you saw her, her hair was either grazing her shoulders or kissing her ears. Tonight, she had it parted in the middle and the bone-straight strands framed her artfully made-up face. Blush lingered on her high cheekbones; fire-engine red lipstick glistened on her full lips and little sparkles glittered playfully on her mascaraed eyelashes.

Two women dressed to the nines were standing a few feet away from Stacie. Their heads were so close together that they looked like Siamese twins. "You know what? You can't take *us* out anywhere, look at her," muttered the one wearing a pair of toe-pinching shoes. "It wouldn't surprise me one bit if I saw her walking out of here with a plate of food. I bet she has a roll of aluminum foil in that Wal-Mart-looking bag of hers."

"Mmm," the other one agreed. "We should tell her to get her ass up!"

"Yeah!" The lady in the toe-pinching shoes hissed to her friend. But neither moved. Instead, one reached into her purse for lipstick. The other grabbed her cellphone and shrugged lightly; who needs a fight on New Year's Eve?

Stacie snuggled deeper into the plush cushions. A satisfied gleam brightened her eyes. This was her type of party. Men, *fine* men, were everywhere for the taking, fine, *wealthy* men, that is. They were like apples on a tree, hanging around for the picking. Atlanta had a lot of them. Not only that, but only the crème de la crème attended Atlanta's Annual Sexy and Sultry New Year's Eve Bash. So far she had spotted the mayor doing her thing on the dance floor, former Ambassador Andrew Young and Denzel Washington huddled together near the buffet, and a former child star working the room like a twenty-dollar-an-hour whore. Yep! This was her type of party.

It was only ten o'clock, but her evening purse was bulging with business cards. Where other ladies had to work for the numbers, men nearly threw their cards at Stacie. She'd hold on to them and sort through them tomorrow morning. Then she'd organize them by jobs—doctors, lawyers, and professional athletes on top, everybody else on the bottom. But tonight, she'd gotten the one number she'd been chasing for the past six months, Crawford Leonard Wallace III. An NBA player and a multimillionaire, his family was well known and respected in Atlanta. Single, six-foot-seven, curly, sandy-colored hair, and hazel eyes, he was as fine as Shemar Moore and sexier than Michael Jordan.

Stacie was so excited that she shimmered, and that's how her best friend and roommate, Tameeka Johnson, found her: stretched out on the couch and wearing a grin so wide that it looked painful. "Whassup with the grin? You look like you just found a million dollars."

"You close, girl. Very close," Stacie crowed gleefully. She didn't say anything for a couple of seconds, but then her secret started bubbling up and she whispered to Tameeka, "You are not gonna guess who I met tonight. You're not gonna guess. I know you're not," she taunted her friend. Before Tameeka got a chance to reply, Stacie blurted out her news and a collective gasp of envy went up throughout the lounge, followed by dead quiet. All ears turned to Stacie.

"Oh, is that all?" Tameeka gave Stacie a dismissive wave of her hand. "I thought you had hooked up with a *ten-incher*. That's cool, girl. So you finally snagged your baby's daddy. He's aw'right, but I've seen *better*." Tameeka sniffed, then turned to the mirror and pretended to check her makeup. She was really watching Stacie's reaction to her reaction and trying to suppress a laugh at the same time.

Where Stacie was drop-dead gorgeous, Tameeka was borderline pretty. The color of creamy peanut butter, five-foot-five, and one hundred seventy-five pounds, she was rarely treated to a head-swiveling, tongue-dropping look from a man. If she was, it was because his eyes zeroed in on her size 44D breasts.

"Meek!" Stacie wailed.

Tameeka couldn't hold in her laughter any longer. "You know I'm only playing, girl," she said. "Whassup? Have you whipped that Stacie magic on him yet?" she teased good-heartedly.

"Oh, I'll do that later," Stacie answered in a voice dripping with confidence. "Maybe *sooner* than later," she said. Then she looked around at the other ladies, who were all pretending not to be listening, and said very loudly, "He's a ten-incher or more," she boasted. "Dude got three legs. I can tell these things. Some women look at the shoe size, I look at the finger width. If he got thick fingers, then he got a thick di—*you know what*. The pants were loose, but it was in there!"

"Girl! You gotta get a piece of that. If you don't, somebody else will," Tameeka threatened.

Stacie gave a short nod. "Hey, what about you? You didn't meet anybody, did you?"

"I did too meet somebody," Tameeka answered defensively, and then suddenly laughed when she realized how juvenile she sounded. "As a matter of fact, I met a *lot* of somebodies. You're not the only one who got it going on tonight," she answered as she bowed her head and hid a nervous grin. Tonight, she'd met her soul mate.

"Oh really? Do tell," Stacie encouraged. "There are a lot of fine men out there. So which bodies did you meet?"

"I'll tell you later," she said, then changed the subject. "So whassup? Why are you sitting in the bathroom talking to me, when you got Mr. Wonderful on the other side of the door waiting to sweep you off your feet?" Tameeka asked, eager to get back to her new guy friend; she didn't want to leave him alone too long, the women were vicious. Something about New Year's Eve turns a woman into a man-stealing, I-don't-want-to-spend-the-rest-of-my-life-alone ho.

"I know, girl! Give me a minute, Meek; I need to run to the bathroom," Stacie called over her shoulder as she rushed past a group of preening women.

Inside the stall, Stacie let out a long breath and frowned. She had promised herself that she wasn't going to do it tonight. The day before she had done it twenty times, and yesterday she'd done it eighteen times, and earlier today she'd done it seventeen. Her face glistened; the makeup couldn't hide the sweat that popped out over her face. Her palms became sweaty and she rubbed her hands together in an attempt to dry them; it didn't work, they only became soggier. She prayed silently to herself that the urge would pass. But it didn't. As she knew it wouldn't. Instead, the urge continued to grow. It seeped into her body like a nasty virus, and there was only one way to assuage it.

"I have to do it," she said in a tortured whisper, then snatched off her right shoe, a red strappy number, and brought it up to her nose. She inhaled deeply, and then took nine more quick sniffs as a calm came over her, blanketing her with a confidence that almost covered her shame . . . almost. The left shoe was next and the smell was even sweeter. She felt reborn. And it showed. Her face glowed; her pulse slowed and a crooked smile graced her face. Eyes sparkling, she pushed open the stall door.

"Let's show the brothas how we do it!" she said as she grabbed Tameeka's arm, then strutted out of the room.

2
Your Expectations Can Become Your Reality

Peachtree Street was overflowing with people, the sidewalks stuffed tighter than Janet Jackson's breasts in a bustier. Rows of vendors and amusement park rides lined the street. In the midst of it all were Tameeka and Tyrell Powell, holding each other's hand, ambling along laughing and talking as if they were old friends, not two people who had just met three hours earlier.

Tameeka was smiling so wide that her lips were hurting, but she didn't care, she was ecstatic. The whole evening felt like a dream. But it was real, the cold wind that kissed her bones proved it, and she shivered slightly and tugged at her wrap. Three hours. That's how long she'd known Tyrell. Tyrell Anthony Powell.

She smiled crookedly. She couldn't believe it when he'd sauntered past half a dozen yardstick-size women and stopped in front of her. She had almost fallen over with surprise when he had asked her to dance.

After their fifth dance together something told her that he was a little interested. But after two hours of sticking to her like half a pound of barbecue ribs, she knew for sure he was feeling her. She shook her head, amazed that a man who looked like him wanted someone who looked like her.

A dead ringer for Gerald Levert, Tyrell was gorgeous. His full lips were totally kissable, but so were his cute ears and his ginger-colored eyes. For a man his size he was light on his feet—instead of walking he glided. She glanced down at his fingers and giggled softly; they were thick *and* wide.

Every couple of minutes Tyrell found himself sneaking peeks down at Tameeka. It was as though she had cast a spell over him, because each time he looked at her, his chest tightened and it felt as though he was breathing through a straw.

Tameeka was telling him a story about growing up with her grandmother. Her face was animated and she'd occasionally let loose a wild, raucous laugh that made him so hard that he felt like he could cut a diamond. She was the most beautiful lady he'd met in a long time, and by far the classiest. The silky fabric of her dress draped conservatively over her full breasts, then dropped down to the tip of her red sandals. Her locked hair was pulled up into a ponytail; a couple pieces had gotten free and gently caressed her cheeks. I'm the luckiest man alive, he thought, and poked his chest out.

Tyrell shook his head, amazed. Three hours ago he had asked her to dance and they'd been together since. He smiled and gave her hand a little squeeze. His smile deepened when she returned it.

They made a striking couple. At six-foot-seven and three hundred pounds, Tyrell dwarfed Tameeka's five-foot-five frame. He was big and cuddly, just the way Tameeka liked her men, and husky enough for her to snuggle in his lap if she so desired. She glanced at him and was shocked to find him eyeballing a group of ladies sashaying by.

Tameeka sucked in a breath of cold air, but it did nothing to cool her down. She exhaled slowly, then, "You like looking at people, don't you?" she lightly teased.

Tyrell chuckled. "Not really . . . why do you say that?"

Tameeka shrugged. "Your eyes seem to have a life of their own . . . at the party . . . walking down the street."

"I like being aware of my surroundings. A man gotta know what's going on," Tyrell answered as he reluctantly pulled his gaze off one of the women, whose legs ended at her chest.

"Oh, is that what it's called?" she asked, cutting her eyes at him. "So . . ." She nodded to the woman in front of them. "What are her legs telling you?" she snapped, arching an eyebrow at him.

"Come on, baby, it's not that serious. I only have eyes for you." He winked sexily, then swiped his thumb over her bottom lip before slipping his hand into hers.

"Corny!" Tameeka retorted, but her grip on his hand tightened.

The blowing wind continued to slice through Tameeka's silk dress and cut her skin as though she wasn't wearing anything at all. She silently cursed herself as she pulled her thin wrap around her shoulders. Stacie had insisted that she wear the flimsy wrap and not the wool coat that she had originally chosen.

"You cold?" Tyrell asked, and immediately felt stupid. He could see her shivering. "We can go back to the hotel if you want," he offered politely, but wished that they could keep walking forever.

"No," Tameeka lied. She was freezing, but she didn't want the night to end. She felt like Cinderella; all they needed now was a horse-drawn carriage. At that very moment, her vision came to life and she giggled as a horse and carriage trotted by.

Tyrell laughed along with her. "Care to let me know why I'm laughing?" He looked down and beamed at her for the thousandth time.

"Oh nothing," Tameeka chuckled, then decided it was too delicious to keep to herself. "Okay, I'll tell you . . . only if you promise not to laugh," she said, peeking up at him through her eyelashes.

"I promise. Cross my heart and hope to die, stick a chicken bone in my eye," he said somberly.

"Boy, you crazy," Tameeka hooted. They both shared a good laugh. Then she admitted to feeling like Cinderella.

"Wasn't Cinderella the belle of the ball?" he asked, and

Tameeka nodded. "Well, you're not only the belle, but you're the queen," Tyrell said, his voice ringing with sincerity.

"That's very sweet," Tameeka said, blushing; at that moment she felt as beautiful and regal as a queen.

"One day we'll take that carriage ride; it's too damn cold—" He stopped and stared down at Tameeka. "Girl, you are freezing your ass off. You killing me with trying to be cute. Here, take my jacket." He slid his tuxedo jacket off and draped it over Tameeka's shoulders. She instantly felt warmer. She inhaled deeply, and her nose was filled with his intoxicating cologne. Thank you, God, she thought. She slid her hand back into his and smiled. His hands were big and strong, just like a man's hands should be, and it felt natural holding his hand, almost as if they'd done it before in some other life.

"You work out?" Tameeka asked. Even though he was big, he was muscular, too. Muscles rippled underneath his tuxedo shirt. He sauntered jacketless through the cold as though it was a balmy summer evening instead of the middle of winter.

"Yep," Tyrell answered, before stopping and flexing his biceps. "Wanna touch?" he whispered as his gaze swept over her body, then stopped on her mouth and Tameeka automatically parted her lips.

"Umm, yeah," she answered, excited by the thought of Tyrell's kiss. Tameeka reached over and squeezed his muscle—it felt like a brick. "Wow, are you a professional body builder?"

"Naw, I'm a bus driver," Tyrell said before he draped an arm across Tameeka's shoulders and resumed their walk.

"Cool, so I got the hookup . . . free bus rides," she laughed up at him.

"I'll hook you up anytime." Tyrell gave her a lazy grin, then squeezed her shoulder. "So what's your nine-to-five?"

"Heaven on earth."

"Yes you are, baby," Tyrell drawled.

"No, I *own* Heaven on Earth, that's my brainchild. I have two employees and I sell everything related to nurturing the spirit. People come to my store when they're stressed out. Last year I grossed—"

"Hold up," Tyrell commanded. "I'm not trying to get in your bank account. Just wanted to know what you did, and I'm impressed. Not only are you a business owner, but you're sexy and smart," he said. "Hey, look, a merry-go-round," Tyrell announced, and pointed to their left. "Let's take a ride." Tameeka hung back; she could see doll-size ladies stepping daintily into the teeny seats. No way me and Tyrell will fit in those little booths, it'll be like trying to squeeze a couple of whales into a Geo Metro, she thought. "Come on," Tyrell insisted, then pulled Tameeka along.

They stood in line, and when it was their turn, she could hear snickers as she and Tyrell tried three different seats before they found one that barely accommodated them. All Tameeka wanted to do was jump off and hide. "Isn't this cozy?" Tyrell asked as he draped his arm around her shoulder.

"I guess," Tameeka answered, embarrassed, but the

music snapped up her words as the ride began. The whole time she sat as stiff as a mannequin; not even Tyrell serenading her with a Luther Vandross song loosened her up. As soon as the ride ended, she pulled herself out and hopped off ahead of Tyrell. "I was feeling queasy," she said in response to Tyrell's raised eyebrow. "Let's go," she said, and gently pulled his arm until he fell into step with her.

Tameeka was enjoying their walk when, without any warning, Tyrell stopped in the middle of the sidewalk and turned to her. "So what do you think about me?" he asked.

"You're wonderful, *fine*, and smart," Tameeka purred as she winked at him and his heart flip-flopped.

"I'm feeling much love. But something's missing," he said, putting his forefinger to his forehead and wrinkling his brow as if he was trying to solve a mystery.

"You're wonderful, fine, smart, and *sexy*," Tameeka whispered seductively.

"Jackpot! Give the lady a free drink."

Tameeka giggled, then peeked up at Tyrell, expecting to see him looking down at her. Instead his gaze was locked on something else. It didn't take a detective to figure out what it was; all it took was one quick glance. She followed his stare; it was glued to the gentle swaying of a passing lady's behind. *Ain't this some shit?* she thought. *He's doing it again!*

Her eyes drifted downward to her dress and she felt like an oversize tomato. She fumed and her hand itched to slap the glassy-eyed look off his face.

"How are the *surroundings?*" Tameeka asked between clenched teeth.

Tyrell shot her a confused look, then grinned sheepishly. "It wasn't like that, baby, all I'm doing is looking."

"So now you admit to looking, before it was being 'aware of your surroundings,' " Tameeka shot at him.

"It's a little of both," Tyrell admitted. "I am a man. Besides, you should be happy that I'm checking out chicks and not dudes."

"What!" Tameeka hissed. "I should be happy that you're looking at women? What kind of messed-up logic is that?" she asked.

"Don't get it twisted," he said in a heated voice. "There are a million women out here showing their asses for everybody and their daddy to see and you don't expect a man to look?"

"I-I-I–" Tameeka stuttered, shocked at Tyrell's outburst.

"Come here," he murmured as he drew her near, and Tameeka rested her cheek on his chest. "As I told you earlier, it's not that serious. Let's enjoy the rest of the evening," he said, dismissing the incident.

Why spoil the perfect evening? Tameeka thought. "Oh, look what time it is," she said, glancing down at her watch. It was one minute to midnight.

"This was nice . . . really nice. Usually I hang out with my boy J and his son Jam. We'd have our butts parked in front of the TV, watching the peach drop and sometimes we'd get adventurous and switch up and watch Dick Clark," he joked, and Tameeka laughed.

"I hear you. I had a *really* good time tonight," she said softly, and the way she said it made Tyrell think that she wasn't treated special on a regular basis.

The countdown to the New Year started and Tyrell peered down at her. "Hey lady, you know what that means, don't you?" he asked, and Tameeka shook her head no. "It means that you owe me a kiss," he said, easing up to her so that her breasts kissed his chest.

"I always pay my debts," Tameeka retorted sassily.

"Then call me Uncle Sam, because here I am to collect," Tyrell announced, then abruptly gripped her waist with his baseball-glove-size hands.

"You are so beautiful," he said, then gently caressed her face with the soft pad of his thumb. As he skimmed her lips, she caught his thumb and tenderly suckled it. She groaned softly. "I've got something else you can suck on," Tyrell drawled, and burst out laughing when Tameeka's mouth dropped open. "Not *that*, at least not yet, but *this.*" He dipped down and brushed his lips against Tameeka's and her hands whipped up his back, clutched his tuxedo shirt, and pulled him closer.

Tyrell slipped his tongue into Tameeka's mouth and she grasped onto it as if it were one of her favorite lollipops. Tyrell let out a soft moan, then pushed against her and Tameeka gasped with delight when his hardness pressed into her. His hands flowed underneath the tuxedo jacket to fondle her breasts, and her body rippled in response. Suddenly heart-stopping fireworks erupted and for a moment Tameeka wasn't sure if they were from her and Tyrell or from the City of Atlanta.

Panting softly, Tyrell pulled away. "Happy New Year!"